THE CARIBBEAN AFFAIR

JACK BARR THRILLERS
BOOK 1

NICK THACKER

FOREWORD
USA TODAY BESTSELLING AUTHOR JAY FALCONER

Admit it. As a reader, don't you just love that pulse-pounding, leave you breathless kind of action-thriller? You know the one I'm talking about. The one with the rich characters that literally jump off the page and come alive, deep mysteries that keep you guessing at every turn, and endless action to satisfy even the most "*die-hard*" fans. So much so that when you're done reading, you can't quite catch your breath, leaving you desperate for the next book to find out what happens next.

You're about to experience all of that and more when you climb aboard *the Caribbean Affair*.

Imagine how your world would be turned upside down if your cruise ship vacation was cut short by a terrorist hell-bent on taking over the ocean liner?

That's the reality Jack Barr and his family face when the *Ocean Voyager* and its crew succumb to evil at its most dangerous level.

What would it mean for the survivors when they realize that their dream vacation is now a nightmare, leaving everyone scrambling to stay alive?

How will Jack Barr turn back this lethal threat to him and his family?

Who will be left standing if they can somehow come together to defeat the terrorist?

Will there be anything left to salvage after the threat is eliminated?

Get ready for a thrilling saga that sets sail right out of the port and won't let you rest until the very end, when you'll be left begging for more.

Welcome to *The Caribbean Affair* by *USA Today* Bestselling Author, Nick Thacker.

WANT FREE BOOKS?

HEAD OVER TO NICKTHACKER.COM/FREE-BOOKS to download three full-length thriller novels!

"COME ON, Dad, you can do it!" Riley shouted.

He shook his head. *The only thing worse than letting my wife see me like this is letting my* kids *see me like this.*

Riley, eleven years old, and Addison, eight, had come along on the cruise. This summer's Barr family vacation was sorely needed. Jack's job at the Central Intelligence Agency under the Directorate of Operations, had been demanding more and more of him of late, and Kate was growing weary of being a stay-at-home mom. She was ready to get back into the workforce, ready for the social life she used to have as an administrator in an HR department of a multinational conglomerate. She was good at her job, and she missed the speed and challenge of it.

The kids were out of school for the summer. Still, their usual circle of friends seemed to all have vanished the day after the final bell, their families deciding to take advantage of the two months of freedom to go on family vacations and trips.

It had taken much pleading from Kate, but Jack had finally

cashed in a week of vacation time to book this last-minute Caribbean cruise.

At first, he had grumbled about it. He was too busy, he didn't want to bring the kids along, they needed time together *alone* — all of the arguments he could think of. And then, eventually, the *real* argument: this was just a band-aid to cover up their true problems. A week in paradise was not nearly enough to get their marriage back on track.

But Kate had not backed down — ironically, one of the traits he loved about her, though he had to admit he had grown less fond of it in situations like these. But she had been right, as always. They needed some time away to bond and rekindle the flame of marriage they had somehow lost in the last fifteen years — with or without kids.

Jack loved his family; his kids were his world, of course. But if he were honest, he wished for just a little more time alone with Kate.

But that was why Kate had chosen this particular cruise, and why Jack had eventually agreed. Leaving out of Galveston, Texas, the cruise liner's seven-day float offered families the perfect escape: a child- and teen-care program that offered fun and entertainment for kids aged three through fifteen.

And unlike the other programs he'd heard of that touted 'age-appropriate entertainment,' the reviews for this particular cruise had been jaw-dropping. Parents were amazed to see that their children wanted time away from their families, and teenagers — normally pre-programmed to assume everything their parents chose for them would be lame — found the activities exciting and fun. Kids met other kids their age, and the childcare program staff acted more like camp counselors, offering a bevy of activities and options but allowing the kids to self-direct. They were present and observant but didn't meddle in the affairs of the kids.

Parents were enthralled that their children had a place aboard the ship, and they were not just an afterthought. For the youngest kids, a full-fledged daycare center took up the back half of the Deck 10 Kids' Zone. Treated like a summer camp, the ship's 'camp counselors' were constantly present and observant, but not overbearing. The oldest kids in the bunch — aged twelve through fifteen — were given nearly free rein of the ship, so long as they had a guide with them at all times or otherwise had permission from their parents to run totally free.

"That's great, Jack!" Kate yelled up at him. "You don't have to go all the way up!"

Jack's mind turned back to the present. He had not realized that in his daze, he had actually *climbed*. He had made it only a few feet, but those precious few feet put him that much closer to the top of the wall.

He wanted to turn and look at her if only to tell her to shut up and let him concentrate. But his eyes were closed, and he had no plans to open them anytime soon. He gripped the plastic protrusions of the rock wall with both hands, his knuckles white. He felt the tension around his waist, the makeshift seat doing its job to keep him suspended fifty-five feet off the ground.

And yet, it was not nearly enough. Jack felt the bile rising in his throat, the anxiety rapidly overtaking his more logical side. He had not been on a climbing wall in years, and even then he'd only done it after being coerced into it by his coworkers at the CIA. The ropes course excursion had been a 'team-building activity,' according to his boss. There had been plenty of griping and groaning about the ordeal, but their supervisor had made it clear the 'scheduled fun' was not optional.

Before that day trip, it had been probably thirty years since he had done any sort of climbing and rappelling. An Eagle Scout, Jack had once completed his Climbing and Rappelling Merit Badge with his fellow scouts, where he had learned — unfortunately — that he had a crippling fear of heights.

The memories returned then, flooding his brain as if he were experiencing them for the first time. He remembered the other boys calling up at him, telling him to 'just do it.' To just let go and let his belay partner ease him down. Some of the more confident boys even tried to shout up helpful tips and tricks, acting as if they had been climbing for years.

Of course, none of it was helpful. His scoutmaster had been quiet and stoic the entire time, knowing Jack better than all the rest. Jackson Barr Sr. had been his troop's adult leader for a few years while Jack was in high school, and he knew his son better than anyone else in attendance.

For that reason, he knew Jack was not capable of hearing anyone else at the moment. He would need to decide on his own, to feel capable on his own.

Okay, Jack, he told himself. *Time to feel capable. Let's get this done.*

HE WAS MOST CERTAINLY *NOT* GETTING this done.

Still stuck near the top of the easiest route available, Jack Barr felt less confident each second.

I could just give up, he thought. *Who's going to care? No one's watching me.*

Except... he knew his family *was* watching. And for some stupid reason, he had decided that he would do it *for them.*

He shook his head, dangling sixty feet above the deck, latched on to the fake rocks for dear life.

Kate called up to him again, this time shouting words of encouragement. They sounded hollow, forced, to his ears. But he also understood that it was mostly his own insecurities coming to bear. She meant well; he didn't need to make something of nothing.

He sighed, trying to focus on his next move up the hard-plastic climbing wall. He and Kate weren't necessarily on the rocks, but the last few years had been tougher than the others. Celebrating their 15-year anniversary, this trip would mark both a celebration of their time together as well as some much-needed rest and relaxation, and, Jack knew, some time for Kate to pry into their relationship and uncover all sorts of issues he wasn't even aware of.

Jack wasn't opposed to the idea of some scheduled soul-searching; he knew they needed to get out of their own heads and just talk through things a bit. They still loved each other, but that love had turned into rote recitations of feelings he wasn't positive were still there; vague maneuverings that fit the mold of what two people in love would look like.

"Come on, dad," Riley said. "Hurry up. There are other people down here who want to —"

"Stop it," he heard Kate say, her whisper-talk louder than her normal speaking voice. She scolded their oldest as Riley giggled, taking delight in her father's discomfort.

"It's okay, honey," Kate yelled, her face tilting upward. "Take your time — there's no time limit on these things, so... I mean, take your time."

He opened his eyes and let his pupils adjust to the bright light of the deck. He let the happy screams of children swimming in the pool just below calm him, the sounds of teenagers and young adults chasing one another in the sunshine put his mind at ease.

Adults down below shouted happily at one another, either already buzzed or well on their way. It was only 9:30 in the morning, but what was time on a cruise ship? He almost laughed. Time didn't matter here, and that was the point — he had all the time in the world to get to the top of this stupid fake wall.

He summoned his strength and looked down at his family. Kate, with her shoulder-length dark brown hair wispy in the gentle breeze, a strained smile on her face as she squinted up into the light. Riley and Addy stood by their mother's side, and he could almost feel the impatience emanating from Riley, his oldest daughter. Addy was a sweetheart, rowdy and always willing to party hard like her mother, but equally ready to console someone if she sensed pain or discomfort.

But she also looked up to her older sister, who meant the world to her. Riley was much more like Jack — much less empathetic, more hard-nosed, and often only self-aware enough to ensure she was taken care of. She wasn't quite *selfish*, but she wasn't as self*less* as her sister and mother. She took after her father more than Jack wanted to admit, but even then, she was a sweet young girl, quickly becoming a young woman.

He had merely blinked, and his daughter had gone from tiny, happy-go-lucky girl to makeup-wearing, interested-in-boys eleven-year-old. But she was an incredible girl, at that. Her friends had shifted over the past few years into a tight-knit group that rooted for one another rather than competed with one another. It had been a subtle shift, but Jack and Kate had both paid attention enough to notice it. It meant that their daughter was growing up and making her way in the world, and they were glad she had chosen friends who would support her rather than hold her back.

Of course, the kid was expressing none of this empathy and adulthood right now. The wry smile on her face told Jack everything. Riley only wanted to get to her and her sister's scheduled events — a movie and popcorn party for Addy and a Deck 10 all-out brawl with Super Soakers and water balloons for Riley. All of that would happen *before* lunch, so they were due at the Deck 10 meeting room by 10 AM.

Riley was about to open her mouth and snap off another

unkind retort, but Kate caught her just in time and pulled at her wrist.

He pulled himself upward, gripping the plastic holds while allowing his legs to do most of the work. This was the easiest climb on the ship's rock wall. It was a route the lanky high-school kid handing out harnesses and helping everyone get hooked up had called 'The Newbie.'

Kate had opted for the medium route — one dubbed 'The *Not* Newbie' — and had sailed three-quarters of the way to the top before tapping out and letting her auto-belay lower her down gently. Jack wanted to do the same, knowing more than three-quarters of the way up the *easy* route would be just as good for him. He knew Kate wasn't keeping track — *she* wasn't the competitive one, he was — but he had told himself that getting to the top was do-or-die.

He wanted his kids to see that he could do it.

He didn't dare look down, feeling his own breath bounce off the rock wall and hit him in the face, only making the sweat worse. His eyes were singed with it, so he squeezed them shut. Three seconds felt like three years, but his feet finally did their job and found the holds they were supposed to find. Now back on track, he stretched his legs outward to a standing position, giving his hands a brief respite.

Then, with a triumphant roar he hoped could be heard in the pool — or at least down by the high school harness handler — he reached up and slammed the bell at the top of the lip with his fist.

Shouts and cheers resonated upward from his wife and Addy. He looked down then, gripping the rope with both hands and waiting for the bit of slack that would tell him he was on his way down the auto-belay system. He also noticed Riley still smirking up at him.

"Good job, *Dad*," she shouted. He could almost *feel* the sarcasm dripping from her voice. "You finally did it. There are only *nine hundred* people waiting to climb now," she scoffed.

Jack ignored his daughter, knowing she was doing her best. When she wasn't coming across as rude or sarcastic, she was actually hilarious.

He felt the pressure of the belay line release and let his feet fall back off their holds. The auto belay system worked like a charm, holding him upright as it lowered him to the ground. He didn't bother trying out any of the rappelling moves he remembered from childhood — no one was watching to see how cool he was, anyway.

The 42-year-old had long since stopped worrying about how cool he appeared to others. Cool, at his age, meant something quite different than it did to his kids.

He smiled as he realized he had just accomplished something he had been terrified of doing. At the ropes course, he had not been able to climb more than halfway up before asking his belay partner to let them down. It wasn't a big deal — he was one of many who didn't make it up the wall that day — but he was the only one in great shape who couldn't do it.

This morning he had woken up a bit anxious, knowing that his family had wanted to try this rock wall. And from watching others yesterday, he knew they would each get to ascend one at a time. That meant he would be doing it *alone* while his whole family and everyone else on deck were watching.

He recalled his dad's words from long ago: "Son, *I* know

you can do this. But *you're* the only one who has to convince *yourself* you can do it."

He reached the ground and Kate and Addy clapped once again, this time Riley joining in with a few slow claps.

"Thanks, kid," Jack said. He smiled down at Riley, then turned to try to coerce a hug from Addy, only to find her already jogging over to the high-school-aged worker to fit her for a harness. She was the last of his family to climb, but her miniature frame would have no trouble scaling whichever wall she chose. They joked that she was the family monkey, capable of climbing anything and everything, and she had the bruises and scrapes to prove it.

Kate walked over to Jack as he watched Addy get ready, and her hand found his. She squeezed it, leaning in close. "You looked good up there, stud," she whispered. "That harness really, uh, isolates your *glutinous maximus.*"

"You mean *Gluteus Maximus?*"

"I stand by what I said," she laughed.

He cocked an eyebrow. "I take it this romantic setting has been messing with your head?" he asked.

"Oh, it has," she said. "Last night, I was exhausted from the drive and just trying to get everyone on board safe and sound," she explained.

"Yeah, I feel that," he said.

"But..." she bit her lip and flicked her eyes away from Jack for a moment. When she glanced back at him, he saw a look in her eyes he had not seen in a long time.

"But the kids are happy," she continued. "Everyone's relaxed now. Tonight, I'm thinking I'm going to feel *very* well-rested. If you know what I mean."

Jack laughed, noticing that Riley had been listening to their entire conversation. The eleven-year-old rolled her eyes and made a fake vomiting sound before walking over to help her little sister.

"Oh, I think I know what you mean," Jack said, returning her smile. "I'm thinking we could even further horrify our children with a live show."

Kate reached around him and smacked him on the butt before joining her daughters.

HOWARD GRAVES MADE that slurping sound as the remainder of his drink left the fake coconut and went into his mouth.

With a satisfying sigh, he leaned back and let the coconut rest on his protruded belly. He hated life in Jamaica, but there were certain perks.

Taking vacation days was easy, considering he was the boss and didn't need to travel anywhere to hit the beach. The vast Caribbean stretched before him, and he let out another sigh as he shifted his feet on the ground, letting the sand tickle his toes.

At fifty-eight years old and rapidly putting on even more weight, he felt like he was already past retirement.

Unfortunately, he had at least eight or nine years left of this madness before he could even think about retiring. Jamaican life was cheap compared to his life back in Miami, but his pitiful salary with Port Authority wouldn't allow him to build up much of a nest egg unless he did his time for another decade.

He groaned as thoughts of work crept back into his previously relaxed mind. He waved at the only server he'd seen attending to this section of the beach — a young man he had not seen in over ten minutes.

The waiter smiled and began jogging over, opening his mouth to ask Howard a question, but Graves simply lifted his coconut. The younger man nodded, snatched the coconut from Graves, and darted off to get him a refill.

"Should have asked for two," Graves said, mumbling as he laid back in the plastic chair lounge chair.

He was especially annoyed since he was the only patron in sight. *Who the hell else are they serving?* he wondered. *It's not like they're slammed with a bunch of tourists.*

Nor would they be, ever. This small slice of the beachfront property was owned by the company that controlled cruise ship access to the port on the side of Jamaica. Howard Graves had been head of security here for eight years already, and before that, he had been a beat cop back in the states. He would be woefully underqualified for a similar job in Fort Lauderdale or Galveston. Jamaica, however, had slightly more lax requirements for its staff positions. An oasis for expats who wanted the easy life, this cruise line was a perfect haven for those who wanted all of the benefits of living in a tropical paradise without putting in the work.

And yet Howard Graves found himself consistently threatening to quit. He hated his job — mostly, he hated the people. Everyone was always so needy, so picky about this or that, and wanted him to do something about it. Just last week, he had gotten into an argument with a low-ranking staffer about how much time off he could take for a death in the family. It's not that Howard hadn't believed the kid — people died all the time

— it's just that he didn't care. Being out longer than allowed meant Howard would have to pick up more work, and that's where he drew the line.

He pulled his sunglasses up to his forehead and risked torquing his upper body to look behind him at the cabana house the waiter had disappeared into, eliciting a groan from his neck muscles. Since most of his work was done from behind a desk, and any meetings or inspections he did need to attend could be reached by using his golf cart, Graves was far more out of shape than he wished. He remembered the good days when he was staying in shape because of the competitive nature of the other guys on the force. Cops in small towns could get away with sitting around eating doughnuts all day, but cops in Miami had to stay light and fit.

He cracked his neck and rubbed against the muscle that had tweaked, knowing it would cause him hell tomorrow morning when he tried to get out of bed.

The young waiter darted out of the cabana house with the speed of an Olympic runner. *He* knew the kid probably made decent money on the other side of the cabana, where the public section of the beach met this private one. Tourists worldwide flocked to the public section to frolic in the sun and sand, but Howard hated tourists even more than he hated employees. The fact that his company maintained this private sliver of beach for its own use was one of the few things he enjoyed about the job.

Graves sighed and leaned back once again, trying to get the most of his brief respite.

JACK PULLED at the collar of his freshly pressed Oxford shirt.

Having been on a few cruises before, he had grown to hate these formal dinners. His day job's dress code already required a suit and tie, and it was one of the few organizations he knew of that still upheld the idea of a "casual Friday." Even still, a casual Friday at CIA only meant he was safe to remove his tie once he got into the office.

So he had been slightly annoyed that Kate had forced him to pack his best suit, citing the ship's written policy for two dinners that week: formal attire required.

"They won't let you in if you're not dressed up," she had told him.

He'd tried to laugh it off, remembering the three other times they had been on a cruise. "On our honeymoon cruise, I *literally* saw a guy in swim trunks and a tank-top waltz into the dining room one night," Jack had said.

Kate just shook her head. "He was wasted, and that one wasn't a formal dinner."

It had not turned into an argument, but that was only

because Jack truly didn't care. He would wear a suit if it meant he got to eat free lobster tail. And "free," of course, now referred to the small surcharge required for each lobster tail at dinner.

When they first married, half the reason to even go on a cruise had been to experience all the food. It was fine dining at its best — world-class chefs preparing meals that were all-you-can-eat gluttonous affairs. Lobster tail, steak, shrimp, whole Cornish game hens, and everything in-between surprised and delighted diners.

But these days, the cruises that still fed people well were all but out of reach for an upper-middle-class family like Jack's. The budget cruise lines, like the one they were on now, had tightened their belts over the past two decades. Now, while the food was certainly passable — and even good after a long day in the sun — it was a far cry from the world-class dining experience it used to be.

So Jack had been annoyed because they now had to pay the same amount for a serious drop in quality, not because his wife was nagging him to wear a suit.

Besides, he looked good in a suit, so at least he had that going for him. Most men his age were uncomfortable if forced to wear more than a t-shirt and jeans, but Jack was used to it. He had spent almost twenty years at the Central Intelligence Agency, landing a job there just out of college. He had fit the persona they were unofficially looking for. He and his buddies jokingly referred to it as the Agency Trifecta: male, pale, and Yale. While he wasn't a *Yale* graduate, he knew he fit what the word implied: well-educated, from the right school with the right pedigree, able to prove loyalty through his family tree.

Jack's father had been a colonel in the Army and had

worked for the CIA for a brief stint. Jack, not wanting the life of not-so-permanent changes of station every three years for his family, had been recruited to the CIA and coveted his office job. While neither he nor his father had worked in a stereotypical espionage or law enforcement role, Jack knew that the acronym carried clout, and people made assumptions based on that. He had grown tired of explaining that he 'wasn't *that* kind of CIA agent.' He was even less interested in correcting people that the CIA didn't have 'agents' — that was FBI.

For that reason, he often told people he simply worked for the state. *Let them draw their own conclusions*, he told himself. He wasn't one to gloat, not one to try to impress. It was another characteristic his father had instilled in him from a young age: let your work and character form people's opinion of you, not your words and antics.

It was just this phrase Jack was thinking about as he watched the other couple at their table. Coming into the dining hall — fifteen minutes late, he noticed — Jack had seen that the man's suit bottom jacket button was buttoned, his first mistake. Second, the suit looked like it had been plucked from the rack of a resale shop. Jack certainly wouldn't judge anyone for that, but the man had failed to have it tailored or altered in any way. He could tell the man was uncomfortable, and whenever he pulled his arms close to his chest, Jack saw the suit strain under the effort.

In Jack's book, being late, wearing an ill-fitted suit, and being out of shape were not reasons to dislike someone. But it was that this man — Mr. Hector Bolívar — had failed to uphold the *second* half of his father's quote: the man simply had not stopped talking about himself and how important he was at his job, the entire dinner so far.

They had finished the dessert round when Jack leaned in, swallowing the cheesecake bite he had just placed in his mouth. "And what was it you said you did, again, Hector?" Jack asked.

The other seven people at the table — Mr. Bolívar and his wife across from them, their two children, and Kate and their kids —stopped chewing and stared at Jack. Riley started giggling.

He saw Kate kick Riley's leg under the table, and Riley stopped smiling.

"I, uh…" The man began.

Kate leaned in and whispered to Jack through clenched teeth. "Are you serious? He's only explained to us like fifteen times." Then, for the sake of everyone else at the table, Kate spoke louder. "Mr. Bolívar is a manager. At a bank."

Jack nodded slowly. *That's right.* He remembered now, as those exact words had fallen from Bolívar's mouth more than once. *I'm a manager at a large bank.* Jack must have been zoned out or purposefully blocking out the man's words and opting for spending more time in his head.

He started to speak again, and Jack remembered *why* he had zoned out. Hector's voice was monotone — the audible version of the color gray — and he knew the words were even less interesting.

Mr. Bolívar droned on, and Riley waited for a gap in the conversation. She leaned over to her parents. "Can me and Addy go sit with those other kids over there?" she asked. She plunged her head to the side, indicating they were supposed to look in that direction.

Jack flicked his eyes over and saw a gaggle of young teenagers laughing hysterically. He saw one of them cutting up a piece of shrimp with a fork, preparing to hand the pieces to the kid on his left, who had placed the fork strategically, his clenched fist hovering above it.

It didn't take much imagination to figure out what they were planning.

Jack followed this teenager's gaze as he plucked the piece of shrimp out of his friend's hand. Sure enough, two tables over, small specks of white and pink dotted the floor. The graveyard of chopped-up shrimp blobs from the makeshift shrimp fork cannon the kids had concocted.

Kate mouthed the word no, while Jack nodded yes.

Riley's smile widened, choosing her father's answer over her mother's, and Kate frowned at Jack. "What? They can't go —"

"It'll be fine," Jack said. "We're right here. They're bored out of their minds, anyway. Let them have a little fun."

Jack shifted and addressed his daughters. "But if that *fun* looks anything like throwing shrimp across the room, you're coming right back over here and hearing all about Mr. Bolívar's job again."

Kate's eyes widened slightly, but Mr. Bolívar didn't even seem to notice that Jack had used him as a potential punishment for his kids. Mr. Bolívar just stopped mid-sentence and addressed Riley. "Actually, if you're interested, there was this time I was traveling for work —"

"No-thanks-not-interested-bye," Riley spat off, rapid-fire. She had Addy's hand in hers and was all but yanking the smaller kid out of her chair. Mr. Bolívar's two children also stood up, looking at their mother.

Their mother nodded, and the four kids dashed off and grabbed chairs at the teenagers' table.

Taking advantage of the pause in the one-sided conversation, Kate reached under the table and squeezed Jack's knee. "I'm impressed," she said softly. "*I'm* usually the one letting our girls run off with people we don't know."

"Is that so?" Jack said, smiling.

Kate laughed. "Yeah. You seem a lot more... loose. Not that you're uptight or anything, but —"

"Yeah, you can just go ahead and say it," he said. "Honestly, no offense taken. I am pretty damn uptight."

"But after last night..." She eyed him with that same mischievous gaze she gave him yesterday at the climbing wall.

"Yes," he said enthusiastically. "After last night, I'm getting very *un*-uptight."

Kate laughed again, then took a bite of cheesecake. Her mouth full, she continued. "Well, if that's what it takes to get my husband nice and relaxed, I guess we'll just have to have a repeat showing tonight."

Jack nodded. "You know, I was thinking the same thing. And since I'm generally uptight *all* the time and pretty stressed *every* day, maybe we can make this a regular —"

"Nope," Kate said quickly. "This is a cruise-ship-only privilege. Back home, I expect full wooing."

CHAPTER 5
JACK

JACK AND KATE spent the remainder of the dinner feigning interest in Hector Bolívar's monologues and watching their oldest daughter flirt with the adolescent boys at the other table.

Hector eventually redirected his monologue toward his wife, whom Jack assumed was used to the verbal onslaught. It gave Jack and Kate some time to catch up.

It was only the second full day of the cruise, but he had to admit that the vacation was going far better than he'd imagined. He hadn't expected to have a *bad* time, but he had gotten the feeling that they would just be doing the same thing they did every other day of their lives: parenting children, trying to earn a brief break from the mundanities of everyday life and generally trying to appreciate the other one enough to not cause an issue.

Once they had gotten settled on board, he had expected Kate to lean in hard on the emotional state of their marriage, thinking she would try to open that can of worms. She was no therapist, but she enjoyed psychological discussions about relationships, human emotions, and everything related. It was a hobby for her, and her and Jack's marriage was a perfect specimen for study.

Jack loved her but didn't share her enthusiasm for the hobby. To him, a good marriage was one where the other was appreciated, shown love, and affirmed. Those things could happen any number of ways, and he felt as though as long as he was doing his best to learn all the new ways he could do those things toward Kate, he was doing a fine job.

So he was surprised that Kate had seemed to have reverted to her younger self instead of diving deep into and unpacking their relationship. She had always been spontaneous, fun-loving, and willing to endure a bit of danger just for the thrill of it. Her personality was almost exactly opposite to Jack's. Jack, as someone who had been brought up prim and proper by a military father and a stereotypical housewife, was much more reserved and calculating. He was interested in following rules because rules made things easier for everyone. He didn't want to cause trouble because it would only cause trouble for everyone. When he and Kate met, she drove him nuts, but he couldn't deny her ability to get anyone around her excited about trying something.

As it turned out, he couldn't deny her at all. About anything.

She had proverbially swept him off his feet, and fifteen years had passed in the blink of an eye. They had grown older, raised kids, and mostly enjoyed life together.

That said, they had also changed, and their marriage had started to stagnate a bit. They had grown wiser in some ways and still felt woefully under-prepared in other ways — namely, how to raise two little girls. And though they had stood together side-by-side through it all, Jack couldn't deny that they had grown apart.

He also couldn't deny that it was probably mostly his fault.

He had given himself to his job these past five years. With the girls getting a little older, Kate had expressed interest in working again, and though he knew she did miss working, he sensed it was about more than that. He sensed she wanted to rebalance the scales, that she wanted him to revert to the father he had been the first five years of Riley's life, attentive and present, able to balance work with home life as if it were a natural thing. Taking a job would force him to work fewer hours if only to be available for the kids.

They sat at the table a while longer and were about to call the kids over to leave, knowing that the staff would kick them out in a few minutes anyway to reset for the next dinner service. Kate tugged on his sleeve and pointed toward the front of the dining hall.

"Look," she said. "I think that's the captain."

"So what?" he asked.

"He's kinda cute," Kate said. "Like, I mean, he's older, but he's... sort of hot."

"Hey," Jack said, giving his voice enough inflection for Kate to know he was joking. Neither of the couple was the jealous type, thankfully. But it didn't mean Jack *wanted* his wife checking out other guys.

He couldn't disagree, though. The captain looked a bit like Rufus Sewell, and his salt-and-pepper beard gave him a bit of distinguished grit.

She laughed, then continued. "I'm kidding. But maybe

he'll come over here? Don't you think it's kind of cool when the captain of the *whole* ship comes down to the dining hall?"

He laughed. "Yep. He's like, 'let's go see what the peasants are doing.'"

She slapped his thigh under the table as the captain made the rounds near the entrance.

"And it's not like he's the *only* person driving the boat. I mean, he has a whole team of people just sitting around waiting for the opportunity to crash this hotel into the nearest rock structure."

"Oh, stop it," she said. "They're not going to crash into anything. They're like, trained and stuff. I think. And besides, there aren't any 'rock structures' in the middle of the Caribbean."

"Well, Cuba would like to have a word."

"Cuba doesn't count as a rock structure," Kate argued. "And we're nowhere near Cuba."

Jack watched the captain as he neared their table, stopping to glad-hand and say hello to all of the guests between them and the front doors of the dining hall.

Jack had seen this before, on their honeymoon cruise. The captain liked to make his guests feel at home. Sort of like how pilots used to come out into the cabin and give kids those little safety-pin wings.

He scoffed. "It's marketing. They all do this; they all try to make you think they are the most important person in the world, so you want their autograph and shit."

Kate slowly rolled her head around. "But he had to go to school to figure out how to drive a ship this size, right? It's a whole thing — the Merchant Marine Academy, I think."

Jack smiled. "Merchant Marine Academy — did you literally just Google 'how to become a cruise ship captain?'"

Her mouth fell open. "How dare you," she said jokingly.

In truth, Jack was a researcher — it was his nature. When she'd shown him the cruise options, he'd read up on *everything* related to it, including how much a cruise ship weighed, how much water they displaced, and — of course — who was in charge.

He knew more about cruise ships than he ever needed to know. Not that he would remember any of it a few weeks from now, but it was still nice to have a few trivial facts stored in his head during the trip. He couldn't help it — his father had been 'Mr. Trivia' all his life, annoying him and his brother with a million facts about random things no one cared about.

Jack watched the captain approach their table. He was wearing crisp whites, this Navy-style suit reminiscent of an actual naval captain. The details came into sharper focus the closer he got. The man looked tired, but his crisp blue eyes belied the rest of his face — sharp, present, and taking everything in.

He looked European. Deep-brown skin, hardened and weathered from years of sailing and being in the sun. The captain shook hands at every table he passed, sitting down for a brief moment at each — no longer than thirty seconds — before rising again and making his way toward Jack and Kate.

"He's coming over here," Kate said.

Jack shrugged. "He's got lots of tables to visit; he won't stay long."

"But we *are* right in the center of the room," she said. "Maybe he'll stay a bit longer here."

Jack frowned at his wife. "Why do you want to meet him

so bad?" he asked. "You want a picture with him or something?"

She giggled. "Oh, that's a great idea. You have your phone with you? Maybe he'll sit on my lap."

At this, Mr. Bolivar joined Jack in the eye roll.

CHAPTER 6
VICTOR

VICTOR ELIZONDO PACED across the floor of his stateroom, wishing there was more floor to pace across. He didn't need luxury, but when it was available, he opted for it. Initially, he had not thought he would need to be aboard the ship for very long — a day, at most.

But as he had prepared for this mission, he had decided that it was far easier to simply book a room like a normal passenger. It would require a fake passport and an alias, of course, but these things were easy to acquire for Victor.

But he had needed to be here, on the ship for the entirety of the cruise, for numerous reasons. Back home in Venezuela, he had a team of fantastic men — men he trusted to protect the cartel's interests. Men he trusted to protect *his* interests.

But this was not Venezuela; they were operating in enemy territory now. Most of his men in Venezuela had a mile-long rap sheet; some were even wanted internationally. He would not risk their lives — or this mission — by bringing them along. To that end, he had opted for newer recruits and a few more experienced men who would not flag international security databases. But he had never worked with many of them, so they would require closer observation.

Some of his men had military training, but in many instances, they had been discharged for aggressive behavior, not following orders, or simply not caring one way or another about the job.

He hated this the most, and it was why some of these younger cartel soldiers would forever stay at a low rank in his organization. He demanded loyalty and could be ruthless if he needed to obtain it. But he preferred men who already understood what they were fighting for — what the work meant.

Hired guns simply couldn't understand that. They were no more than human triggers.

Still, there were some advantages to having a handpicked crew made up of less-experienced members who *weren't* mercenaries — they could more easily blend in with the *actual* crew very well. They were smart enough to know that they would have to do both jobs for the first few days of the cruise so as not to elicit suspicion from anyone else. They each had different stories prepared, as well. According to the fake papers they'd used to come aboard, most of them had been assigned this ship from another ship in the Integrity Class fleet, while others claimed to be either new or in for just a summer job.

He knew that crew members of these cruise ships turned over regularly, which was by design. Wages were the most expensive line item on the balance sheet for these cruise companies, so they did everything they could to keep them as low as possible.

Victor paced around the space between the bed and the

wall three more times, thinking through the next phase of this journey. It aggravated him to no end that he had had to come and clean up this mess.

If it were up to him, he would not have come in the first place. As one of the top leaders of the Venezuelan *Vínculo* cartel, Victor Elizondo carried enough rank and power in the organization that he rarely had to do things as risky and exposed as this mission. There were plenty of lieutenants he controlled who would have killed for an opportunity like this one — one that would be in the public eye and almost guarantee a promotion.

But yet, he was *not* at the top. He still had to take orders just as much as he had to give them to those below him.

And the orders had come, and they were simple: *Book a cruise on this ship. Figure out where the shipments are going. Figure out who is stealing from me.*

The simplicity carried with it a certain weight. The leader of the *Vínculos* was not to be trifled with, and he did not dole out trust and responsibility on a whim. Victor had earned his way here, and he needed to prove himself still worthy of that honor.

So he needed to familiarize himself with the plan. Better than that — he needed to *internalize* the plan. It was his, but there were still a few details left hanging. He needed to ensure that those details would be taken care of and that contingencies were built in. No plan survived first contact with the enemy, and the element of surprise was only useful the first time.

He paced, not because he was worried about the plans failing, but because he needed to ensure that he had seen every last option. Every possible outcome, within reason, needed his mind's eye watching over it, working through options.

He *would not* fail.
To fail would mean death.

CHAPTER 7

JACK

"GOOD EVENING," the captain said upon reaching their table. "I'm Captain Phillips."

Kate snorted, covering her mouth with her hand a bit too late. Jack flashed her a glance that he hoped said, *'shut up right now.'*

The captain waved it off. "Don't worry about it," he said. "After the movie came out, it became a running gag around here. Besides, my name is *José* Phillips, so our last names are where the similarities end."

He was of course referring to the movie, based on a true story, called *Captain Phillips*, starring Tom Hanks.

"Well, you're both *captains*," Mr. Bolívar said. "That's a pretty big similarity."

"This is true," Captain Phillips said, somehow not appearing annoyed. "May I?" The captain motioned to the empty chair beside Jack, where one of Mr. Bolívar's children had been sitting earlier.

Jack nodded, then mumbled something unintelligible. He had tried to say, 'sure, no problem,' but he was so shocked that the captain would even *want* to sit down that the words came out discombobulated.

The captain sat, placing his cap on the table. He grasped Jack's shoulder and squeezed as he shook his hand again. Jack examined the man up close, focusing on his attire now. It sure *looked* real. He wondered if there was a special 'ship captain' store where one might acquire the naval-style whites.

"Oh, we get a special showing," Kate asked. "But don't you have to say hello to everyone?"

The captain glanced at Kate, his eyes moving up and down. It was a little lengthy of a glance for Jack's taste, but he didn't blame the captain for noticing how strikingly gorgeous his wife was.

"Well," the captain said. "I *am* supposed to meet as many people as I can. Our passengers are our business." He winked. "However, building real relationships with our customers, like you all, is also important. I like to meet the people who have taken such good care of us over the years," he said.

Jack almost rolled his eyes. It sounded like such a hokey canned marketing response, although he suspected there was truth to the statement. He had read that the captain of a cruise ship was like the CEO of a large company. Hundreds of staff and crew were aboard, each part of one of three departments: Engine, Hotel, or Deck. Each of those three departments had its own director, and each of these directors reported directly to the head honcho — the man seated next to him now.

He had assumed that captaining a cruise ship likely involved more than just steering a big wheel and shouting out, 'full steam ahead' or something like that, but he had been shocked to learn that the captain had their fingers in just about every aspect of the ship.

And the captain's position wasn't just a figurehead position, either. The man had probably graduated from a four-year maritime university, then spent the next fifteen to twenty years working up the ranks, hoping to be in the right place at the right time to land the coveted role of captaining this vessel.

From what Jack had read, the job seemed harder to get than trying to become a brain surgeon, and the pay was not nearly as good. He had seen stats before they left and was shocked to learn that cruise ship captains made anywhere from only $100,000 to $150,000 per year, depending on the size of the boat, their expertise and experience, and how generous the cruise company they worked for wanted to be. It was good money, but Jack could think of five better-paying jobs for the work and dedication involved.

"I hope you all have been enjoying your time so far," the captain said, phrasing it like a question.

Mr. and Mrs. Bolivar nodded quickly, like good students. "Oh yes — oh yes," Mr. Bolívar said. "We *love* cruises. We don't get to embark on them as often as we like, considering my job as a manager at a — "

"We're having a great time," Kate said, smiling as she cut off Mr. Bolívar. "We're sort of celebrating our fifteenth anniversary, actually," she added.

Jack frowned at her. *Why offer all this information?* he wondered. *Are you hoping he'll have a chocolate cake put on our bed?* He knew it had been an option when booking the cruise, but he had opted to save the money — they'd have plenty of cake every night after dinner.

And it's not technically *our fifteen-year-anniversary cruise,* he thought. *It's a fix-our-fifteen-year-marriage cruise.*

"That is absolutely wonderful," Captain Phillips said. "I

celebrated my own twenty-fifth anniversary with my lovely wife last month. She was able to come with me on a five-day cruise to the Bahamas. And before you ask, no, I did not have to drive."

They all laughed, but Jack felt Mr. Bolivar's was genuine.

"I've always wondered," Kate said, leaning toward Captain Phillips. "What's... uh, *down* there? Like, in the crew quarters?"

Captain Phillips frowned, then smiled. "What do you mean? There are rooms, much like yours. And there is a crew mess hall, some recreation rooms, and a gym." He paused, now addressing the rest of the table. "To be honest, I don't get down there as much as I would like."

"I mean, are there like... *secret* hallways?"

Jack shook his head and smiled. Kate had always had a flair for the dramatic. She loved secret passageways and hidden rooms. She loved to fantasize about what might be tucked away, out of sight of the general public. It was part of the reason Jack had wanted to plan a Europe trip that involved a lot of castle-hopping — castles were the perfect example of secretive, ancient places, and they would allow her imagination to run wild.

Captain Phillips laughed louder, a guttural chuckle that was infectious. "No," he said. "I'm afraid not. The ship is well-mapped, and while the crew decks are off-limits to our passengers — for safety reasons, of course — you can see a cutaway view of the entire ship in our gift shop."

And you can buy *one for the low price of one million dollars,* Jack wanted to add.

Jack was about to force himself to engage in more small talk when he noticed two men rushing toward the captain.

They wore all black, and they were clearly part of the crew or staff. They hustled over, and one whispered into the captain's ear, making sure to do it on the side of the captain away from Jack so he couldn't hear. The captain's stoic expression never faltered, but he stood and shook Jack's hand once more.

"I do apologize," the captain said, clearing his throat. "I must attend to something somewhere else. I am truly sorry to cut off our conversation."

"That's okay," Mr. Bolívar said from across the table. "I know how it is, you know? Being busy and everything. I can't seem to get a minute to myself at work, either! Go steer the ship away from the iceberg!"

At this, Jack actually *did* roll his eyes. It seemed the captain shared his disdain for Bolívar's joke as he stared at Bolívar for an extra second, blinking, before turning away and walking briskly out of the room, the two staffers on either side of him like professional bodyguards.

"Really, Hector?" Mrs. Bolivar said, nudging her husband with her elbow. "A *Titanic* joke? In the middle of the Caribbean?"

Bolívar shrugged. "It was just a joke," he said.

Kate squeezed Jack's knee, and he looked up at his wife. The mischievous look in her eye had returned.

"What's up?" he asked, almost afraid to hear the answer.

"Oh, nothing," she whispered. "Just... the whole *Titanic* thing gives me an idea."

Jack rolled his eyes again and let out a sigh. "Well, I can't wait to hear this."

CHAPTER 8

JACK

"KATE, COME ON," Jack said. "We can't leave them alone!"

Kate made a face. "*You* come on. They're old enough now. And they're asleep!"

"That's part of the problem," Jack said. "What if they wake up, and we're gone? They'll freak out. Addy will lose her *mind*."

Kate ignored Jack, and he chased her down the hall. They had left their room, 'just to get a drink,' Kate had explained.

He had begrudgingly gone along because — well, hell, because they were on a *cruise*. It was like being in an airport: the normal rules didn't apply. 8 AM on a Tuesday? Grab a drink!

But he had assumed they would *just* grab a drink at the bar nearest to their room, a poolside cabana-style bar and grill open all night. It was only a hundred feet away from the exit at the end of their hallway, so they wouldn't even need to take an elevator to get there.

But Kate, as usual, had other plans. She wanted to do something *fun,* and that always meant it would be something that would cause undue anxiety for Jack. He didn't understand why *he* had to suffer whenever Kate wanted to be spontaneous. Why couldn't they *spontaneously* just order room service and watch a horror movie?

He reached the end of the hallway Kate had led them to, drink in hand. There were two 'pretty and fruity' drinks Kate had wanted to try at the bar, which were her two compulsory purchase keywords, so they stayed for one drink, then ordered the second. Kate had sworn she would not leave the first drink mug behind — it was a 'collector's item,' according to her — but Jack had not said anything when she'd done just that.

The bartender had tried to remind him, but Jack had waved it off — there was no room in their suitcases to pack the stupid gigantic plastic mugs, anyway. The bartender laughed, then winked at Jack knowingly as they left, Kate pulling him back toward their room greedily.

But they *hadn't* gone back to their room. She'd pulled him to the elevator, and they had descended to Deck 3, the lowest accessible deck to passengers. Now, she was on the hunt.

"Kate, come on. What's the plan?"

"There doesn't *need* to be a plan, honey." She turned and smiled at him, then kissed him. "That's part of the problem."

"The *problem*?" he asked. "What the hell does that mean?"

She shook her head. "Sorry, I didn't mean — you know what? Never mind, I *did* mean it. *You. You're —*"

"*I'm* the problem?"

"No, I mean *you* always need a plan!" she said. "Why? I mean, we could plan all of this out, and you know the first time I go off-script, you'll freak out, but you'll follow along. We *never* stick to the plan."

Jack started to heat up. "And that's because you *refuse* to stick to the plan! You *have* to do things your way."

She raised an eyebrow, daring him to step into the grave he had just dug.

"Look," he said. "I mean, I'm sorry. I don't mean 'your way,' really. It's just... we're two different people. We want different things. Right?"

"I don't know that we do, Jack."

He took a long, well-needed sip of his piña colada. It was on the strong side, and judging by the wink he'd received from the bartender, he wasn't sure if it meant the guy had been rooting for him to score with his wife or if the bartender was trying to hint at him scoring with *Jack*.

"Yeah, that's fair," he said. "We're on the same page. We always have been. With the big stuff — kids, finances, our future. But our personalities are different. That's why we're here, right?"

"Here?"

"On this cruise, Kate. We're here to figure *this* stuff out. We're different enough that it's become a problem, right?"

She frowned, thinking for a moment before answering. "Yeah, I think that's about right. But you know what? As soon as I stepped foot on deck, I realized that only the big stuff matters. We're together *because* we're different, in spite of it. We work *really* well together, Jack."

He stopped, taking a step back. He smiled. "Yeah, I feel that, too. But... why go through all this trouble, then? Why'd we spend four grand on a cruise vacation if you realized we're good immediately upon getting here?"

She laughed. "Oh, we are *not* 'good,' we're just 'going to be okay.' I just realized when I got here that this trip isn't going to be something we'll use to dig into the things that are *wrong* with our marriage — 'cause there aren't that many, honestly. We'll use this time to get to know each other again. And that will help us remember the *good* things about our marriage because *those* greatly outnumber the bad things."

Jack's smile grew. "Whew," he said. "I honestly thought you were just waiting to corner me and read me some new *Psychology Today* article you found. And then we'd have to discuss it and figure out how we 'manifest our insecurities,' or something like that."

"Actually... I did bring some magazines with me. You'd *love* this one article about —"

"Hard pass."

She giggled again and then leaned in for another kiss. "Look, Jack. Every marriage has problems. But I realized that *all* of ours seem to stem from us just not really *being together* a lot lately. I miss you. *We* miss you."

"Yeah, I miss you guys, too."

"So there's no ulterior motive. I just wanted to do something that *forced* you to be away from work long enough to remember *why* you work in the first place."

A door slammed at the opposite end of the hall, and the elevator dinged at the same time. Two staffers stumbled out of the opening doors. "This... isn't... our floor," the first one said, a thick South American accent making it difficult to understand him.

They were obviously drunk, and the second one, no more than a kid, smacked his hand against the wall to hold himself up. "Yes... yeah... man. Yeah, this is... us."

He burped, then collapsed just outside of a room.

The other guy, a bit older than the kid, just shook his head.

"Okay, bro... your funeral. Victor's... gonna... gonna kill you. I'm not... waiting around for that."

He turned, performing an inebriated one-eighty, and returned to the still-open elevator doors.

When they finally closed, the hallway once again quiet, Kate looked up at Jack.

The eyes are back, he realized. "Kate — what are you about to do?"

"I said there was no ulterior motive coming down here," she said. "But that was a lie. The universe just made it very clear that I now *do* have an ulterior motive. I can go find another mug. The one I left back at the bar!"

Jack was surprised she even remembered this.

She started toward the passed-out kid.

"Kate... no," Jack said. "Let's get back to the room. We can ask the bartender tomorrow; I'm sure he'll remember us. The girls —"

"The girls are fine," she insisted. She crouched down and felt around the kid's side. Suddenly her hand shot upward, triumphantly. In it, Jack could see a keycard.

"This'll get us to the lower levels," she said enthusiastically. "And then, *anywhere* we want to go. And I can find a *different* mug. You know... you know they have different mugs *each day?*"

Jack groaned.

"Come on, honey," she said. "It'll be *fun*. I didn't think we'd get this lucky. I want to explore! And earlier, when I said I wanted to find a car and recreate that *Titanic* scene? I meant it. "

Jack scoffed. "Right..."

"Hey, Kate *and* Leo were in that scene, remember? So I won't be having *all* of the fun."

He shook his head but walked toward Kate, who was now nearing the elevator with her prized find clenched tightly in her hand.

She turned to Jack, dropping her pretty, fruity drink to her side. She immediately turned on the 'doe eyes' look that made his knees weak.

"Jack?" she asked. "Will you be my Leo?"

CHAPTER 9
JACK

THEY HAD NOT FOUND a car yet, but their search was not over.

So far, the lowest of the two crew- and staff-only decks seemed completely devoid of life. They had seen a few black-clad service staff hustling through the forward port-side hall-way, but Jack and Kate had been able to duck behind a tower of what looked like airline food service carts to stay out of sight.

Kate had poked around, looking for the 'secret passageway' she just *knew* the captain had lied about, but had come up empty-handed.

Jack was getting tired and knew the alcohol was getting to his wife's head. She was getting *handsy*, and while he was indeed benefiting from that handsiness, he didn't want to be caught in the crew-only area with his pants down. Literally.

"Just a few more minutes," she said, her words starting to slur a bit.

Kate had always been a lightweight, and in their younger years, it had made these cruises a *lot* of fun. They always paid extra for the all-inclusive drink and beverage packages, and while these days — like the food — it wasn't *truly* all-inclusive, it was a worthwhile expense.

Kate fell to the side, leaning heavily on Jack. He pulled her in, looking down at her and noticing her chest rising and falling steadily as she breathed.

Let's get you back to the room... he thought, the idea of it only exciting him more. It would be a tricky play, getting her back while she was still awake enough to... do stuff.

"Let's look over there," she said, suddenly wide-awake and bouncing across the hallway toward a door marked *Theatre Access*.

"No, let's not," Jack said. "I think we should start heading back."

But Kate already had the keycard up and on the lock. It clicked, flashing a tiny green LED light, and she pulled it open.

"After you, handsome."

He groaned. *We better not get caught,* he thought. He didn't think they would kick them off the boat — they weren't stealing or doing anything wrong. But... rules. They weren't supposed to be here, and he didn't want to explain himself to the friendly captain they had just met.

Plus, his wife was a bit on the *intoxicated* side. *If she gets close to the 'kinda hot' captain now...*

He pushed the thought away as Kate pushed him into the room. It was dark, but there was enough light coming in from the open door to see that they were in some sort of antechamber. Like a green room for a stage, which is probably exactly what it was.

The door had said *Theater Access,* after all.

He stopped and waited, but Kate was already moving past him toward a door standing open on the opposite side of the room. She walked through, not a care in the world about getting caught.

For a moment, Jack wasn't annoyed — he just wished he had some of her ridiculous confidence.

He knew his wife could turn on the charm and get them out of any situation they might get into. A cute, short girl like her usually had no problem brown-nosing whatever authority figure wanted to get them in trouble. Add to that they were on a cruise ship and alcohol was involved, and Jack had no doubt she'd be able to get them out of trouble, scot-free.

"All right, Kate," Jack said. "That's far enough. It's getting late; we should get back to..."

He stopped as he crossed the threshold into the next room. Kate was there, standing in the doorway, staring.

He, too, stared. They had entered a bigger room — not the theater they were supposedly accessing, but another antechamber of sorts. Where before the room was closet-sized, this one was the size of a gymnasium.

And all along the walls, stacked to the ceiling of the two-story room, were crates.

"What are they?" Kate asked.

She was swaying, and Jack was sure she was just staring straight ahead because her mind was not quite working properly at the moment — she wasn't stunned to see the crates here because she didn't *know* they were here. If he had to guess, she was probably seeing double and had simply stopped in the doorway because if she'd moved forward, she'd have fallen on her face.

"No idea," Jack said. "But let's get you back to the room."

"I want to check..." she burped. "Check them out."

"No, Kate. We don't need to check out the crates —"

She darted off, running, somehow still upright, and reached the first crate she could find. It was metal, but with a wooden top. She pulled the heavy lid back a bit, the alcohol in her system making it a humorous affair for Jack.

He watched, shaking his head. "What's in it?" he asked. He was not curious; he just wanted to prove to her that it was nothing of concern.

Kate backed away and frowned. "G — guns," she said.

"Wait, what? Guns?"

She nodded, pulling the lid back in place. "Yep, full of guns." She laughed as she walked back over to Jack. "Lots and lots of guns."

Jack rolled his eyes and shook his head.

"What do you think is... is in the rest of them?" Kate asked.

"Just... stuff. They're all full of *stuff*, Kate. They're crates on a cruise ship, so they're probably all full of 'cruise ship juice.'"

"What's 'cruise ship juice?'" she asked, her words starting to slur together.

He sighed. "It's... nothing. I'm just making a joke. Like gas, or food, or whatever a cruise ship eats to keep moving."

She laughed, a slow chuckle at first, then a full-on belly laugh. She hiccupped in the middle of it and fell backward.

...right into Jack's waiting arms. *Perfect catch*, he thought, silently high-fiving himself. "Come on, babe. Let's get you up to the room."

She made a disgusted face, but her eyes were closed. *Window of opportunity is quickly shutting*, he thought. He pulled her back into the smaller room.

"I don't... I don't *wanna* go back."

"No?" he said. "But I have something I want to show you."

She let herself be carried over the threshold and into the hallway once more. "Show me?" she asked, frowning, still with her eyes closed. "Like... what is it?"

He chuckled. "You'll just have to trust me."

"What... *is it*... Jack? Are you being gross? Will I like it?"

Yeah, but I'll like it more, he thought, grinning. "Yeah, I think so. Come on."

He pulled her to the side, reaching the same tower of food carts they'd hidden behind before. Just as they reached them, Jack heard an elevator opening.

He yanked Kate around the back of the tower once again. "Hey —" she started.

He clamped his hand over her mouth. "Shh, stop talking for a sec," he said. "We've got company."

For her part, Kate stopped talking, opting instead to completely fall asleep that exact second. He grunted as her full weight fell into his hands, nearly losing his balance. He hoped she wouldn't snore — she didn't normally, but alcohol made things weird.

They stayed silent as the three people exiting the elevator walked past them. They were in a hurry, discussing something quietly. He watched them a bit, trying to push the buzz away so he could focus. They all had darker skin than his, but still were all different shades. One man had freckles covering most of his skin and looked at least twenty years older than the second-oldest person. All of them were men, and their eyes darted left-to-right as they walked, as if looking for something.

They spoke in Spanish — he heard the words *shipment* and *delivery* a couple of times, but the rest of the conversation was too quiet for him to make out the details.

Weird, he thought. *What delivery are they waiting on in the middle of the ocean?*

They would reach Jamaica some time overnight, he knew, so perhaps they would be docking and receiving a delivery then? More food, perhaps? Or alcohol?

Still, it seemed strange — these cruise lines had a very good idea of how much to pack to keep their thousands of passengers sated and happy, so he couldn't imagine that they *already* needed a refill. But whatever, he told himself — he didn't run a cruise ship.

The three men turned a sharp left and headed straight for the door Jack and Kate had just left. *Theater Access.* They opened it and disappeared inside. One of the men raised his voice now that they were out of the hallway, and Jack thought he could make out a few of these words, still in Spanish.

"...Going to kill him..."

Hmm, Jack thought. *That guy seemed pissed about something. One of their crewmates must have messed up. Sucks for them.*

He waited a moment longer, then lifted Kate's now-lifeless form and forced her to walk toward the elevator. As they rose back to their own deck, he wondered what cruise ship discipline entailed.

CHAPTER 10
JACK

JACK WOKE THE NEXT MORNING, mildly annoyed. Kate had not exactly *promised* him anything, but he had dragged her back to their room after their romp belowdecks with the intention of messing around a little bit — and, maybe, hopefully, letting it lead to something more.

And she *had* told him she would be relaxed, implying that much fun would be had after the kids were asleep.

Instead, he had plopped her onto her side of the bed, where she had immediately rolled over and started snoring. He had just let out a deep sigh and gotten into bed as well, deciding to give up the fight and read a bit before falling asleep.

When she woke up, she immediately apologized, but her focus was on getting the kids to their program. They were currently walking across Deck 10, the kids in tow. Riley, always an early riser, had been annoyed that her parents were only just starting to come to at 7:30.

Kate pulled up next to Jack as they walked. "I know you're mad," she said from behind dark-tinted sunglasses. "I'll make it up to you, I promise."

Jack raised his eyebrows, smiling. "Yeah? Not sure I trust you. Only *two* of those 'pretty fruity' drinks, and you were *beyond* gone."

She slapped his chest as they walked across the expansive deck to deposit the kids in their program for the morning.

"It wasn't *those* two drinks," she said. "It was those two drinks, *plus* the three I had at dinner, *plus* the bottle of wine we shared on the deck, *plus* —"

"I get it, I get it," Jack said, laughing. Riley was walking with Addy about fifteen feet in front of them, clearly trying to get to the drop-off location in a hurry. She kept turning back and motioning for her parents to speed up, but Jack enjoyed the leisurely pace. He hadn't gone overboard last night, but he had definitely gotten a bit buzzed. Enough to enjoy himself, but these days it meant his body would complain about it the next morning.

The plan was to drop the kids off at their area and return to the room for a couple of hours of napping.

Or... something else.

He was tired, and he was sure Kate could use a couple more hours of sleep as well, but he had not-so-subtlety dropped the hint that she could 'make it up to him' after they ditched the kids.

Many of the ship's passengers were lined up like cattle at 'muster,' waiting to be siphoned out into one of the barges that would take them the rest of the way to the Jamaican shore. They had reached port last night, but in this case, Jack had been amused to learn that 'port' only meant 'anchored in the middle of the bay.' Since their ship was one of a few in the world's largest cruise ship class, the Jamaican port on this side of the island nation could not handle docking it ashore like the rest of the ships.

Jack and Kate knew the drill from a handful of cruises they'd been on before. Passengers flocked to the muster stations moments before the doors opened, causing a hectic mad dash to the shore, where they would spend the day. Jack and Kate hated the crowds, so they often waited an hour or two before disembarking.

And they also knew the best way to handle excursions: to not do any officially sanctioned ones at all. Rather than pay an exorbitant premium to the cruise company for something they could buy separately, they had opted to only do a couple of hand-picked excursions for the girls, and none of them would be on the island of Jamaica. Instead, here they wanted to shop and hang out at the beach. Since they would be docked at port all day, they had plenty of time to do just that.

It was 8 a.m., so there was no rush to get down to muster, just to wait in the ever-lengthening queue.

Kate grabbed Jack's hand and held it as they walked toward the Deck 10 kids' drop-off zone. Addy's and Riley's excitement was electric. It made sense that Addy would be excited — she had been placed in a group she'd immediately hit it off with, and didn't have to hang out with her sister or parents all day. She felt safe but could also enjoy time with new friends her age.

On the other hand, Riley was usually against any adult-mandated fun. Typical for her age, so Jack had been surprised to see how quickly she was moving toward the drop-off and check-in area.

But Kate had explained earlier exactly why their oldest daughter was in such a hurry. "There's a boy…" she had said.

Jack nodded in understanding but silently hoped he could

get an eye on this boy while dropping his daughters off. He was sure there was no harm in an eleven-year-old's summer fling, but a dad had to be a dad.

As they walked, Kate seemed to sense this in Jack, and she turned to him. "You're not going to, uh, *talk* to this boy, are you?"

"Ha," Jack laughed. "Riley's eleven! What's the harm? It's not like it's a real fling or anything."

Kate arched an eyebrow. "Actually... he's thirteen."

"Thirteen! What? I didn't — so *that's* why she didn't tell me!"

Kate giggled. "It's fine, honey. She's growing up, and like you said, it's not like this is a *real* fling. Just..."

"Just, what?" Jack asked.

"Just don't be weird."

They reached the check-in station, and one of the older counselors, a guy named Darek, gave Riley and Addison a high five. Riley rolled her eyes at the guy, but she returned the high-five nonetheless.

"Me?" Jack said. "Weird? I'm not going to be weird."

"Bye, Mom! Bye, Dad!" Riley and Addy said in unison. They dashed off behind the counselor, who was still scribbling their names on a sheet of paper. They disappeared down the hallway and to the left, where the main meeting hall for all the kids was located.

"Guess you missed your opportunity to be weird," Kate said smugly.

"I wasn't going to be weird!"

With a wave toward the counselor and a quick "have a nice day," they left the station and started walking back across Deck 10. Deck 10 was the largest of the open-air decks, stretching from the fore to the aft of the ship. Two towers of smaller decks were stacked up near the front and back of the boat, going up to Deck 17 in the front and Deck 15 in the back.

On their first day on board, they had taken a quick jaunt around each of the upper decks, mostly to show Riley and Addison, who had never cruised before, what a cruise ship was all about. They had seen the Deck 12 spa and gym, as well as the stairs leading up to the bridge. On the back half of the ship, Decks 10 through 12 were exclusively for kids, and the whole area acted like a cruise-within-a-cruise. Three full decks just for children and adolescent passengers, separated into age-based groups.

The setup made it seem like the kids' own little paradise. Inside, flanking each side of these back decks were two gigantic movie theaters, one inside for when it rained, and one partially open-air. Aside from these entertainment options were multiple mini-golf courses, food options, and even a makeshift mall-like shopping center for older kids.

"So," Jack said. "Back to the room?"

Kate laughed, leaning into him as they walked. "You mean for a *nap*, right? Because you're *so tired?*"

"Yes, definitely. A nap. *That's* what I'm excited about."

And that's when he heard the *boom* of a far-off explosion.

WHAT THE HELL WAS THAT? Victor wondered.

A moment ago, a heavy-sounding *boom* rattled through the walls of Victor's suite. It seemed to have come from the ship, far down below.

He turned to his right-hand man, Raul. They shared a two-bedroom suite with a connecting door between them. At the moment, Victor and Raul had been mapping out the next phase of their plan, ensuring everything was in place for when the moment was right.

But right now, the moment was *not* right.

"Did you hear that?" Raul asked.

Victor nodded, but he was looking toward the door of his room.

"It sounded like —"

"An explosion," Victor said.

"Was it ours?"

Victor shook his head. *It had better not be.* He shook his head faster, trying to push the negative thoughts out. *No, we remain in control either way.* "If it was, we will hear about it very soon. Do you have men on Decks 1 and 2?"

Raul nodded. "Yes, of course. Should I have them contact you?"

"No, we cannot take the risk of having them blow their cover. They are not trained as well, and I do not want anyone asking any questions."

He felt the ship shift beneath his feet. Up here on the forward section of Deck 13, he could feel little other than the gently swaying of the ship as it moored in the bay. Since the Jamaican waters during this time of year were incredibly still, it was as though he were simply standing in a hotel room on land.

"I can run down and check myself," Raul said. As Raul, like each of Victor's other men, was working as a crewmember onboard the *Ocean Voyager*, he had a job as a line cook for the executive officers. It was one of the best jobs on board, as it was a consistently small cast to cook for and included plenty of time off.

But Victor had placed Raul there not because of his cooking skills — he had none — but because by having an inside man in the officers' mess, he could keep his eye on the real target: Captain José Phillips.

Captain Phillips was a man Victor needed to keep close watch over, but he did not want to raise suspicion just yet. Victor had a job to do, and he could not babysit the *Ocean Voyager's* esteemed and capable captain.

"No," Victor said, shaking his head. "It's early. Let's wait and see what happens. There is nothing to do now but wait."

"But sir, if it was —"

"If it *was* ours, then the damage has been done. Our time-line may be advanced, but the plan remains the same. Besides, we only invite more work for ourselves by investigating early. There will be crew looking into it, so we can simply check the internal feeds and stay informed."

Raul did not seem convinced.

"I know you trust me, Raul," Victor said. "I need you to believe that trust now. This does not change our ultimate plans or goals, no matter what happens. We are still ahead of schedule, but even if this does slow us down, *we* hold all the cards."

Or at least, we will, he thought.

"Yes, that is correct, sir," Raul said. "Of course."

"And don't worry — I know fear of the unknown is common, but remember: we *still* hold the element of surprise. I intend to hold that for as long as possible."

"Even if our method of revealing that surprise is now gone?"

Victor smiled. "This was not supposed to be our surprise, Raul. This was merely the *catalyst*. If we are now forced into motion, so be it. What are they going to do? Stop us?"

"Of course not, sir."

"Right. For now, the best we can do is wait. We will get news of what this is all about from both the crew and our men. The only thing we need to do is prepare for a contingency. To ensure we can move forward, no matter what may have changed."

"Anything you need me to do?" Raul asked.

Victor thought for a moment. At first, he began to tell his lieutenant no, that there was nothing to worry about. But then he paused and looked at Raul.

"Yes," he said. "Yes, I think there might be something you can check into for me."

Raul waited.

"If there was foul play, I need to know who it is. I want to know *immediately* if another faction on this ship is working against our mission."

"Right, yes."

"Find them and kill them."

CHAPTER 12

JACK

"JACK, WHAT WAS THAT?" Kate asked. Jack didn't respond. He was busy watching everyone else on deck and their response.

He knew he hadn't imagined it — it *had been* an explosion, he was sure — but it felt somewhat validating to see that everyone else had felt it and heard it as well.

A couple wearing only swimsuits lounging on chairs near the pool in front of him started looking around anxiously and whispering. Two others on the far side of the pool jumped up and began walking toward the ship's edge.

He looked at the water in the small pool. It was sloshing up and over the edge, lapping on the deck. A large man holding a drink was frowning into the water as if the source of the boom had come from the bottom of the pool itself.

"Jack..."

Jack stepped forward now, following the couple walking toward the edge. Kate was there by his side, though she had stopped speaking. He thought he heard a scream or a shout from somewhere else, perhaps on one of the lower decks? It sounded faint and muffled, and he couldn't be sure it was not a scream of joy. Perhaps a kid in another pool on another deck.

The kids. He felt his heart race, his fatherly instincts kicking in and clouding his judgment.

Everything is fine, he told himself. *There was an accident somewhere belowdecks, but they'll get it under control.*

More people were gathering along the edge of the ship, on both sides of Deck 10 now. Jack and Kate reached the port-side railing and peered over.

There was nothing to see but water and the bright white side of the ship's hull.

He heard others talking amongst themselves, wondering what had happened and hoping everyone was okay. He felt himself calming down then, forcing his training to kick in and let his mind clear enough to operate properly. The CIA didn't employ only operatives — spies — but they *did* insist upon a certain fitness level in all their officers. And they did a great job training their employees to handle the real issues: the *psychological* ones.

Jack was no super-soldier, but he had done a brief stint in the Army, moving to the CIA immediately after and landing a cushy desk job at the DO. Thanks to his Army mindset and the attitude at Langley, he kept his body in near-perfect shape and often sparred with other officers in the massive gym beneath their office. He knew hand-to-hand combat, kept his weapons training up-to-date, and generally tried his best to stay healthy.

But he was also *very* well-trained in handling his own psyche. He meditated daily, got plenty of sleep, and never stopped trying to improve his mental acuity.

He needed these skills now, if only to supersede his instincts.

Kate weaved her hand through his arm and pulled him close to her. He knew she was experiencing the same thoughts. *We need to find the kids. We need to make sure they're okay. I know they're okay, but I just need to see them...*

He turned back to look at the open deck and was about to recommend they walk over to the kids' area — if only to prove to themselves that everything was perfectly fine and that their kids were having a normal, fun day. With any luck, the kids hadn't even heard whatever had caused the explosion and were wrapped up in their own game, movie, or whatever else they were doing.

Kate had turned around with him as if on cue, probably knowing what he was thinking as well. Before they could begin to move, a surge of people appeared from the cafeteria just beyond the set of double doors on this side of the deck. Throngs of people began bumping into him and Kate, pressing them back against the railing.

He heard Kate suck in a sharp breath of air and noticed that she had gotten elbowed by an overzealous flip-flop-wearing old man with a towel wrapped around his waist. Jack pulled Kate closer, trying to help her, but realized he had only made it worse as they had now given up those few inches of precious space they'd previously been using. They were compressed down even more as people continued surging around them.

"Come on, guys," he said. "What the hell?" But no one reacted.

He heard shouts from the mob: "What's down there?" "I don't know!" "Nothing, everyone needs to just chill the hell out."

A kid, probably eight or nine years old, began crying, and Jack saw that he had become separated from his mother. He pressed into the crowd, starting to feel frustrated and out of control, and peeled apart a group of college kids. They didn't want to move out of his way at first, so he started pressing more forcefully. One of them responded to his behavior with an obscenity and a quick "Hey, man!" but Jack didn't care. He reached the kid, still dragging Kate behind him, and grabbed the young boy's hand.

"Hey, bud," he said. "It's okay. I see your mom."

The kid looked up at Jack with huge eyes, pleading. He spun the kid around and pushed him gently through the group of people that had caused him to get separated from his mother. Thankfully, the people there seemed to finally understand what had happened and moved out of the way as best they could.

But the wall of human life still grew denser as everyone had to see what was going on for themselves.

"I think I felt the deck shift again," he heard a girl say.

Another responded. "No, you're just imagining things. Everything is completely fine!"

"Yeah, that's why we heard a damn *explosion*, idiot."

The boy's mother, already growing frantic, pulled the boy in and lifted him awkwardly. He was too tall to be held, but Jack understood the natural instinct well. Satisfied he had done his good deed for the day — and had gotten his fill of looking at nothing, he kept moving in that same direction: away from all the people.

People were curious animals, and there was nothing more curious than an explosion on a cruise ship.

Kate didn't argue as he pulled her along; the longer they were stuck in this mob, the more anxious both of them would become. He pulled her through the still-open doors of the cafeteria. A few people were still eating, apparently the type of people who simply could not bother to be interrupted while eating. And across the sprawling cafeteria, he saw groups of crew and staff, wearing either all-black or all-white depending on which category of staff member they fell into, all huddled together in pairs or threes.

"Something *did* happen," Jack mumbled.

"What?"

Jack shook his head to help clear his thoughts. "I said, something definitely happened. The crew is trying to figure it out, too. Look."

"Do you think —"

He nodded quickly. "Yes, of course. The kids are fine." The words came out perhaps too harshly, but he had wanted to assuage his own fears as much as hers. "They're tucked away on the back of the ship in their zone. Whatever that was, it came from down below."

"How do you know?"

"I don't know for sure," Jack said. "But it *had* to have been from down there. I felt the ship vibrate and rock a little bit, but if it was from up here, we would have seen something. Windows blowing out, smoke, something. It seemed so far away."

He pulled Kate through the cafeteria and to the doors on the opposite side. He hoped the mob of people on the starboard side of the deck was at least starting to disperse.

"Yeah, that makes sense," Kate said. "I definitely felt it, too. It really did feel like it was from far away. Maybe it wasn't even on the ship at all?"

Jack shrugged. "I guess it could have been something underwater. Seems like that would feel about the same to us all the way up here. But still, there's nothing out here except water. We're twenty minutes by boat from the Jamaican coast, so if an explosion took place on the island that was big enough for us to feel out *here*, we would have seen something over the *land* — smoke or whatever."

The ship groaned; a shredding sound grated on Jack's ears. He moved his hand to hold on to Kate's instead of keeping her arm wrapped through his, and together they stepped out onto the ship's starboard side. The groaning noise continued; five full seconds of noise and even the patrons still chowing down inside stopped and frowned at one another. At the very end of the groaning noise, the ship listed to the side a bit. Jack felt his stomach fall and his feet lose their place on the deck.

A whole new slew of screams rose simultaneously as people and crew members alike fell, smacked into walls or each other, or reacted to the terrifying feeling of weightlessness.

The movement ended only a second after, but Jack looked up and down the ship and then back at his wife. "Kate, am I crazy? The ship looks like it's tilting to the side."

She nodded, wide-eyed, still looking out over the water on the starboard side toward the island of Jamaica. "No, you're definitely *not* crazy. Look."

She pointed down and out, and Jack saw a huge ripple, like an underwater zipper, running the length of the ship moving outward. It was a small wave that could only have been caused by the ship's movement — the rest of the Jamaican bay was pristine, still. He watched the wave recede into the distance, then heard another groan as the ship moved again.

He squeezed Kate's hand, not wanting to state the inevitable, but knowing he had to say it.

"Kate, the ship is sinking."

KATE FELT bile rising in her throat. "Oh, my God. Oh, my God." She repeated the words a few more times, unable to help herself.

She tried to calm her nerves by closing her eyes and gripping the railing. Thankfully the masses of people along this side of Deck 10 were broken up much more evenly, and they didn't have to pass through a veritable mob to reach the railing.

She dropped Jack's hand, preferring the hot, hard railing of the ship.

"It's okay," Jack said, his voice calm. "It's going to be okay. We just need —"

"We're going to get the kids," Kate said, pulling her hands off the railing. She had not meant to snap at him — he had not done anything wrong, of course. But her emotions were starting to get the best of her.

She took a few more deep breaths and repeated her mantra silently in her head. *Oh my God, oh my God...*

"Look, I could be wrong," Jack said, shrugging again. "I don't know anything about ships other than what I researched before we came aboard. Maybe that *was* it — maybe it *was* an explosion, for whatever reason, and it let in some water. But they have, like, blast doors and stuff. They can just shut down certain compartments, right?"

Kate shook her head. She hadn't wanted to admit it, but when Jack uttered the fateful words, she knew them to be true. "No, Jack. You're right. The ship *is* sinking. That's what we felt. I'm positive. It's not normal."

Jack forced a smile, but it didn't match his eyes. He reached up and massaged the back of her neck — normally a sort of 'magic button' that immediately calmed her down. This time, however, it did nothing. She pulled away, turning toward the stern of the ship.

"Come on," she said. "I'm checking on the kids. I know there's a protocol for all of this, so if we *are* actually sinking, we need to get close to a lifeboat, and I want to make sure the girls are with us."

Jack nodded and she started walking, doing her best to dodge the growing amount of foot traffic on Deck 10. It seemed that because this deck was the first and largest open-air deck, it became the unofficial meeting place. It was the only deck on which the entirety of the ship's passengers and crew could stand together.

Still, this deck was packed with all sorts of things that made gathering as one cohesive body very difficult. Multiple pools and hot tubs, cafeterias and dining halls, and of course the Kids' Zone squarely in the center of the back of the ship all made collecting together and becoming one blob of humanity nearly impossible.

But it wasn't for lack of trying. The deck was filling up

quickly as more and more guests and crew had come up on the elevators or stairs to see what was going on.

The fact that they were all curious but detached told her that the explosion probably wasn't as bad as she had initially thought. No one was franticly rushing toward the lifeboats. The explosion had probably happened on deck one or two, she thought. And it was probably small enough not to warrant a ton of concern for our safety.

She recalled her and Jack's little excursion down there last night, ending with...

She frowned as they walked, dodging the family of five standing around, looking helpless. *I actually have* no recollection *of how last night ended*, she realized. *Wow, I must've had a lot to drink.*

She remembered that Jack had been quiet about it this morning, not really giving her a clear picture of what they'd seen or done. But that was not uncharacteristic of Jack — he often tried to pretend things like that had not happened. It's not that she thought he was a 'party-pooper,' but...

Well, yeah, she thought. *He* is *a party pooper.*

And she did remember dinner, so she figured, during her loosened-up state of inebriation, she had told Jack something that had gotten him worked up and excited, only to disappoint him when they returned to the room, but hey — that was marriage, right?

And that's not what mattered now — obviously, there were bigger issues to deal with at the moment.

They were about halfway across Deck 10, near the largest pool and adjoined stage, where prior to now, some band or musical act had been performing constantly, all day and almost all night.

She saw some of the musicians sitting on the edge of the stage, checking their phones. A few other crew members dashed around on the stage, looking busy but not actually doing anything.

The drummer or a drum tech was busy unscrewing the tops of cymbal stands, taking them off, and carefully placing them in boxes.

Interesting, she thought. *The only reason you start packing up your instrument is if you're done playing.*

And since they were only on day three of their seven-day cruise, she found it very interesting that these musicians were done playing.

What do they know that we don't? she wondered.

It did not bode well for their situation, and it gave her even more impetus to get to the back of the ship.

There was another litany of screams and shouts as the deck shifted once more, this time complemented by a loud *cracking* sound. Nothing fell or broke that she could see, but she knew that this ship was not made to sail on its side. Something structural — something likely very important — had broken somewhere, either in the internal architecture of the ship's hull or a column or post out here on one of the decks. The ship tilted more to her left but stopped again a moment later.

"Okay, I *definitely* felt that one," she said.

Jack mumbled something, but she ignored him. This was a nervous tic of his — something he had always done when he got worked up and was trying to solve a problem. Usually, it was something he did when he was trying to figure out a problem at work, inevitably one he had decided to take home with him. He would sit on the couch next to her, his laptop open, mumbling to himself about this or that.

It was her turn to drag him along, then. He was focused on whatever problem he was trying to solve in his head, and she was trying to focus on the only problem she knew she could solve — she needed to get to the kids.

"Kate, I —"

She tried to listen, but her hearing was strained as a gaggle of older teenagers darted in front of them, all laughing and joking. She had forgotten what it felt like to feel immortal, to feel like every problem in the world was a problem for someone else.

These kids still had their innocence, still had the outlook and optimism she knew every teenager experienced. They didn't know how dire the situation was.

No, Kate. You *don't know how dire the situation is. These kids could be right — this could all be nothing.*

She wanted to believe that it was all nothing, that somebody had made an egregious error that had somehow tilted the ship a bit, an accident, and that within a few more minutes, everything would right itself — literally and figuratively — and they would be on their way.

But the rational part of her brain knew this was just wishful thinking.

Something bad had *absolutely* happened, and it was causing the ship to sink.

CHAPTER 14

GRAVES

HOWARD GRAVES' day off had ended way too soon. Now he sat at a desk, facing a mountain of paperwork he wasn't sure he was going to do.

He had worked this job long enough to know which of the papers *actually* had to be filed or turned in to the right places and which ones could be... well, forgotten.

He was sick of all this shit, sick of playing gopher for the cruise liner's board members and senior vice presidents. Each of them thought they ran this operation, and each of them was equally wrong. *He* ran this operation; without him, all of it would fall apart instantly.

Though his job title was Director of Security, over the years — and thanks to an aggravatingly overachieving previous security lead — the job had swollen into the *tour de force* that it was today. He didn't like it and longed for three or four protégés who would take on these burdens themselves, but he did not have the budget to make it happen.

He hardly had a budget at all, in fact. Most of his job was spent managing his direct reports, barking at them for one reason or another, usually because they were doing something wrong. He found it insufferable that good workers and laborers were impossible to find on this damned island. But it was not just a problem exclusive to Jamaica — he had also hated everyone he had worked with back in Miami. Most of the cops there had been lazier and more incompetent than he could have imagined.

He slid a few stacks of papers from one side of his desk to the other — manifests for all the ships coming into port this week. Nobody ever looked at them because there was never anything to look at. Endless names of people, their ages, and where they hailed from. Who cared? It's not like any real Person of Interest could get past Port Authority and get on a boat using their real name, anyway.

He sighed and rubbed his temples, wondering if he would be able to steal away for a few hours later this week and get a massage from the cute Jamaican girl in town he'd been seeing. He had gone in on a whim a year ago, and the hour-long Swedish-style massage had become somewhat of a ritual for him. The older — and heavier — he got, the less effective the hour-long massage was, and he had complained to the girl numerous times. To her credit, she had gotten much more aggressive with his back and shoulders, though he sensed it was damn near killing her to keep it up.

Whatever, he thought. *It's her job.*

The thought of visiting her again was a fantasy he decided to explore for a few minutes. He closed his eyes and leaned back in his office chair. The plastic wheels and reclining mechanism squeaked and squealed, but he pushed back farther.

Suddenly the chair's front wheels leaped upward, and he felt himself falling. He squawked and grasped for the table's edge, barely catching it with his left hand at the last moment. He held on tight and pulled himself back up, breathing heavily.

He cursed and shook his head just as someone knocked on his office door.

"What!" He roared. He was not in the mood for something else to go wrong, for somebody to be managed and shown how to do their job.

The door opened a crack, and he heard a voice — a young woman who technically worked for the directors of the company as well, but that he had sort of commandeered over the years as a secretary — poked her head in.

"Excuse me, sir?"

"Hurry up, Sally, I'm busy," he said.

"Yes, sorry," Sally said. "Sir, there's been an incident."

He rolled his eyes. "And what sort of incident is it this time?"

"The *Ocean Voyager* — the new ship in the *Integrity* class?"

"Yes, I am of course familiar. It docked last night. Passengers have been arriving all morning."

"Yes, sir, that is correct. However, something... Something's happened. An explosion, we think."

"A — a *what?*"

Howard felt his palms growing sweaty, the acid reflux already beginning to build in his throat.

"Yes, some of the passengers claim to have heard a boom or something emanating from belowdecks. We weren't sure if it had even come from the ship but then, it..."

Graves's eyes were bugging out of his head. "Then it, *what?*"

"It seems to have listed to the side a bit, sir," Sally

explained. "It's not actively sinking right now; we don't think. Likely because it's in the —"

"The Shallows, yes, right. No, it probably won't sink very much at all after this, but that doesn't mean it's not going to cause some major damned problems for us. And plenty of headaches for me."

The Shallows was indeed the shallowest section of the bay, on average. But maneuvering the massive hull *past* The Shallows was impossible due to a tall reef growth that had taken hold around the inner bay. The smaller ships could pass easily, but these larger boats were forced to stay out past the reef.

He began massaging his temples again, harder this time, trying to invoke his massage girl as he did. *Come on*, he told himself. *Not like this. Don't do this to me now.*

A situation like this was far more than he wanted to tackle alone. It was far more than he wanted to tackle, ever. Running a cruise port for a large cruise company was no easy task, and that was only if everyone else working with him and for him did their jobs appropriately. They rarely did, so there were already plenty of headaches to go around.

"Sir, we don't believe there have been any injuries, but of course, we are waiting to hear from the ship itself."

"Yeah, right. I don't care about any of that. EMT and Coast Guard can help out. Tell me about the explosion. Where was it?"

She frowned, then shook her head. "We don't know, sir, it's — we're still trying to figure out —"

"Wait a minute," Graves interrupted, realizing something. "Who is *we*? Why am I just now hearing about this?"

"Sorry, sir. It just happened — and there were plenty of crew members on the docks who saw it and were dealing with passengers, so I've been trying to make the rounds and let everyone know what's been going on, and —"

"I am the *only* one who needs to know what's going on!" Graves roared. "I should have been informed about this the moment it happened. Does no one have a damned radio on?"

She swallowed, then glanced down at her feet before looking back at Graves. He kept his eyes on her but felt along his desk for his own walkie-talkie. He felt the knob and quickly clicked it past the 'on' position and turned up the volume. Immediately, it sprang to life with choruses of updates and emergency protocol shortcodes.

His frustration grew into a fury.

"Get out," Graves said, pulling his fingers up to his temples once more. "Just *leave*. You've got a job to do, and so do I."

Sally left, closing the door hard. He thought it sounded like she may have even slammed it.

CHAPTER 15

KATE

SHE HEARD one of the older teenagers trying to explain to his friend. "Nah, man. This is the shallowest water for miles. It's only like, I don't know, forty or fifty feet deep. So even if we do sink, we're not going down that far. I bet the tops of the decks around us will still be out of the water."

"And you're okay with that?" The girl asked, giggling after. Kate heard the strain in her voice, even though she had tried to laugh it off.

The kid shrugged. "Doesn't matter, anyway. The crew will start handing out lifejackets and sticking us in those boats."

Kate followed the kid's gaze and saw the long line of small lifeboats against the wall.

As they walked and got closer to them, she realized they were anything but small. Each lifeboat could hold up to 150 people, and this ship had about forty boats total, each held in place by the davits, which would swing out and lower them to the sea after being filled with passengers and crew. She remembered the famous dilemma suffered by the *Titanic* way back in 1912: not enough lifeboats for everyone on board *simultane-*

ously. The *Titanic* had been designed according to procedure at the time — enough boats to ferry passengers to safety, *not* to accommodate all the passengers at once.

It was a mistake the shipping and cruise industries would not make again.

The fact of the matter did not help her feel good right now, however. The teenagers split off from her and Jack, and they had a stretch of about twenty feet in front of them, relatively free of people before they would reach the last third of the ship. She picked up her pace, taking advantage of the empty straightaway. Jack kept up with her, and while he was silent at the moment, she knew he was still in his own head about something.

"Jack, it's okay, honey. You can't fix a sinking ship."

She wanted to encourage him and put his mind at ease, but her mind was racing. She didn't blame him for wanting to fix this — it's what he did. He liked to say that his job was a 'professional fixer.' CIA life was not glamorous, at least when the job took place mostly in an office like her husband's. But he seemed to really enjoy the types of issues and problems he got to solve at work.

He could only tell her about a handful of them, and even then he had to use snippets of stories and change people's names in order to not cause a security blunder. But she knew he was good at his job, and they appreciated him for it.

They were about to reach the home stretch — about fifty feet away from the kids' check-in counter they had left only minutes earlier — when a group of seven or eight crew members burst out of a door just to their right.

It was a crew-only entrance and exit, a door leading into the bowels of the ship, one she had not noticed before. There were photographs on the wall depicting beach scenes and island life, but otherwise the entire hallway was bland. Doors, like the one the crew had just exited from, pockmarked the hallway between the pictures.

The crew immediately surrounded Jack and Kate. "Ma'am, sir, we're going to need you to come with us."

Kate felt the anxiety rising again, her face beginning to flush. "No, I —"

"Ma'am, it's okay. We're going to get you on a lifeboat and then over to Jamaica. It's only about half an hour from here."

The group started moving them along, pushing them opposite the direction Kate wanted to go, but there was nothing she and Jack could do. She wasn't about to start throwing punches on innocent crew members, though she secretly wished her husband would. Even a brief break in the group, and she could sprint over to the check-in station.

"I have kids... my kids are —"

But she couldn't get a word out. Another crew member, a beefy man with a buzzed haircut, stepped in front of her. He grabbed her wrist, perhaps a little too hard. "It's okay," he said. "I *promise*. We're going to start corralling everybody toward the lifeboats, but we have to follow this protocol."

"But my *kids*," she said, this time landing on the final word with some more confidence.

The beefy guy nodded before she was even finished. "I understand; I really do. Trust me — we're going to get every-body into lifeboats, including the children. They've got their own procedure down there, though."

They pulled her and Jack along as her frustration grew. *Why isn't Jack saying anything?* She nudged him with her elbow as they passed another set of pools and hot tubs just behind where the stage was.

"Actually," Jack began, suddenly coming to life, "if we can just —"

He tried to pull to the left, but two crew members there nudged him back in with Kate. *What the hell is this?* she wondered. *This all seems really forceful. Why are they treating us like this?*

"Sorry, sir. Captain's orders. Protocol says we can't leave anyone if we see them; that's why we're all here to escort anyone toward the lifeboats."

To his credit, the man grabbed on the shirt of an older man who was leaning over the railing, looking at the tenders making their way back from Jamaica. The man looked up, surprised, but fell in line as they walked. Two of the crew members on Kate's left grabbed the teenagers from before. There were a few utterances from the group of kids, but they too obeyed orders and fell in.

They didn't have far to walk — they had passed many lifeboats already, and Kate assumed they were supposed to meet at this crew group's designated sections. They had gone through a quick training session immediately upon embarking. They had all stood around on this deck, tightly packed in numbered sections painted on the white walls behind them, while a crewmember explained how to use the lifejackets and how to get into the boats.

Never in a million years did she think she was actually going to have to do that.

"What about our lifejackets?" she asked then. "Aren't they in the rooms?"

"There are plenty more on deck, hidden in compartments along the wall."

"And also plenty in the lifeboats themselves," a female crew member added.

A few quick nods all around, and they continued their journey. Two crew members stopped at a section marked 237, and they pulled the teenagers and another group of about fifteen passengers into that section.

"Don't we have assigned sections?" Kate asked. She remembered they were supposed to meet at a certain spot, though she couldn't remember exactly how to get there now. There was too much else going on in her mind to care about details like that. Besides, she knew Jack would remember the section number for the rest of their life. He had always been the master of memory — as long as the information was trivial and useless.

He had remembered what she had been wearing when they had first met, though to this day, he had a hard time remembering her birthday or their anniversary.

"Too late," the buzz-cut man said. "This is, uh, a different protocol."

"You have more than one 'the ship is sinking' protocol?" Jack asked.

"Just keep moving," the man said. Kate thought she heard a tinge of frustration in his voice. She eyed him, wondering if he would actually stoop to using force to pull these passengers where they needed to go. He certainly looked like he could if he wanted to. She remembered the scene from *Titanic*, where a man shot at passengers to keep them corralled and not panicked.

She almost laughed. *Yep, that will do it,* she thought. *Nothing like shooting people to get them to stop panicking.*

They reached section 234 and stopped. "Okay, you two: with me."

Jack and Kate looked at one another before realizing he was talking about them. Kate saw that they had collected about thirty more people, all milling along like cattle in a cattle chute. These thirty people, all ages and demographics — were corralled and told to stand in this section for a few minutes while the crew members got their boat ready. More and more passengers made their way to their section, and Kate noticed that the crew did, in fact, seem to have a good protocol. A group of people would make their way over, where they would be immediately told to move to a certain section.

Kate saw a couple of lifeboats beside them already starting to lower, the massive arms of the davits swinging out and over the Jamaican bay.

"Don't you have to check our names and stuff?" she heard a man ask.

Buzz-cut shook his head. "They'll do that at port, where it's easier to keep things moving quickly," he explained. "Protocol right now is to get everyone off the ship, stat."

Kate heard mumbling around her, more questions and answers, all of them guesses and speculation. No one knew what was really going on, and no one knew the extent of the damage. Would the ship actually sink? Were these waters too shallow for that to happen? Sure, maybe a couple of decks would fill up with water, but if the massive cruise liner hit the bottom of the Jamaican bay, would they simply stop there, tilted to the side?

Not that it would be a simple thing, either. Millions of dollars would be lost trying to salvage the huge boat, and perhaps a billion in total damages when all was said and done.

The most important thing, she knew, was to keep all of the passengers safe. So far, they seemed to be doing that well. A bit overzealous, perhaps, but they were moving right along and keeping things positive. She heard the chains of the davits starting to lower her lifeboat a bit, getting them ready for passengers. The hatch on the side opened, and a crew member — a petite, blonde-haired girl — poked her head in, then came back out and addressed the crewman standing next to her.

"Support systems, check. Onboard equipment, check." She then turned to everyone else and raised her voice a bit. "Okay, here we go. Everyone stay calm, and let's fill this baby up!"

The crewmember had an accent, Ukrainian or Russian. She was joined by a male crew member, and they looked to be brother and sister. Blonde hair, blue eyes, mid-20s.

She knew the crews of these ships often hailed from other countries, both because it was a good, decent job for people all around the world and because it was cheaper for cruise companies to hire from countries that had lower standards of living.

She felt Jack squeeze her hand. "Let's just get in first, then we can sit back and figure this out."

She scoffed. "Jack, what do you mean? Figure *what* out?"

He seemed surprised for a moment, as if she should have been privy to all of the conversations he was undoubtedly having in his head. Then he snapped out of it. "Oh, right. Sorry. I just — something about this seems weird. Fishy."

"I don't care about any of that shit, Jack. We need to get the kids. If they're going to meet us in port, I want to be the first boat there."

Jack nodded. "Of course, yeah. You're not wrong about that. Let's get to port and make sure we get eyes on the kids. That's priority one. It's just..."

He was about to speak again, but the words trailed off as they were funneled into the open hatch of the lifeboat. They sat next to one another on the port side of this little boat, near the back of it. It was fully enclosed, likely to ensure buoyancy in case of large waves and, Kate guessed, to prevent its occupants from losing their minds if they *saw* such a wave. There was, however, a tiny porthole on the angled top of the boat, and two people — a man and a woman — were taking turns looking through it.

"Okay, people!" said the Ukrainian cheerleader. "Let's sit down and get those lifejackets on, please."

Jack helped Kate with hers, getting all the straps where they needed to go. Before working on his own, they sat down for another few minutes while everyone else got into the boat. They were crammed in here like sardines, but Kate figured that was protocol. No reason to worry about comfort — this would be a twenty- or thirty-minute boat ride, anyway. Their crewmember closed the hatch then, and the light inside dimmed. Sunlight came in through the porthole, which was now cleared and unobstructed by viewers.

Of course things are going to be okay, she told herself. *These people train for just this event.*

She swallowed, then went through the plan in her mind.

We'll get to shore, and we'll get the kids. Then we'll figure it out from there. A cruise ship sinking in shallow waters was a massive problem, but it was not *her* problem. So what? When all was said and done, they would be in Jamaica, a perfectly acceptable place to have a family vacation. She and Jack loved Jamaica — she remembered their honeymoon trip here, running through different parishes and visiting rum estates and distilleries.

It actually sounds nice, she thought. *We'll have the kids with us, so we'll just hit the beach. Maybe we'll even find —*

"You okay?" Jack asked, squeezing her leg.

She nodded, for the first time since she had felt the explosion actually believing it. *I* am *okay,* she told herself. *Everything's going to be just fine.*

She leaned her head sideways, parking it on Jack's left shoulder. The lifejacket stunk a bit like burnt plastic, but she also smelled Jack through it. She smelled his cologne, still fresh from that morning, and she nestled in close to her husband.

We're going to be okay.

CHAPTER 16

JACK

SOMETHING IN JACK'S mind suddenly clicked.

Something's not right.

He still couldn't place it, but it was related to everything he'd seen. He could not even remember *what* he had seen, or more specifically, what things he had seen that were causing his subconscious to start trying to get his attention.

Something about last night? Down below? Talking to the captain?

At his day job, Jack was a fantastic problem-solver. He had an uncanny ability to make connections where others swore there were none. He could see all of the pieces of the puzzle at the same time, see how they fit together, and then deliver the results. He had been repeatedly lauded for his efforts by his boss or coworkers.

He knew it annoyed the hell out of some of the more competitive agents, but he couldn't help it.

Now, though the puzzle was not clear, he knew there *was* one. Enough of the pieces had been overturned and displayed as if on a table in his mind. He could see there was something to figure out. Something to solve.

"Kate, something's not right," he said suddenly.

More and more people filled the lifeboat, and he knew they were getting close to capacity.

An elderly couple across from them frowned, a quizzical expression showing on the woman's face.

He lowered his voice to a mere whisper. "I just... I don't know. I feel something *weird*."

"Well, we're in a lifeboat wearing lifejackets and just got off of a sinking cruise ship," she said. "That definitely feels *weird*."

He shook his head. "No, not like that. There's something else. Something I didn't realize I was trying to put together. But I'm starting to now."

"What? Starting to put what together?" she asked. He noticed the older man across from them lean in a bit, looking the other way as if pretending he wasn't trying to hear what they were saying.

"Well, for starters, last night — you may not remember any of it, but I do. That room we found? The one with the crates all stacked up? You opened one, looking for the cup thingy."

"Yeah..." she said, clearly trying to remember. "And I found guns, right? Like, the sort of thing they'd need to use for security?"

He frowned. "Maybe. Yeah, I guess. Honestly, I didn't believe you. A box of guns — on a cruise ship? But then *this* — the ship sinking. I mean, that doesn't *ever* happen. Sure, there was the time that idiot captain crashed into some rocks because he wanted to wave to his girlfriend or whatever, but there's nothing like that out here we could even crash into."

"I thought an explosion caused us to start sinking?" Kate asked.

He nodded again, harder. "Yeah, yeah. That's exactly what I think it was, but... Why? Why the hell was there an explosion — a *bomb* — on a cruise ship?"

She did not seem to like that answer. "How do you know it was a bomb, Jack? Maybe it was an accident?" She offered. "Like an engine blowing up or something?"

He squeezed at his temples; his eyes closed. *Something isn't right. And if Kate was right about the guns...*

The sense was growing within him — he didn't know what it was, but he knew something was not right about this whole situation.

"I have to get out," he said suddenly.

"What? What do you mean, you have to get out?"

Jack stood up, earning glances from the other people crammed around them.

Kate pulled at his arm. "Honey, come on. Sit down."

He brushed off her hand but sat back down, taking off his lifejacket. He leaned in close, talking directly into her ear. "Kate, I can't explain how or why I know this, but there's something going on. Something *really* fishy. Something bad."

"Jack, you're scaring me. Let's just get to shore and —"

The voice of the petite crewmember carried through tiny, crackling speakers. *"All passengers, prepare for launch."*

He shook his head. "No, you get to shore. We don't both need to be there, right?"

"I'm not going alone."

"Kate, you're their *mother*. You can do this. Get the kids, and you'll be fine. Everyone on board will be there, so it's not like you'll be alone in Jamaica. Find the Bolivars if you can; I think their kids were also in the kids programs."

He felt Kate growing agitated, but he had already made his decision. "I just... I need to look around. There's nobody on board now, right? The ship isn't going anywhere, we haven't felt it list or even move a little since the last time, and you heard those teenagers. This is the shallowest water around, so it's likely possible the boat has already sunk as far as it's going to go."

"Jack, this is crazy talk," Kate said. "How am I going to get a hold of you?"

"We're right off the coast," Jack said. "I'll have cell service. Let me just get to the room and get my phone. Once you get to shore, ask someone for one. Get one with an international plan if you can, and —"

Kate shook her head, balling her fists. "Jack, you're acting *insane.*"

Jack needed to act. He heard the davit chain whirring to action. They would start to lower in a moment, deck by deck, until they hit the water.

One of the crew members seated down the way stood up and began walking the length of the lifeboat. Jack needed to act fast. Without saying goodbye to Kate, he darted across the floor to shouts telling him to sit down, to relax. He hit the hatch full-speed, smacking his palm out onto the latch. His body weight and shoulder launched the hatch open, and he continued moving right through the open hole in the boat.

"Sir!" the tiny crewmember shouted. Jack only had a few seconds to crawl out of the hatch before the crewmember was at the door. He reached through and held onto the rubber railing lining the lifeboat. When he had fully exited, Jack swung the hatch closed; his feet were already moving. With the door closed, he kept his hands in place on the rubber grip while his feet stretched out to reach the hull of the cruise ship.

They were moving past luxury balconies now, about five feet away from the wall. He forced himself to not look down, knowing that just because he had successfully climbed *The Newbie* yesterday did *not* mean he was now a professional rock climber.

Besides, he was still deathly afraid of heights.

The hatch clicked and started to open, but Jack jumped out at the same time. He lunged forward, pushing his upper body off of the raft while letting his legs fall forward onto the balcony. Since they were coming down to it, he didn't need to push toward the cruise ship as much as just let gravity do its thing.

He landed on his feet, then crashed sideways into one of the patio chairs on this balcony. He knew from a previous trip these balconies could not be locked from the inside or outside, since they were part of a private room. He reached for the door handle, still reeling from the fall, and pulled it open.

Before stepping back into the room, he turned and faced the crewmember, still descending wide-eyed on board the lifeboat. She was furious, but Jack just waved at her.

"Sorry — forgot my phone."

CHAPTER 17

CARLOS

CARLOS RUBIO SAT in the stiff chair of the lift. It was a forklift with a crane attachment. It was much larger than an actual forklift, a purpose-built machine designed to lift the myriad boxes and crates in the warehouse and move them around quickly and accurately. But since not every box, crate, and cart that needed to be loaded onto the ships docking here in port were the same size and shape; this machine had been fabricated to assist the dockworkers with moving everything around safely.

Almost everything that would eventually end up on the ship already had attached casters, which made them easy to load up or down a ramp, but some ships — like the *Ocean Voyager,* the massive *Integrity*-class ocean liner one out in The Shallows now — weren't able to get close enough to the docks to allow the dockworkers to roll everything down into the ships' bellies.

Carlos' job was simple — he told his family and friends that his job was to 'move things around.' There was more to it than that, of course, but the basics were just that. Boxes and crates inside the massive warehouse here in Jamaica needed to eventually find their way onto a ship. Every day he had loads of massive, heavy boxes that were either full of food and supplies and needed to get back to a waiting cruise ship, or empty and needed to get back to a resupply charter ship.

He drove this lift daily, hardly having enough time off to eat a sandwich and chug a bottle of water. The cruise company ran its labor crews like donkeys, squeezing them to get as much output as possible, and rarely giving them a raise. Some argued that the perks outweighed the difficulty of the work — things like the private beach next door and a workout center attached to the back of the facility. But those perks were pointless when Carlos could never seem to get a day off in the first place.

His direct supervisor — Howard Graves — was a barrel-chested man who walked and acted as though he were far more appreciated than he actually was. Carlos had heard that the man was an ex-cop from Miami, and he certainly had the swagger to prove it.

But the man had gotten fat and lost his edge, and his laziness had caught up with him over the years. Instead of working hard himself, Graves worked everyone else hard. The only times he'd ever seen the man was in his golf cart, the poor thing loaded past the breaking point, shouting at employees and staffers.

Carlos sweated with exertion as he delicately maneuvered one box of foodstuffs to another ledge. Driving this thing wasn't physically taxing, but it was hot in the warehouse. And it annoyed him to no end that it seemed he was the only one Graves trusted to do it.

Graves had recruited Carlos two years ago from the surf shop at the port where he'd worked previously. Since Graves seemed to act like he was in charge of everything here, Carlos had been excited to potentially work directly for a man he considered to have more clout than anyone else around.

But the honeymoon phase — if there even was one — had ended very quickly. Within two weeks, Carlos realized how much of an asshole Graves really was. He made more money driving the lift instead of working in the surf shop, but was it even worth it?

"Aw, crap," he said. He groaned again as he noticed the stack of boxes he had been working on was not actually pushed up against the back wall. That meant there were *two* rows of boxes and crates he needed to move before the evening shift took over, rather than just one. He was going to have to hustle if he was going to get it done in time.

Cruise companies were essentially logistics companies that ran floating hotels. They were adamant that everything needed to move swiftly and smoothly for the passengers on board to meet their every need.

Of course, Carlos couldn't afford to go on one, though he had spent plenty of time inside the ships. He often had to deliver some boxes directly and into what he and his coworkers called 'The Belly of the Beast.' The cavernous interiors on the first few decks of most cruise ships were where most of these boxes and crates would end up before the voyage. A separate team of deck crew would handle the logistics of transporting each box or crate or other item where it needed to go *during* the voyage, so Carlos's job was to simply get the boxes inside. Seeing cruise ships come and go every single day out in the bay had normalized the size of the floating vessels, but every time he got to get closer to one, he realized just how massive they actually were.

Carlos was driving another box across the floor when Graves himself rolled in. At the moment, there was nobody else in the warehouse. Graves, straining the tiny tires of his little golf cart he rode around in, approached Carlos and did not even wait for him to turn off the noisy lift before shouting over the roar of its engine.

"I need you down here, now," Graves shouted.

Carlos frowned but did as he was told. He flicked off the ignition switch and jumped out of the large machine. He walked to the cart, waiting for Graves to exit and stand.

He didn't. "You're still SCUBA certified, yeah?"

"Of course, sir," Carlos said. Long before his employment with the cruise company, Carlos had been one of the island's most qualified SCUBA instructors. He had tried his best to maintain his gear and training, though he'd only been in the water a few times in the past couple of years. There simply wasn't enough time.

"Good," Graves said. "I need you to suit up."

Carlos cocked an eyebrow. "Sir? I am in the middle of my shift, and —"

"All of this shit can wait," Graves said. "There's been an... incident, and we will most likely need help *underwater* as much as we will above water. I've got patrol boats on standby, and the Jamaican Coast Guard — not to mention the rest of the JDF — will be flying in here and trying to take control of everything."

Carlos knew it was the Coast Guard's and Jamaica Defence Force's job to take control of a situation out at sea, if there was a big incident. But for smaller situations out in the bay, it got a little trickier. Since the ships themselves were owned by a cruise company that most likely were not flying the Jamaican flag, and since they were close enough to the company-owned coastline, there was always a little bit of power jostling between the companies and the Coast Guard, as well as any local law enforcement that might want to get involved.

But he didn't know what the situation was, so it was hard to say whether Graves was overstepping his bounds or simply trying to get ahead of the situation.

"What's going on, sir?" Carlos asked.

"Later," Graves said, dismissing him with an open-faced palm. "Just need you to be ready. You have gear here?"

Carlos shook his head.

"Doesn't matter," Graves said. "You should be able to find everything you need down in the locker area in the PA bunker. Go there now and suit up. I'll have one of the boats get your tanks ready."

Carlos couldn't believe what was happening. "I'm sorry, sir — you want me to go get ready to *dive* into a dangerous situation?"

Graves waved off the question again. "It's not *dangerous*, per se. We just got a... situation with one of the new cruise liners that came into port last night. You'll probably be hearing all about it once you get out there, so I won't waste your time. All the passengers are on their way to the docks as we speak, but I want to make sure we are prepared with a diver in the water."

Carlos's eyes widened. "A cruise ship... And you're only sending one diver?"

Graves shook his head. "No, of course not. That would be stupid. I've got five others ready to go, or at least on their way.

They'll be in the boats as well, waiting at Dock 3, and I expect you to be there. Twenty minutes?"

"Yes, sir."

Carlos watched as Graves rolled away in the golf cart, the man's massive frame taking up both of the seats. He exited the lift and walked toward the door, following Graves. He left his machine dormant in the middle of the warehouse floor. It was a breach of safety protocol to leave it there, but Carlos had not heard his boss tell him to park the lift, and if he was going to make it to the docks in twenty minutes, fully loaded, he needed to haul ass to the locker area and find this gear Graves had told him about.

What could possibly be happening that had his boss so spooked? He believed Graves that he would find out soon enough — certainly, somebody outside would be shouting and pointing, explaining what they thought had happened. Had two ships collided? Maybe a big one hit a smaller boat or yacht. The smaller vessels, often captained by amateur pilots, sometimes had no idea how to maneuver through these shallow waters. There were areas that were far too shallow for any boats, and the cruise ships had to stay in designated lanes.

For that reason, some of the smaller yachts often found their way into the designated shipping lanes and had to be not-so-politely told to leave by Port Authority.

If there had been such an incident, he couldn't imagine it being the cruise ship's — and thus the cruise company's — fault. Captains of cruise ships were rarely allowed to drive into port alone. Usually another boat would sail out and deliver a 'port pilot,' a maritime ship pilot with specific experience in each port who knew the channels and protocols and could handle parking the massive luxury cruisers.

A ship like the *Ocean Voyager* would not need a port pilot, as it would have stayed anchored out in The Shallows, away from the reefs, where tenders would ferry the passengers and crew to the docks.

It didn't matter — he had a job to do, and although he was certainly anxious about what was going on out there, he was also excited to potentially get in the water once again. He did love diving, and he was still very good at it. He longed for the day when money didn't matter as much, and he could retire and spend his time floating around the reefs and shallow areas of the waters around his home country.

Carlos smiled as he thought of this. *This day just got a whole lot more interesting*, he thought.

And, hopefully, a whole lot more fun.

CHAPTER 18
JACK

IN ONE FLUID MOTION, he pulled himself inside the room and slammed the balcony door closed once again. He saw the open hatch, the crewmember inside leaning outward, bug-eyed. Jack's acrobatic stunt had apparently impressed her, but he did not dwell on it.

He strode through the lavish room and reached the door to the hallway. Throwing it open now, he leaned out and saw that the hallway was completely empty.

It was very likely he and Kate had gotten into one of the first lifeboats to fill up, so there should still be people milling about on some of the decks. Besides that, he knew some crew members or staff would be walking the halls quickly, checking every last room for any occupants trying to stay behind or otherwise unaware of what was going on.

The longer he waited, the emptier the ship would become.

But he didn't have time to wait. Jack needed to get back to his room quickly and *then* figure out how to stay out of sight. He reached the elevators at the end of this hallway but knew that taking them would only alert anyone above or below him to his presence. He figured these elevators were also connected to some sort of security grid, letting the team know which floor each elevator was currently on.

Stairs for me, he thought. Jack reached the stairs a moment later but heard talking from somewhere beyond the doors. He darted into an offshoot of the hallway, one of the little nooks overlooking the floor below. He stood quietly behind a massive flowerpot, waiting. The voices died down, but he heard their footsteps now. They came to his floor, then continued past, downward.

Jack waited another few seconds, then tiptoed over to the closed doors. He opened the door, thankful that it was not squeaky, then stepped into the stairwell.

He felt better moving stealthily up and down the stairs, as he would be able to hear anyone entering the landing above or below him almost immediately. And unless they were sneaking around, as well, their footsteps would give them away.

He took one flight of stairs, then exited onto his floor. He didn't see anyone here, either, though he knew that could change in an instant. Jack ran the twenty-five or so feet to their room, holding out the keycard from his back pocket at the same time. He saw the green light and heard the click, and within another two seconds he was inside his room, catching his breath against the now-closed door.

Think, he told himself. *Figure this out. Kate will get to the kids if they are already on a lifeboat. But I need to make sure they're gone first. That they got to their boats safely.*

There were other things he needed to check — whatever it was his subconscious was yelling at him about — but he knew the kids were the priority.

He walked over to grab his phone, satisfied that he at least had the beginnings of a plan.

Jack was about to leave the room, cell phone in hand when something caught his eye.

There, on ,the edge of the nightstand next to Kate's side of the bed, he saw the keycard she had swiped. Unlike his passenger card that only let him access this room, this was the same one that had gotten them access to the lower decks last night.

And the one that would, hopefully, grant him access to *any* place on the ship.

He walked over and picked it up.

For a moment, his rational mind argued with him. *What exactly are you going to do, Jack?* it asked him. *Who do you think you are, James Bond?*

I'm just going to look around, he told himself. *I'm going to check on the kids, make sure they got on a lifeboat, then I'll head down and see why my subconscious mind is screaming at me.*

He took one final glance around the room, then left.

He didn't know if the crew in the lifeboat had any sort of radio or walkie-talkie on their person, but had not seen anyone carrying one. He hadn't seen one in the boat itself, either.

That told him they would be moving to shore first, then informing whatever authority needed to know that there was still a castaway onboard the cruise ship.

Unless they ran the engine hot, driving flat out and risking bumping and jostling the old people inside, he figured they'd proceed more cautiously to shore. That meant he had fifteen or twenty minutes before Kate and the others reached the dock. He didn't know what would happen after someone alerted them to his presence here, but he knew the clock was ticking.

He ran up the hallway and back to the stairs, finding them silent and empty once again. He took them two at a time to Deck 9. While the kids had been on Deck 10, Deck 10 was open and had previously been filled with people getting on lifeboats. He could move down this hallway without being seen far easier. And, if he heard anything or saw someone, he now had a keycard that would supposedly get him into any of these rooms. Satisfied that this was a safer bet, he moved forward.

He reached the doorway to Deck 9 and opened it slowly, peeking out. Seeing nothing, he stepped out and started jogging down this long stretch of hallway. This was the most vulnerable he had been so far, and if someone happened to leave a room on either side of the hallway, from any side on the ship, they would see him.

He ran faster, reaching the opposite side faster than he had thought possible. Feeling slightly winded now, he stopped just inside this stairwell before taking the stairs two at a time. He reached Deck 10 and immediately heard a noise.

More talking, coming from just outside the stairwell doors on Deck 10. He ducked to the right, hoping the shadows would hide him if the doors swung open now. He listened, trying to hear clearly through thick wood doors.

"He's going to kill us if we lose any of the product," he heard one of the people hiss.

"He *needs* us, at least for now. Fifteen of us, against the entire crew and passengers? There's no way he can move the rest of it alone."

There was a pause. "Yeah, but he just successfully got *rid* of all the passengers and crew."

"The explosion?" the second person asked. "You think he did that on purpose?"

"Of course he did," the first person said confidently, his voice louder now. "He had to have done it on purpose. Right?"

There was a longer pause, and the voices moved away from the door, likely toward their actual destination.

Who were these people? Jack wondered. *Crew? Or had another group gotten on board this morning?*

He didn't have time to think about it right now, nor did he have enough information to figure out what they were talking about.

Time to make sure the kids got away, he thought.

THE RIDE to the cruise docks was a bumpy one. Kate had never traveled to port like this before, and she suspected that the lifeboat had been built for stability and reliability, not comfort. The elderly couple across from them held each other tight, and she wondered how they were holding up. She couldn't help herself — she had always had a maternal bent and an instinct for taking care of others. It was part of why she and Jack worked so well together — it wasn't that he didn't care about the kids, because he certainly did, it was just that he always was so focused on providing for the family, worried about keeping them all safe at all times, that he tended to be a little more detached emotionally.

She felt that she picked up the slack well. She knew that girls often latched onto their mothers out of human nature, but that instinct would wear off as the years went on. She had always done her best to build a solid relationship with them now in these younger years, to hopefully allow them to feel safe and secure talking to either of their parents as they grew older.

She turned her attention to the porthole to her left. She stared through it, into the blue sky, dotted with clouds, for what seemed like hours. She knew only minutes had passed since they'd been dropped off and started driving, but finally something passed across the view outside the window. Some sort of barge or fishing boat, its extended boom arm casting a shadow over the smaller lifeboat. It was impossible to tell if that meant they were close, but it gave her the sense that they were near the docks.

Twenty or thirty minutes had passed since they'd boarded the lifeboats. It had been an excruciating amount of time, silently waiting and wondering, and it had not been helped by the fact that the crewmember who had seen her husband jump out the open hatch had chided her during the early minutes of the trip.

"He's going to be in huge trouble," she had told Kate. "If Port Authority or the Coast Guard get their hands on him, he could actually go to prison."

At first, Kate had argued. "He's just trying to help, and he's scared," she had said. "He wanted to make sure our kids got into a boat safely."

If any among the other passengers were on her side, they didn't speak up. The journey had been long and awkward so far, and except for the arguing, mostly silent. The others had not seemed to care much about what was going on, probably realizing that everything was totally fine and they were safe. Worst case, they would have to spend a few extra days in Jamaica before flying home. Sure, they would never see their stuff again, but Kate thought little of worldly possessions. A few suitcases full of clothes was nothing to cry about.

The boat bumped into something a few minutes later, and a few startled people jumped up in their seats, expecting the worst. She stayed seated as the boat bumped a few more times, and she heard sounds of shouting from somewhere up above. She looked out the porthole, and then the hatch opened. A dark-skinned man peered in, smiling a toothy grin. "Hello, everyone," he said in a thick Jamaican accent. "Usually, we don't meet under these terms, but: Welcome to Jamaica!"

It seemed as though the crew had practiced for just such an occasion, as the disembarkation process was swift and smooth, with little fuss. Lines were cast out, the lifeboats hauled toward the docks, and friendly Jamaican dockworkers greeted every boat. Even the elderly couple was helped off the boat with extra care.

When it was her turn to leave, she walked up the short stairs and poked her head out. The bright Jamaican sun was piercing, and she had to squint to see. She stepped a foot onto the dock — a wooden structure that seemed to extend as far as her eye could see in one direction. Along its distance, she saw what seemed like thousands of lifeboats bobbing up and down, each of them spilling their passengers onto the wooden deck before turning around and giving space for another lifeboat to dock.

She had been in one of the first lifeboats to reach the dock, which meant she was closer to the main bridge and walkway that separated the city from the port. She turned in that direction and walked, feeling strange suddenly as the gravity of the situation hit her. She had no bags, not even a phone or purse, and she was in a completely different country.

Shouts arose from her left, and she saw a large Jamaican woman wearing the Port Authority uniform waving her hands, trying to get peoples' attention. She told them to follow her into the main Port Authority building behind her, where they were gathering more crews to help with the disembarkation process.

Usually the kiosk stations she saw would be open, ready to check each passenger's ID or passport, as they got back *on* the cruise ship after a day of fun. Since passengers were required to prove they belonged on the boat, they needed to check in before returning to the ship.

This cruise a 'closed-loop' cruise, one starting and ending at the same American port, but she knew everything was different now. This was far from a normal situation, so all bets were off about what the Port Authority workers here would require of them.

She knew that exceptions had already been made today, and she wondered what the bureaucratic red tape would be like. Would they let her even *get* to her kids?

With that charge in mind, she walked over to the first group of lifeboats that had beaten hers to shore. The people inside had just gotten out and were walking toward the Port Authority entrance, following calmly behind the Jamaican woman. Another group of PA staffers spilled out from another door and were laughing and smiling, waving at the new arrivals and motioning for them to follow along.

Wow, she thought. *For an emergency situation, they are really turning on the charm.*

It made sense, however. No one had died, to her knowledge, and there was no reason to be solemn or scared.

She could see clearly that there were no children among the groups that had already left their lifeboats. Deciding to get a good look at everyone coming into port, she turned around there and waited, letting the people pass around her. The dock stretched out for what seemed like a mile out to sea, and people began clogging up the walkway. Eventually, a sort of queue was formed, all of the people walking toward her and the Port Authority building to be gathered and counted.

She had a sudden pang of regret as she realized that count would number one fewer than it should. She knew her husband wasn't the *only* one still aboard the massive cruise ship, but eventually, it would come out that someone had broken out of their lifeboat and jumped back onto the sinking ship.

As the petite, college-aged crewmember driving their lifeboat had explained, Kate was sure he had broken all sorts of maritime laws, though she had no idea what they would be. Surely they could excuse it all as the actions of a temporarily crazed man, hell-bent on finding his children?

She didn't see her kids anywhere, but there were thousands of people now walking toward her, including children and teens. She waited, letting them move around her, before she had a better idea. She walked back a few paces and stood on top of a concrete bench that had been built on the deck of the pier. With her view now higher, looking down toward the people walking by her, she could easily see the tops of the heads of them all.

If she did see any smaller people that fit the size and dimensions of a kid, they were already with their family in every case. There was no large group of children or teenagers by themselves anywhere in sight.

Her heart was racing, but she knew it was just a matter of time. Her kids *would* get off one of the boats. They *would* be corralled into the line and follow their crewmember right to where she was standing.

Surely they would be here any minute.

Even if the kids had been the last to leave the ship, she *would* see them. And she would stand here until she did.

CHAPTER 20

JACK

JACK PULLED his phone out of his pocket and turned the screen on. He was at the stairs' exit leading onto Deck 10, now only 50 feet or so from the kids' check-in counter. For the moment, he was alone and isolated. No one knew where he was, and he hoped to keep it that way as long as possible.

By his calculation, Kate would still be on her twenty-minute journey toward the dock, so there was no reason to expect a call from her yet. And he knew she wouldn't call him right away.

For one, she didn't even have a phone with her. Jack had considered grabbing her phone from the room, but the lifeboats had already disembarked, and he had no need for two of them. Besides, he had told her to borrow a phone when she got to shore, and he knew she would be able to do just that as soon as they landed.

But the first thing she would do — the first thing *anyone* would do — once she got to shore is look for the kids and secure them. She would pull her hair out looking into every last lifeboat to find them, which he knew could take upwards of half an hour if things moved quickly.

But he had also stopped here to take a moment to look at his phone, make sure it was working, and go through his plan. He needed a rest. He was in wonderful shape, but that did not mean he was a marathon runner or an Olympic sprinter. He was a forty-two-year-old man who ran a few miles a day, every other day of the week.

Running up and down the stairs, into his room and back, all the way up and down the hallway twice — not to mention his parkour-like escape from the lifeboat itself and the sheer terror he was feeling throughout it all — meant that he was now starting to breathe quite heavily.

If he intended to keep up this stealth, intended to duck behind doors at the drop of a hat, he needed to take as much time as he could to catch his breath.

The kids were waiting on him, so he didn't want to take too long. If they were still there in their designated section, he needed to figure out why they were and how to get them off the boat. He hoped that because they had their own secure facility, nearly impenetrable by anyone other than paid staff and counselors and parents during emergencies, he assumed that a protocol existed for getting them all off the boat safely. Perhaps there were a few lifeboats just for the kids? Maybe they had all been corralled onto one muster station, so that they could do a headcount and make doubly sure that all kids were present and accounted for.

He gave himself three long, deep breaths, already feeling his heart rate begin to normalize. It was still elevated, but it wasn't bursting out of his chest anymore. He could breathe, and it seemed like his legs were now warmed up, prepared for anymore exertion he would force them into.

With his second wind carrying him along, he carefully pressed open the door and stepped out onto Deck 10. He glanced around, seeing the same long, open hallway he and Kate had previously been walking down less than an hour before. He turned this way, hoping there were no more hidden staff members tucked behind these nondescript doors.

He walked now, opting for the more silent approach. He was still very much at risk of being spotted, and though he had the keycard at the ready, he didn't want to take the chance of calling attention to himself by making too much noise.

He reached the check-in station and found the stand empty. Not unexpected; there was no reason for any parent to be checking in their kid right now while their boat was sinking. He stepped around the stand and walked deeper into the hallway; toward the room he had seen his daughters turn into earlier.

He paused near the next turn, listening for any sound that might tell him who was here, and where they were hiding.

Instead, he heard nothing. He let out a breath he hadn't realized he had been holding. It meant — he hoped — that the counselors and staff had, in fact, gotten the kids off the boat. He heard no shouts or screams of laughter, no loud bass drops from a movie a few doors down, and no running sounds of footsteps as kids and staff pounded around this deck and the two above him.

But he had to be *sure*. He had to at least check the rooms large enough to house them, since that was where his subconscious was telling him to go. He still did not understand what it wanted from him, why it had forced his hand back in the lifeboat.

He felt his father's presence then, urging him forward, telling him to have faith in his own instincts.

Just like at work.

Jack hated to admit it, but he was a far better desk jockey than a field agent, and he likely always would be. He had a knack for figuring things out, which he had leveraged into a very successful career with the Justice Department. There was rarely a case that came across his desk that he couldn't solve or at least make progress on.

But the difference with those cases was that in each instance, the case was *already* a puzzle someone had started putting tougher, *already* offering him all the details and questions that needed to be answered.

Here, in the middle of the Caribbean on a boat, he had no idea what he was supposed to be looking for. Was he poking around to find what had caused the explosion? Was he here to ensure the boat wouldn't sink any further? Or was he just simply a scared father, trying to get a handle on the situation so that he could keep his kids and family safe?

If it were anything but the last option, he was woefully unprepared and inexperienced. Who was he to measure how buoyant a cruise ship would become after an explosion? And he was no cop, no soldier. He was not trained to kick down doors, run at the enemy, or play private eye and snoop around for clues. He had been in those classes, but at the time it was all just theory.

He wasn't *that kind* of agent.

No, he had the suspicion that he was just here to check on the kids, as much as his gut told him otherwise.

He meant what he had told Kate — that the ship was most likely done sinking. For whatever reason, it had not listed anymore, nor had it sunk any further beneath the waves. He hoped that meant the damage was done, and he could move about unopposed. Now either way, there was no question in his mind that he would be able to safely get off the ship when he was done here. Even if he had to swim, plenty of other boats and small ships would be coming to check on the cruise ship in the near future. Any swim he would have to take would not last long — maybe half a mile.

He reached the doorway that led into the larger hall, where the kids started their day and would be corralled for meetings or larger events. This was where they had first dropped the girls off when they showed them the space, and from here, they would be split into groups and taken to their respective areas on one of the three decks.

He hesitated at the door, squeezing his eyes closed and saying a quick prayer.

Please, do not be here. Please, make this all a waste of my time.

He hoped that the girls and the rest of the kids were not behind these doors. If they were, it meant something had gone *seriously* wrong. If they *weren't* here, it meant they had successfully been taken to lifeboats and placed inside, safely on their way to the Jamaican port where they would be reunited with Kate and the other parents.

Please be a waste of my time, he said again, silently.

He pushed the doors open.

His heart caught in his throat. Something nagged at the

back of his mind, but he pushed it away, needing to know. He stepped through the small antechamber leading into the larger room, a miniature hallway with another set of doors just beyond. He pushed these open as well, then immediately looked into the expansive space.

There were no kids inside.

JACK LEFT the children's area and hustled back to the Deck 10 aft stairs. He still had not seen anyone else, though he had heard a few voices chattering loudly as they walked around. It was eerie how quiet the ship was — he had never been on a cruise ship alone, of course, so it was very strange now to be in such a large place with few other people around.

A day near the end of their last cruise had rained, and they had returned to Galveston early. As it had been January, the rain had been cold, chasing everyone off the deck and down into the internal areas of the ship. He and Kate had walked outside then, feeling how strange it was to be alone in such a large space.

But this was different — it was summer, and the weather was perfect. The Jamaican sky and bright sunlight pierced every nook and cranny on Deck 10, hardly casting any shadows at all.

The ship had stopped moving for the time being, but he wondered if and how the tides would affect it further. He wasn't sure what time that would be, but he assumed he had hours before anything changed drastically.

He did not, however, have hours before Kate and the others reached the shore and word got out that he had scrambled back on board the ship. Besides that, he saw there were still crew members running around, trying to put out fires — either figuratively or literally. And this whole place would soon be crawling with Coast Guard and SWAT teams, or at least the Jamaican equivalent. He wondered what sort of protocols and plans the cruise ship had for situations like this.

Of course, they had trained and prepared for a bomb on board. The unfortunate consequence of living in modern-day America was that nowhere was truly safe from a terrorist attack — or a stupid person being reckless. It could have been any number of things that had caused the explosion, but he felt safer knowing the captain and his teams would have worked through the protocols for just such an event.

He was descending the stairs, aiming for Decks 1 and 2. If the ship had taken on a lot of water, the boat most likely would have shifted even more to the side. He was no expert, but he had to guess that safety compartments on one or two where the explosion had been had automatically or manually been closed, shortly after the blast.

That meant — he hoped — Decks 1 and 2 were not completely flooded. A relatively small hole in the side of the ship should not be a death sentence. Dozens of major naval disasters over the course of history had proven that. He didn't know what sorts of safety features a cruise ship like this had, but he knew it had them.

Not surprisingly, he found the stairwell doors to Deck 2 locked since everything below was crew-only. He pulled up the stolen keycard and was happy to see the green LED light appear and hear the clicking sound as the door unlatched. He pulled it open slowly, as he had all the other doors, doing his best not to announce his presence. He did not need to get caught and thrown off the boat, or worse — turned into whatever authority would be here soon.

Immediately upon walking out onto this deck, he could sense that there was much more activity down here. He heard voices deep in conversation, almost shouting at one another, though he couldn't make out the words they were saying. Somewhere behind one of the doors on this level was a large group of people, and he saw a couple of crew members darting back and forth in the hallway on the opposite side of the corridor near the ship's bow. None of them looked in his direction, but he did not want to stay out in the open for long.

I just want to figure out what's going on, he told himself. He knew he should just go back up to Deck 10 and try to catch any of the lifeboats that might still be leaving. He doubted there were any left for passengers — it seemed as though all of them had been corralled and taken off the ship so far by now, but he knew there was still crew here that would need to leave at some point. He thought he had heard of inflatable lifeboats for the last of the crew and officers leaving, and he wondered where those might be located.

He wasn't sure what the plan was at this point — should he check every room? Why would the kids be down here, below the waterline, in the first place? His conscious mind knew it was stupid, but there was something in him telling him to poke around a bit. He figured he wasn't looking for the kids as much as just trying to figure out why there had been an explosion. It was his professional bent to look into things, to piece things together. He had learned to trust his gut, but he had still surprised himself by jumping back onto the ship.

He swiped the keycard over the keypad on the first door to his right, and it swung open inwardly. He stepped inside and saw that he must be in a section of the hallway designated for the crew. Four beds lined two walls, one bunk bed on each side. The rest of the room was sterile, white and bare, with no decorative features or stylistic additions the passenger suites had. A few photographs and pictures were taped to the walls near each pillow. He saw some posters of a rock band he didn't recognize on the wall across from him, and duffel bags and suitcases jammed underneath the bunk beds.

And that was it. There was nothing else in the room. Whoever these people were, they lived out of a duffel bag or a suitcase for months on end. They shared a room with three others, working day and night to scrape by and send whatever tips and earnings home to whatever country they had come from.

It was sort of sad — the cruise company always made it seem like working for them was a glamorous affair — that their exotic crew and teams had been handpicked from special places all around the world, when in fact they were simply just people trying to eke out a living, practically begging for tips.

He sighed and was about to leave the room when he heard his cell phone start to ring.

"Shit," he whispered. He quickly tapped the volume button to shut off the ringer and put it on silent mode as he pulled the phone up to his face.

It was a number he didn't recognize, but that was what he had expected. He could not answer it fast enough. He pulled the phone to his ear. "Kate — is that you?"

There was sobbing on the other end of the phone.

"Kate!" he said again, louder. "Kate, is that you? Talk to me!"

"Jack..." she finally said. "Yeah, it's me. Where — where are you?"

Jack shook his head, then answered verbally. "I'm — I'm still on the ship. Kate, the kids — you're with the kids, right?"

He once again felt the bile rise in his throat as his greatest fear — the one he had been ignoring, trying to stifle this entire time — came back to life, this time with a vengeance.

Kate responded slowly, robotically, as if reading from a script. "Jack, no. The kids never made it here. We've all checked every single lifeboat multiple times. No one has seen anyone who was in the Kids Zone get out of any of the boats."

Oh, my God, he thought. *Shit. Oh, shit.*

He started pacing, breathing quickly. Jack felt like his world was crashing down around him. He didn't care about anything else at that moment. His entire existence shrank to the size of two small humans, eleven years old and seven.

Where are they? He started shaking; he heard Kate shrieking into the phone — the sobs now taking over, controlling every fiber of her being.

What is happening? Why would they not be there? Or upstairs, still in their zone, waiting to be taken to a boat?

His gut had been correct, though he had been woefully incorrect about *why.* Sure, there had been an explosion which he was still curious about. But he had been brought here seemingly against his own will, not to figure out what the explosion was all about — but because it knew there was something fishy going on, and his own kids had been pulled into it.

Kate was talking again, asking him something. He wasn't sure what he even mumbled in response — his mind was already elsewhere, already racing with the possibilities. *Where could they be? Can I possibly find them on this huge ship?*

He heard her say okay, then the phone call disconnected. He reached down and clicked the call off from his end as well, then shoved it back into his pocket.

His breathing now was slow, steady. He must have been inadvertently already trying to calm himself down as he talked to his wife. He had not realized he had been doing it but was thankful he had.

His mind felt clearer now, the fear and shock of it all *clarifying* his thoughts rather than muddying them. Nothing else mattered to him anymore. The explosion could wait, the others back at the docks could wait.

Now, there was *one* mission: he *had* to find the kids.

I HAVE *to find the kids.*

Nothing in his life — his *entire* life — meant more to him right now than his current mission. He needed to find the kids and get them safely off the ship.

Jack ran through the chain of events that had led to this moment. Upon dropping them off at Kids' Zone, he and Kate had made it almost all the way back across the deck when they heard the boom and felt the ship start tilting, taking on water somewhere down here.

Almost immediately, the crew members had dashed into action, corralling everyone and getting them onto whatever lifeboats they could find.

He had assumed that the same actions were being taken by the counselors and crew staffing the children's area and that the kids had also reached a lifeboat. He and Kate had assumed that they would all get to Jamaica simultaneously or close enough.

There was simply no reason for the kids to still be on board, but where else could they be?

He had checked other rooms in the children's area and

found no one. Then, he had gotten a call from Kate giving him the worst news he had ever heard in his life.

Something was definitely wrong, and he sensed it was something sinister. He had inadvertently put himself right in the middle of it.

Standing inside this crew room forced him to catch his breath, though he wanted to start out into the hall and start cracking skulls, asking anyone and everyone where the hell his kids were. But he knew that was a bad idea — there might be a few actual crew members milling about, gathering belongings or checking for other passengers, but if what he believed were true — that there was *another* group on board, one with more nefarious goals — he couldn't take the risk of just running around like a crazy person.

He had heard the people from inside the stairwell, as well: 'fifteen of us against all of the crew and passengers,' the voice had said.

Fifteen of who? Jack wondered. *What were they doing here? What were they trying to accomplish?*

And how in the hell were his kids involved with it?

Jack squeezed his fists tightly, enraged as the adrenaline surged through him. He reached out and gripped the edge of the bathroom counter to steady himself.

There were far too many rooms and hidden spaces on this luxury cruise liner for one man to check alone, at least in a reasonable amount of time. He had to scratch that idea.

His next best idea was to check the larger rooms he knew about — the theaters, dining halls, cafeterias — any accessible space he knew of that was large enough to hold that many children.

But then again, how many kids had been enrolled in Kids'

Zone that day? He knew some parents would have taken their kids to shore with them for excursions or to hang out on the beach. There were probably fewer than a full roster of kids signed in today.

So fewer kids meant less space required to hide them all. That meant his options of spaces to check had just skyrocketed once again.

And besides, if they *really* wanted to hide the kids, they could just separate them into a bunch of rooms just like this one, then guard the doors.

He hated to admit it, but a needle-in-a-haystack search for his kids was not his best option at the moment. He would still look around, keeping his eyes open and his ears up, but the best thing he could do right now was act like a detective. If he could figure out what was *really* going on, the deeper meaning behind all of this, and what these people's goal was, it might help him get to the bottom of this.

But there was no way in hell he was leaving this ship until he knew his kids were safe, so he might as well put himself to work. If he was going to be useful at all, it was in being the eyes and ears for everyone back onshore. Thanks to the cellphone in his pocket, he had access to the outside world, though it was difficult to know what to do with it. Right now, in the chaos of the unfolding drama, he could talk to Kate or call out to whatever authority would listen.

As time went on, however, whatever these people were working toward would make it less likely for him to be able to get a call out. He knew that the ships' communications tower allowed two-way conversations, and the cruise company — constantly looking for ways to nickel and dime its passengers

— charged exorbitant fees for cell phone service and access, even while at port.

And he did not have an internationally unlocked phone, which meant he was currently beholden to the ship's tower for all communications.

Somebody, at some point in the future, might be watching that very tower for any communications going in or out. If he was on the phone then, or even sending text messages, they would find it immediately. He didn't know if it were possible, but he even thought they might be able to block his number from communicating in the first place.

So having a conversation with the outside world was not going to be an option for very long, and it was risky even now. He wondered if there was already somebody paying attention to inbound and outbound calls and Internet access and had overheard him or at least seen that he had had a conversation with Kate.

He needed to get somewhere safe. A place he could think and plan out his next moves. It was only a matter of time before word got out that he was still on board, and as the port crew siphoned through the ship's manifest and determined who exactly was accounted for and who was not, they would probably know his name in short order. Perhaps Kate was even working with them to get her husband and kids back, and she wouldn't know any better — she had no way of knowing that something else was going on aboard the cruise ship.

If she told them his name and Port Authority communicated this with the group of people on board, it could be disastrous for him.

He opened the door just a crack, waiting next to it and staying out of sight in the small bathroom. He heard voices, but they sounded like they were still coming from a ways down the hall. He was about to leave the room when he heard the stairwell doors open, predicated by the telltale click of the locking mechanism. He ducked back into the bathroom as two people exited the stairwell landing and started walking down the hallway. He couldn't hear their conversation.

When they passed, he silently closed the door once again and let out a breath. *This is not going to work,* he thought. *I'm too exposed, too obvious.* He looked down and noticed for the first time the way he was dressed. A t-shirt and swim trunks. Flip-flops.

Not exactly a detective outfit.

He suddenly had an idea. Jack walked over to the tiny in-wall closet inside this crew room.

Come on, he thought. *Just this once. Give me a sign that I'm on the right track.*

He pulled open the closet door and let out an even deeper, satisfied sigh. *Yes,* he thought. *Exactly what I need.*

Staring at him from inside the closet was a full lineup of crew outfits — all black, complete with black-soled tennis shoes sitting at the bottom of the closet at waist height. He pulled out the shoes first, glad to see they were around his size. Not perfect, but he wasn't planning a long career in cruise work. But it meant that the clothes inside — at least some of them — should be a good fit.

Jack pulled on the slacks and found them a bit loose. *They'll have to do.* The black button-down shirt came next, and to his surprise, he found it fit pretty well.

Okay, he thought optimistically. *We're making progress.*

He slipped on the shoes and laced them up while sitting on

one of the bunk beds. Before standing again, he noticed something from the corner of his eye.

There, tucked underneath the top of the bed, pinned to the underside of the mattress, was a badge.

Juan Ortega, El Salvador.

He whistled softly. *Well, I guess I'm going fully undercover. I hope I look like a Juan enough to pass as Juan.*

He pulled the badge off the bed and put it on his new shirt, trying not to laugh at his terrible pun. Then the thought of it reminded him of his daughters, who always groaned at his amazingly clever 'Dad jokes.'

This is just Phase 1, he told himself. *I have to do this to find the girls. I'll look around and see what's what, and this will help me move around without people noticing too much.*

He knew he was doing it for *them* — for Kate.

But if something *really* went sideways, something terrible happened — was he going to die for what might be a stupid idea?

Was he throwing his life away for nothing?

CHAPTER 23

JACK

JACK BARR, now moonlighting as Juan Ortega from El Salvador, left the crew members' room and walked confidently down the hall. He wasn't sure how he would pretend to fit in, but he figured among the fifteen people he was actually worried about, there would also be normal cruise ship crew members milling about, working on closing shop before disembarking.

If he could busy himself with a random task whenever he saw someone, it might buy him enough time to figure out who they were and what they were doing. Or if they were part of the group that might have the information he was looking for.

His first step was to get down to the opposite side of the hall, where he and Kate had been sneaking around the night before. He didn't think he could easily access the same room where he had seen the guns in the crate before, but it couldn't hurt to try. Besides, the end of the hallway was where some of the crew seemed to be gathering at the moment. Whatever they were doing, it was down there. He walked toward the area, nodding at two crew members walking in the opposite direction as he passed. Neither of them batted an eye. *Okay*, he thought, *so I definitely pass as a Juan. Good to know.*

He hoped his outfit wasn't somehow signaling to the world that he was a musician, magician, or some other entertainer and that he might be asked to perform to prove his identity. He couldn't carry a tune in a bucket, nor could he play an instrument to save his life.

And he really hoped he would not have to even *be* in the position of having to save his own life.

He saw the towers of crates, still stacked, behind which he and Kate had hidden. He approached them, walking slowly and calmly. There were other crew members around him now, all men. There were either no women on duty right now in this area of the ship, or he was walking amongst the fifteen men who were supposedly plotting something. Still, no one seemed to care that he was approaching.

If it were the case that these were the very men he had heard about earlier, no one had recognized him as *not* a part of their group yet. That told him they might not be as well-organized as he had thought. Perhaps this was not some sort of elaborately planned coup but simply an accidental explosion, and the 'fifteen' he had heard about were just someone's poker group.

Still, he didn't make eye contact unless it would have been awkward not to. He waited by the towers, pretending to read the small text on the side of each box. All of them were food — the text just lists of ingredients that would be found inside, mostly baking items with the occasional pot or pan required for a specific dish thrown in.

Finally, the hallway cleared enough for him to approach the door. This was the same Theater Access door through which he and Kate had entered the night before. Four of the men in the hallway had just entered in, but he waited until the three crew members still in the hallway were looking in the other direction or moving into a room, then he swiped his keycard and opened the door. He stepped inside the smaller green room and was about to walk into the larger hall where the crates were stacked when he heard shouts.

"Do it, now!" A man's voice shouted. It sounded gravelly, as if the man speaking were in his late forties or fifties, strained but gritty like he was just about to lose his voice.

There was a pause, and then Jack's ears took in an explosion of sound.

He was horrified to recognize the sound as rifle fire.

Multiple assault rifles began firing all at once, and amidst the rounds leaving the chambers, he also heard screams of death and agony coming from the larger room.

He did not dare poke his head through for fear that the guns would turn on him next.

He smashed his hands over his ears, amazed by how loud the sound was even from up here.

The guns died down after a few more seconds, and the grizzly voice continued. "We need to get this done quickly, men. Find the rest of them, *now*, and eliminate them. The last lifeboat left with its crew on board, so the only ones left are the inflatable rafts on 10 and the fore section of 11."

There was another pause. "And make sure the crew that *is* still on board — the crew that has seen you all — *does not leave.*"

Jack did not hear any response except the sound of pounding footsteps. They thundered through the theater's warehouse-like back space and grew louder.

Oh, shit, Jack thought. *Shit, shit, shit. They're coming up here.*

He raced back to the door and pulled it open quickly, turning to shut the door as softly as possible. He wanted to make sure no one had heard him in the antechamber, but he needed to hide — fast.

He was hoping to get into one of the rooms across the hall nearby. Of course, they would probably be checking all of the rooms, but what other option did he have? None of these doors were opening, so he had to assume that the crew had not heard the gunfire.

He whirled back around and found himself face-to-face with a wide-eyed young man, hair disheveled and hanging down to his shoulders.

Jack glanced down at his badge. *Giuseppe Peralta,* from Florence, Italy

"Who — who are you?" Giuseppe asked in accented English.

"Jack." He saw Giuseppe's eyes dart toward his own badge. "Sorry — I'm borrowing this outfit."

"What was that noise?"

Jack's breath caught in his throat. He was standing directly in front of the door, and he knew men were on their way, about to spill out into this exact space. "I need you to follow me," Jack said quickly. "We need to hide. Now!"

Giuseppe stood there, still wide-eyed. "Were those... were those *guns?*"

Jack started to panic. "I'm not kidding, man. Get down here *now!*" He pulled the kid with him around the stack of boxes just as the door smashed open, the crashing of the men within spilling out into the hallway. The kid started to argue, but Jack clamped his hand over his mouth and wrapped his arm through the crewmember's own and held it in place by clamping onto the back of his neck. It was not a perfect hold, but Jack was stronger than this wiry little guy, so it wouldn't take much.

Jack whispered directly into the kid's ear. "They shot a bunch of us in there," Jack said, taking on the persona of Juan once more. "I — I didn't see it, but I heard it. *All* of it. With any luck, though, they'll start checking the rooms, and we can just hide here for a minute."

Jack felt Giuseppe start to shake, and felt a tear hit the top of his finger, but he held his hand firmly in place. He could not take the chance of letting the kid spoil this hiding spot. The two men who had burst forth from the greenroom immediately started working their way up the hallway, skipping the tower boxes Jack and Giuseppe were hiding behind entirely. He assumed that they thought the crew would still be in their rooms doing whatever they had been doing previously, ignorant to the massacre that had just taken place. There was no reason — yet — for anyone to be hiding.

The two men worked swiftly on opposite sides of the hallway, using keycards that were attached to auto-retracting belt clips. At each room, they smacked them against the locking mechanism, then pulled open the door. They waved their rifles out into the room for a second or two, then pulled back into the hallway and moved to the next door. After three doors, the man on the right began firing into the room. He heard a shout, followed by a sickening silence. The man shot another burst of rounds into the room, then pulled back and let the door close. He didn't even hesitate before moving on to the fourth door.

Giuseppe was sobbing now, his head and chest moving up and down roughly while Jack held him in place.

"It's okay, kid," he said. "We're safe right here. For now."

Jack wasn't sure he believed his own words, but what choice did he have? This kid was a loose cannon — his cries would easily alert the men to their location.

Jack and Giuseppe waited for an excruciating amount of time while the men performed their horrific duties. They did not fire into very many rooms, maybe ten or twelve along the entire course of the hallway, eventually opening the room at the far end Jack had previously been hiding in. Finding it empty, they left through the stairwell on the far side. At this point, Jack could barely see them.

Finally, after twenty minutes, Jack released Giuseppe's mouth. Thankfully, the kid did not immediately start screaming or crying loudly. He waited, then twisted a bit so his eyes could lock onto Jack's.

"Who were those people?" Giuseppe asked.

"Beats the hell out of me, kid," Jack said. "And I'm not sure I want to find out."

"We need to get off the boat. We need to find —"

Jack nodded but cut him off. "*You* need to get off the boat, yeah. But I need to stay a little while longer."

"What? Why?"

Jack took a deep breath, letting it out slowly to calm his nerves. "Because," he explained. "I need to find my kids."

JACK HAD TRAINED with assault rifles before, both in the Army and as qualification required for his current job. He was a great shot, but most importantly, he knew his way around a weapon and had developed a respect for firearms. He didn't love the idea of having to *use* them — part of why he appreciated his job riding a desk — but right now, there was no desk in sight. He was in the field, and a trustworthy weapon was exactly what he needed.

He turned back to Giuseppe. "There are probably still men in that room," he explained. "But I need to get my hands on a weapon. It's the best way I can think of to protect myself. To protect you."

Giuseppe's eyes seemed to grow wider. "Can't I just... leave? There is more lifeboats, yes? I know my way around the ship, and I can use crew-only access elevators to get to Deck 10."

Jack shook his head. "Somewhere, there are life rafts, from what I heard. But no, you can't leave yet. We need to get you up to the deck unseen, or they're going to kill you too. I can't take that risk."

Giuseppe swallowed but nodded. It seemed he understood how dire the situation had just become. Suddenly, he started sobbing once more. Jack was confused but then looked down. The kid's black pants were wet around his crotch and leg.

Giuseppe was about to speak, but Jack cut him off again. "Listen, kid," he started. "No one is *ever* prepared for a situation like this. *No one*. Got it? So the fact that you did what you were supposed to do — you got out of the way, and you hid, means you're still alive, and you should be proud of yourself for that. Don't worry at all about that mess; it means nothing."

Giuseppe did not stop crying, but Jack's words seemed to have calmed him down bit.

Jack couldn't wait any longer. He stood up, walking around the side of the tower of boxes. "I need you to follow me — and by follow me, I mean I need you to stay right on my ass. Soon as I open that door, you're walking through it, got it?"

Giuseppe nodded immediately, standing up and wiping his eyes. He had to be uncomfortable, but Jack knew that was the least of his worries at the moment.

The hallway was now devoid of any other crew members, and Jack absolutely hated that he knew exactly why that was.

But the fact that everyone was dead meant the hall was quiet, and that gave him the ability to move to the Theater Access door again without being seen or heard, so he did just that. He knew this movement was going to be the riskiest one yet — anybody could be waiting behind this door now, guarding it for any crew members who may have survived and wanted to escape. But Jack didn't know his way around these decks — if there was another entrance to the theater access warehouse, he didn't know where it was.

He clicked his keycard, then winced as he opened the door. He was basically announcing his presence, but he had to take the risk. He *needed* a weapon if they were going to get out of this alive.

He waited, Giuseppe right on his ass as he had requested, and Jack pulled the door open a bit wider. He heard nothing and saw nothing, though the room was still dark inside. He stepped in, letting out a breath when he realized they were alone. Giuseppe followed close behind, and together the pair moved toward the opposite door.

Here, Jack held his hand out and whispered to Giuseppe. "I need you to wait in here for a minute, okay? Maybe hide behind that desk or something?"

Giuseppe nodded again and walked hesitantly over to the desk. Jack didn't blame him. It was terrible cover, useless if anybody actually came looking for them in the room. Jack saw a box of fabric rolls, each about four feet tall. He pulled it over and slid it in front of Giuseppe's hiding spot. It still wasn't great, but it did the trick — Jack could not see Giuseppe in the shadows now unless he was looking for him there.

Hopefully though, Jack wouldn't be long. He stepped back toward the door leading into the larger space and tested the handle. There was no keypad on this door, and he was glad to find it still unlocked. He hoped that meant the two men who had exited from here were on a one-way mission — clearing out the floors room by room, methodically and thoroughly, so they wouldn't miss anyone. They had taken the stairs at the far end of the hallway, so Jack hoped that meant they would be continuing upward, deck by deck, and not coming back this way anytime soon.

Jack winced at the implications. *They're killing everyone here,* he thought. *At least, all of the adult crew.*

He did not let his mind continue to the next obvious thought.

I'm going to find the kids before they can do anything, he thought.

He opened the door and stepped through, knowing that this was the moment he would be shot if it was going to happen at all. Nothing he could do about it now, really, so he figured he might as well just embrace it and hope for the best.

Happily, he found himself not shot upon entering the larger room.

In fact, it looked completely empty. He let out a breath.

He stepped in and started down the stairs toward the crates. He and Kate stood right here only a day ago, but the room's contents made the room look a world apart from how it had been.

Three of the crates were open, their heavy wooden lids leaning against them. Weapons and ammunition were sprinkled on the floor, laid out in rows and organized. Rifles, sidearms, and ammunition boxes covered a blanketed space around the first box as if the men had torn into it, taking only what they wanted and leaving the rest.

And why not? No one else would be coming for them — these men had full control of the ship.

Beyond the boxes, splitting the room in half, was a massive metal door extending from the ceiling of the level above, sealing off whatever was behind it. The door seemed to split the stage — directly above Jack's head — in half horizontally.

He knew exactly what he was looking at. A blast door — a metal wall that could be lowered, which compartmentalized the ship into smaller spaces.

This must be close to where the explosion had happened, he thought. The floor was not wet, and there was no sign of water having been in here, so Jack assumed that this massive door was simply one of many — a preparatory compartment meant to prevent flooding in case another compartment flooded.

He wondered if the captain had lowered this door manually or if there was some sort of automated system in place. He knew much of the buoyancy and sinking prevention of a ship was due to the many compartments that extended up the hull. Any breach would flood only a certain amount of compartments.

But an explosion — that would cause far more damage, and the compartments would be totally blasted through, allowing water past them and into the main deck areas.

He did not know what he would find if he somehow made it beyond this door, but he assumed there would be smaller doors similar to this one, each holding back seawater.

Jack examined the huge door for a moment longer, frowning as he heard a strange humming sound. It was in the distance, sounding as though it might be coming from somewhere on the *other* side of the door. It was irregular, too, like the sound of an engine revving up and slowing.

Weird, he thought. He did not inspect it further — it was probably just a pulley or chain on the other side of the blast door malfunctioning.

Jack turned his head back toward the staircase he had just ascended and immediately threw a hand over his mouth.

Holy shit.

He backed up against the wall of crates. "Oh, my God," he said softly.

JUST PAST THE STAIRWELL, there looked to be an orchestra pit, currently covered by a sliding wooden ceiling — the front of the stage floor above.

And in that pit is where the bodies were.

At least twenty black- or white-clad crew members were sprawled on the floor. Blood was pouring out of the bullet wounds that had taken their lives.

Jack felt tears coming to his eyes, and his hand clamped tighter over his mouth than it had previously been on Giuseppe's.

He needed to run. He needed to get away from this. Maybe he could just get upstairs and dive off the edge into the water. It was still broad daylight outside, so there was little danger he wouldn't make it to shore. He could just simply ignore all of this and wait for the authorities to come in and fix it.

But no, there would be no 'fixing' this. These people were *dead*. Killed by whoever the hell was running amok on this cruise ship.

Whoever had his kids.

Jack was starting to piece this puzzle together. He still didn't know the *why* behind it, but he was starting to understand the *how*. He was starting to understand a bit about what was going on. There was certainly more to understand, more to uncover, but the puzzle pieces were culminating in his mind's eye.

A small terrorist group wanting to make sure whatever they're doing here is not seen.

They're killing any crew still here.

But what are *they doing?*

In any other situation, and any other day, Jack would have absolutely run for the hills. He absolutely would have gone overboard — would have tried to escape this madness. He would *never* attempt this — whatever it was he thought he was doing — alone. There were teams for this sort of thing. Operatives and agents, as well as officers and analysts that he worked with, who could put together a plan of attack...

That's it, he thought.

Before, when he was just snooping around, there had been no reason to call this in. How could he explain himself? That he ignored a crewmember's order and jumped off a lifeboat and back onto a sinking ship, for what?

And then, when he'd realized that these men were killing people, he had not assumed anything — there were crazy assholes everywhere, and just because some were going on a mass shooting spree did not mean the CIA needed to get involved.

But this was now... different. This *was* a terrorist attack, at least of some sort. These men had a *purpose*, a goal.

He reached down and picked up one of the assault rifles. He recognized the rifles as the M4 carbine, firing 5.56 NATO rounds, made by any number of manufacturers. Currently in use by almost all American military branches, it was a very popular weapon.

And now he knew why it was here. These men were preparing for an all-out war. If any of the other crates he and Kate had discovered here were full of weapons, it meant they expected to arm a *lot* of people.

Jack saw that all of the boxes of ammunition would fit the gun, but he did not see any clips and didn't want to load a magazine by hand, so he clicked off two extra fully loaded mags from two other M4s and stuffed them into his pockets.

Two extra magazines — a total of sixty rounds — would have to be it. They were bulky and awkward in his pockets, which were already sagging and threatening to fall down, but he didn't care. He was armed, and he intended to stay that way.

CHAPTER 26

JACK

AS HE STOOD up and shifted to get comfortable, rifle in hand, he did his best to not look at the mass grave to his right. He turned slowly in the other direction, toward the wall of crates, and continued turning until he was facing the stairwell again. And just then, the door opened.

"Giuseppe, I told you to —"

Jack's eyes widened as he saw that the person who had opened the door was *not* Giuseppe.

Jack backpedaled, hitting the wall of crates and twisting around the first one he found that was not stacked tightly against the wall.

The intruder opened fire upon realizing that Jack was not a member of his team. The rounds pinged off the crates, some getting lodged in their wooden lids, and Jack kept his head down.

Shit. I'm stuck here, now. While he knew his way around an M4, he did not have *this* sort of training. He didn't know how to clear a room, how to stay hidden under pressure. He had never fired at anything but a piece of paper or a range target before, either.

The best he could do was lift his rifle and try to fire off a few random shots, hopefully landing some in that direction. He had seen that move in movies — though he had to admit it was usually the bad guys trying it, and the bad guys always lost.

He sat alone behind the crate, the tears still welling in his eyes, as he heard the slow footsteps of the person entering the room and standing on the landing. They fired their own M4 every few seconds, a few short bursts at a time, keeping Jack pinned.

It's okay, Jack thought. *I have no intention of poking my head out and making a run for it.* There were only about thirty feet of space between the shooter and Jack, and the man literally had the high ground.

Jack felt his throat tighten, his heart racing beyond a level he was able to control.

This is it, he thought. *I'm going to die down here, acting like some commando.*

He wanted to stand up, to at least try to fight back before the guy just walked around the crates and shot him point-blank. But he was too scared, too terrified and horrified by what he had seen already.

He squeezed his eyes shut, his finger tightening over the rifle in his hands. He dared a peek around the side of the crate.

The man lifted his gun to fire at Jack again, and he pulled his head back just as he heard a loud *thunk*. It sounded like metal hitting something softer, and a second later the man fell, the sound of his heavy body crashing down the stairs.

The mercenary let out a groan, and Jack heard the sound of his rifle clattering farther down the stairs.

He waited for another few beats, then turned and peeked around the side of the crate he was hiding behind.

Giuseppe, standing on the landing while holding a fire extinguisher, smiled at him.

His pants and left leg were soaked with urine, but the kid stood triumphantly.

Jack looked over at the man who had fallen and saw that his eyes were blinking.

Jack took aim and fired, placing a single round through the man's cheek and neck. The man made a disgusting gurgling sound as he died. While Jack had not exactly gotten him right between the eyes like he had hoped, the shot had clearly been accurate enough to get the job done.

He hated doing it, but it was his life — and Giuseppe's — or this guy's. And this guy had probably been one of the men executing these poor souls in the orchestra pit.

"Giuseppe... *thank you*," Jack said, standing and starting to walk toward the stairs. "You saved my life, kid."

"You saved mine, first," the kid said in response, shrugging it off.

Jack hustled up the stairs and gave the kid a quick embrace, ignoring the dampness that had now traveled to his own pants. He pulled the kid back into the room and closed the door.

"How did he not see you?" Jack asked.

"He was not looking for me," the Italian said, shaking his head. "I got lucky, I guess. It's dark in here, and he just ran through as if he knew you were —"

"Oh, shit," Jack said suddenly.

If *this* guy had come rushing back, it might be one of the guys from earlier. He didn't recognize him, but then again he had been hiding behind the stacked boxes, not trying to examine the killers.

But if this was one of the guys from the hallway...

His thoughts were silenced by the sound of the outer lock disengaging.

Someone was coming into this room. Jack pressed Giuseppe into the corner where he had hidden him before and spread his own body out, covering him. He lifted his rifle and waited for the door to open. There would only be a second, but that brief second would be Jack's only opening. The man on the other side would be vulnerable during that time, as he got around and got his body in front of the doorway and let his eyes adjust.

The man started to speak, likely calling out to his partner about why he had heard gunshots, but Jack didn't hesitate. He pulled the weapon up and fired three quick rounds on the rifle's burst mode, aiming upward with the kickback, landing at least one round into the man's body.

This man fell also, and Jack saw that he was dead on impact.

Good riddance, Jack thought.

CHAPTER 27

JACK

"WE NEED TO HIDE THE BODY," Jack said.

Giuseppe's eyes widened once again. "Mr. Jack — you want me to..."

Jack saw that the kid was extremely shaken, so he told him to stay hidden. "Don't worry about it," Jack said, sighing. "I'll take care of it."

The man was large, weighing probably 250 pounds, most of it muscle. It took some effort to pull the guy into the antechamber area and then onto the stairs' landing, but he was relieved when Giuseppe actually stood up and picked up the man's feet, which were dragging behind and slowing Jack down.

Jack tried not to look at the guy's face, his lifeless eyes staring straight up as he pulled him along, his hands holding under the man's armpits. He reached the stairs and then pulled the man over the first one, relieved that gravity was now help-ing. The floor down below was slicker, and Jack made short work getting the guy past his comrade and behind the crate Jack had previously been hiding behind.

He repeated the process with the other man, setting them side-by-side, their bullet wounds and bleeding bodies on display.

It wasn't a perfect spot, but it would work temporarily. All of the bloodstains up above and on the floor down here could easily be assumed to be blood from other crew members they had slaughtered.

At least, he hoped.

Jack was under no illusion that he was still here unbeknownst to the rest of the others. By now, someone had surely told the leader of this group that there was a passenger stowaway somewhere on the ship.

And what of the captain and bridge crew? He didn't know the protocol for the officers in charge of the boat, but he had a feeling they would be the last to leave. Maybe this group *had* waited for the captain and his officers to leave on their lifeboat... or maybe they intended to use them as hostages.

He didn't have enough information to decide what to do next, so he stuck to the original plan — he needed to find his kids.

Sure, Giuseppe was a risk, but there was no way he would leave him behind to get killed. It was clear from the look on the young man's face that there was no way he would be able to handle a gun, so that meant Jack was now the guy's personal bodyguard and escort.

"Where are we going?" Giuseppe asked. "Can we not just stay here? We can shoot anyone who comes in. And surely *somebody* will be coming to help us soon, right?"

Jack arched an eyebrow. "You sure about that?" he asked. Then he smiled. "And by *we*, I think you mean *I* can shoot anyone who comes in. What happens if two or more of them come at us from opposite directions? If we barricade ourselves in here, we only have one gun and trust me — it's not like the movies. We won't be able to shoot our way out."

Giuseppe swallowed, seeming to not like this response.

"No," Jack said. "I need to find my kids. And that means we can't sit here hoping and praying like it's some tower defense game."

Giuseppe nodded, then stepped forward, closer to Jack. He could almost feel his fear, it emanated from his body like heat.

"Since these two goons were in charge of taking out all of your crew members in this hallway, I'm going to assume that the coast will be clear — that any other goons will be in different hallways. If it's not, well..." Jack didn't really have a good answer for what would happen if the coast was not clear. "We'll just have to improvise, I guess."

He led them out of the theater access area and into the hallway once more. He was careful to step over the puddle of blood where he had shot and killed the second man, and he was pleased that Giuseppe did as well. The last thing they needed was to leave giant red footprints wherever they went.

He closed the door behind him, his senses on high alert. He had to assume everyone remaining on the ship — everyone alive, that was — was hostile. This group may only have fifteen — perhaps now thirteen — people, but they were all heavily armed and clearly would shoot at anyone dressed like Jack and Giuseppe.

Maybe it was *a mistake dressing up like a crew member, after all,* Jack thought.

He kept his rifle up, hustling down the hallway. The expansive corridor now seemed to stretch twice as far, every second that passed giving Jack more reason to worry. They reached the door at the end of the corridor, the one behind which Jack had hidden and changed into this crewmember's clothes. He wondered where Juan Ortega was now — had he gotten off the ship safely? He hoped the man had been up above, on Deck 10, helping the passengers and eventually finding his way into one of the boats. He tried not to think of the dozens of crew members and staff that were now dead or bleeding out in their rooms in this hallway.

He also tried not to think about all the *other* hallways just like this one — however many people had stayed behind, for whatever reason, were probably dead.

He still hadn't seen *all* fifteen members of this group, and he had only heard a few guns firing at once in the orchestra pit area earlier. So it was entirely possible that these two men he had killed were the only two gun-toting bad guys killing everyone inside, but he found that hard to believe. More likely, these two were just a pair of many, all dispersed by whoever's gravelly voice he had heard, told to go kill any of the remaining crew.

He passed the room on the left and used his keycard to unlock the stairwell doors. He pulled Giuseppe inside the dark landing and waited, listening for any voices or noise. Hearing nothing, he took the stairs two at a time to the next landing — Deck 2. Behind these doors, he pulled out his phone and saw that he had missed some notifications. Most were calls, which he would not have risked answering anyway, but one was a text message.

It was from a different number than the one Kate had called him from before, but the first two words told him it was his wife.

> *Jack, it's me. I'm using another passenger's phone, but they're letting me hold onto it for now.*

> *Let me know you got this.*

He pulled the phone up to his face and sent a response. He didn't feel comfortable talking aloud, so he sent a text response instead.

> *I got your note. Still on board, searching for the kids.*

What more could he say? What could he tell her that would not cause her to freak out? Surely he could not just tell her that he was being chased by assault rifle-carrying mercenaries? That he himself had shot and killed two of them? The only *possible* way to ensure he didn't cause even more unnecessary stress for his wife was to withhold facts. He knew she was worried about the kids, and that worry would have nearly consumed her by now, so he didn't want to pile on.

Still, it was nice to have some connection to the outside world. He wondered if he could have Kate get him to somebody who might be able to help.

> *Can you find somebody in charge? A police officer or Coast Guard person? They might be able to help me.*

He wasn't sure they *could* help him, but the more people out there who knew what was going on in here, the better. After all, as much as he downplayed it, he *did* work for the Central Intelligence Agency, so he had plenty of experience with identifying terrorist groups. These guys certainly fit the bill from what he had seen thus far. They knew how to handle weapons and were not afraid to use them. That meant they could easily be mercenaries — work-for-hire soldiers paid by whoever was in charge of this operation.

But the operation seemed to be progressing in a way that fit the profile of a terrorist operation. He still didn't know their motive — or even what they were fighting for — but they were clearly working toward some goal. They had waited until most of the passengers had gotten off the ship — surely not out of kindness and compassion, but because Jack knew it was impossible to corral that many people. Statistically speaking, every additional hostage in a situation like this added an exponential number of layers of complexity. A group of fifteen men, even if each of them had a weapon, would still only be able to control two or three people apiece.

He knew that *they* probably didn't know that, but they probably did not need to try to corral thousands of innocent people. They weren't trying to cause terror for terror's sake — they *wanted* something, which meant leverage. That meant hostages.

Jack also knew those hostage situations rarely played out as they did in the movies — eventually, people panicked — in some cases even losing their fear of death entirely, and simply started to make a run for it, as if they were operating on autopilot. He had seen it countless times in post-op reports. A gunman thought he or she had control of a room full of hostages just because they were holding a weapon. But eventually, if the situation progressed far enough and there were enough innocent lives at stake, the hostages realized that they had safety in numbers. Sometimes they would band together and fight, or sometimes a few of them would spread out and try to make a break for it.

The gunman would inevitably start frantically shooting whoever and whatever they could, either running out of ammunition or getting overtaken by the hostages.

Yes, these situations often did end with lives lost, but it was rarely a complete massacre.

Unlike the crew members who had been executed downstairs, he thought.

Jack knew they fit the profile of terrorists, at least in form. They were methodical, purposeful in their every move. They had absolutely been planning this. He wondered if they had brought the weapons on board themselves? Had they somehow snuck them into the storage warehouse behind and below the theater? These were questions he felt himself trying to answer. As much as he did not want to be working right now, it was his job — he couldn't help trying to put two and two together.

But he forced these thoughts out of his mind. It was not time for that. Right now, he needed to get to the kids, and get in touch with someone on the ground who might be able to help.

CHAPTER 28

KATE

KATE PUT the phone back in her pocket. She was still standing near the family that had given her the phone, and its owner — the mother of the three kids huddled around her and her husband — had told Kate she could keep it.

"A phone is a small price to pay to get your kids back," the woman had said. She knew the woman was being genuine, but it still felt hollow and forced to Kate's ears. Unlike her, these people still *had* their kids safely with them.

She had found a few other parents looking for their own kids as well, though they were all busy calling anyone and everyone they could, and some of them had told Kate that they would stick together and eventually make their way to the Port Authority building for screening. Kate could not bring herself to follow along — her husband was still on the *Ocean Voyager*, and if there was a chance he could find the kids, she wanted to be out here.

She was not above stealing and piloting a lifeboat and driving back out there, either. Petty crime in a foreign country was also a small price to pay to get her kids back.

But for now, she waited. Jack would call when he was safe and had more information. Or he would text. There was nothing she could do now but wait on the docks, where all the action was, and try to track down someone who looked like they were in charge.

No more lifeboats dotted the bay except for those that remained moored to the docks, and all boat traffic had been steered away from the tilted cruise ship out in the distance. No one had the full story, but Jamaican authorities had told boats and watercraft to steer clear of the cruise liner.

Thousands of people were still huddled on the docks and port entry area on the Jamaican beach, and Kate could already see news crews and amateur journalists making their way over. They had somehow gotten through the Port Authority security, but that didn't surprise her. This whole debacle would be international news in mere hours, and she was sure that in a twisted way the cruise company and Jamaican Tourism Board knew they could make a killing from a disaster like this.

But she wondered if the news crews knew about the missing kids yet. It was possible, she figured, but unlikely. They seemed too calm, simply reporting on the wreck out in the bay. As the story unfolded for them as well, they would eventually be appalled — but then very excited — that a juicy twist in the story had been handed to them on a silver platter.

For Kate, the twisted story was purely gut-wrenching. *Where the hell were they?* she wondered. If they *were* still on the ship, why weren't they being put in lifeboats? Were they waiting somewhere, scared? Had they been told help would come, only to be forgotten?

And if they weren't on the ship, she knew they hadn't reached the shore. So where were they? She had examined the insides of every single lifeboat multiple times, checked behind every corner, behind every docked yacht and sailboat, and asked anyone and everyone she could find who would listen if they had seen the kids. On top of that, there were the other parents with missing children, as well. She wasn't crazy — it was not just her kids who had disappeared.

She had even seen Mr. and Mrs. Bolívar, their dinner partners, from afar as well, but their kids were present and accounted for. She watched as the kids walked with their parents toward the entrance to the Port Authority building.

She had heard from a group of twenty-somethings that the passengers were allowed to leave, so long as they checked their names against the manifest and showed some form of identification. But since everyone had been removed from the ship so quickly, most people *had* no identification on them. That had led to a huge bottleneck, and a large line just outside the Port Authority main building. Some Jamaican authority or another was trying to check every last person coming into their country, making sure they were cleared to be there.

Under normal circumstances, there would not have been trouble at all. Kate knew everyone aboard the *Ocean Voyager* had had to have an up-to-date passport to even disembark, but she figured a situation like this would cause all sorts of new bureaucracy — if there was a chance for bureaucratic red tape, there would be lots of it. She could imagine the stress and anxiety in there now. Police and Port Authority workers were trying to maintain order and keep everyone calm while also ensuring they knew who was coming into their country.

She had even heard another group on the phone with an airline, trying to explain the situation and telling the person they had better get more planes gassed up and ready to go.

The man calling had seemed frustrated, so she assumed it was not going well. He wasn't wrong for calling, either — all of the airports on the island were about to be slammed with passengers just trying to get home immediately, not wanting to try to enjoy themselves after their cruise had ended in disaster.

All of this, though, was like background noise to Kate, who was nowhere near ready to try to get into the country and fly home. Her motherly instincts had kicked in long ago, and she was willing to go on a rampage to get to her children, if that's what it took.

She was feeling especially frustrated that no one seemed to be in charge here — she had seen the red shirts of some of the crews from the gift shop and surrounding kiosks, and a few police officers walking around out on the docks, but no one seemed to have any contact whatsoever with the ship.

CHAPTER 29

CARLOS

CARLOS PULLED THE REGULATOR AROUND, fitting it more comfortably inside his mouth. He kicked smoothly, rhythmically, as he propelled himself through the water. He had gone without the extra weight belt, wanting to remain somewhat buoyant but also not have trouble fighting with the natural tendency to float to the surface. Graves had ordered him to stay underwater the entire time, adamant that he not so much as risk even a single bubble catching someone's attention. It should not be a problem if he stayed deep enough. It was in the middle of the day, so if anyone were directly above him, they would easily see his lithe shape working its way toward the massive cruise ship out in The Shallows.

He still did not know why Graves had sent him here, what his boss wanted him to do when he got there. The man's only instruction had seemed purposefully vague: "just check things out."

It was unhelpful, but he didn't argue — he would take any excuse to get into the water again. *Far better than driving around and babysitting crates and boxes.*

Plus, the weather today was phenomenal. A few clouds pockmarked the blue sky, and plenty of sunlight lit the shallow bay. He saw many schools of fish happily darting back and forth, looking for a meal, and larger versions of the same looking for the pool itself. It was a constant game between them, and though it was beautiful to human eyes, he knew everything in the water was at risk of being eaten by something larger.

Sharks were not common here, nor were dolphins, as there was usually too much boat traffic this close to shore. Farther out was where they typically would frolic and play and where the sharks would hang out by the reefs, looking for a snack.

But today, he would not be that snack. There were very few dangers to Jamaican divers, and sharks were not among them. Today, there was nothing to worry about — he could simply enjoy the weather, and appreciate the strange request from his boss.

He pulled his arms up and put them into action now, letting them add power and control to his speed.

He swam like this for about twenty minutes, not even growing tired. Though he drove the lift most days, he had stayed in decent shape.

He saw the partially submerged hull of the cruise ship up ahead. Even from here, he could see that it was situated at a slight tilt. The bottom was not quite touching the sand, which meant the ship was still buoyant. It had taken on a lot of water, but its compartments had held thus far. The sandy ocean bed was about ten or fifteen feet below the hull's pointed bottom.

He slowed as he drew near the forward section of the southward-facing cruise ship. He didn't know what he was looking for exactly, but he figured he would know it when he saw it. Perhaps Graves had just sent him out here to examine why the ship had started taking on water. He had heard rumors of an explosion, probably accidental. If Graves had wanted to start an investigation as to what had caused this, he should have sent Carlos with an underwater camera.

No matter — Carlos would do as he was told. Worst case — and likely what Graves had been thinking — there was nothing much to report. Just a breach in the hull, but the ship's partitions would have halted further sinking. In that case, he would just swim back to shore and report his findings. Graves probably needed Carlos to check it out so that he could tell the cruise company exactly what was going on — that there was no reason to worry, everyone was safe, and — perhaps most importantly for a man like Howard Graves — that it wasn't his fault.

He started on the starboard side of the ship, not expecting to see anything noticeable. Based on the direction the boat was listing in the water, he assumed the breach would be on the port side of the ship. But he wanted to be thorough — if there were anything to see here on this side, he would find it.

He swam up the length of the ship toward the aft section, and saw the two massive propellers as he rounded the corner. Neither of the 'screws' was spinning, obviously, though he did see a stream of bubbles rising from the center of each Azipod shaft, telling him that the engines were still running. *So the ship still has power,* he thought. *Whatever has happened on board, it has taken down their communications, but not all of the power.*

He continued to the port side of the ship, still not seeing anything out of the ordinary other than the tilt of the boat itself.

About one-third of the way across the port-side, nearing the front of the boat, he saw it.

A brutal scar, almost perfectly circular, with dark burn marks around its edges.

He stared bug-eyed through his mask at the hole. Carlos had never seen anything like this before, and though he had seen a few sunken vessels on some of his dives, they were almost always either deteriorated old fishing boats or small dinghies that had just begun the slow process of turning into a reef. Boats regularly sank around the shores of Jamaica — bad news for the fishermen and tourist companies that owned them, but great news for divers and snorkeling tourists wanting to explore a new fish hideout.

But he had never been in the water so close to a massive luxury cruise liner, and he had certainly never seen a breach in one's hull. This was, without a doubt, the cause of the ship's listing. Though it was still buoyant, he was not surprised that the ship had settled to one side — water was extremely heavy, and part of this cruise ship was filled with it. He crept forward in the water, feeling strange now as if he were the first to see a terrible car accident.

There was a slight flicker of movement to his left, beyond a large reef gathering about a hundred feet distant, but he ignored it. The rare shark that came to explore these waters was so unlikely to threaten humans that he had not even given it a thought.

He had a job to do, and he intended to complete it. The brutal scar of an explosion marring the otherwise pristine exterior of the ship was not enough to give into his trepidation.

Carlos was fearful now only because it was a situation he had never been in before. He remembered the early days of learning to dive — all the information he had to keep straight, like how far he could descend, how slowly he had to rise to prevent the bends, all of it. Those were not even fears that registered in his mind now.

He took a deep breath from the regulator and moved again toward the open hole. There was about fifteen feet of space between himself and the breach in the hull, and he slowed to a stop to take his time approaching it.

After a moment more of examining the surroundings, ensuring it was safe, he crept forward.

CHAPTER 30

KATE

KATE HAD FINALLY DECIDED to leave the dock area to look for someone in charge. She was now walking toward what appeared to be an employee entrance for the cruise line's offices here at the port.

She was ready to raise hell, so whoever was just beyond that door was going to get an earful. As she stepped close to the door, however, it sailed open, and a huge man fell out of it. He looked to be mid-fifties, his hair disheveled, shirt halfway untucked.

But she didn't care how he looked — all she noticed was that he was wearing a badge stating that he was part of the security team here.

"Sir!" she began, hurriedly spilling out the words as fast as her mind would let her. "My kids aren't here — they didn't arrive, and I —"

The man held a hand up and continued walking past her rudely. "Sorry, lady," he said. "Got a lot of other shit to do."

Kate whirled around and grabbed the man's milky white

elbow, cold and flabby. She dug her fingers into the fat, and the man yelped in pain.

"Ouch! What the hell!"

She marched back in front of him and stared up into his eyes. "If it sounded like I was asking you a *question*, my apologies. Let me start over." She paused, taking a breath. "*I. Can't. Find. My. Kids.*"

The man sidestepped her once more and started huffing as he walked away again.

Kate was about to smack the shit out of him, but she knew he was — so far — her best hope at getting help. Once more, she marched directly in front of him, then stopped.

He didn't. She felt herself falling backward, but caught her balance at the last moment.

This man literally *just tried to walk through me,* she realized. He was doing his best to move quickly, but she could tell it was a strain for him. His fat torso seemed balanced on top of toothpick-like legs, making him look almost comical in any other situation. She wondered who the hell this guy was — he clearly was not the best and brightest this security team had to offer.

"Who the hell do you think you are?" she yelled.

He didn't stop, but he shouted back over his shoulder. "Howard Graves, Director of Security. And director of everything else," he muttered.

It wasn't much trouble for Kate to keep up by walking slowly, so she caught up with the man, now breathing rapidly from his apparent exertion.

"Look, I really just want some help," Kate said. "*Please.* You're supposed to be in charge of all this? Well, missing kids are a part of this."

He seemed to have heard this for the first time. He stopped, eyeing her. "What do you mean your kids are *missing*? They weren't on the lifeboats?"

She shook her head open. "*No*, that's what I've been trying to tell you. I got off over half an hour ago; my lifeboat was one of the first ones here. I've checked every single damned lifeboat multiple times, okay?"

He backed away, his palms out. "Okay, okay. Geez, lady. Don't have to get all snippy with me."

"*Snippy*?" Kate asked, incredulous. "I'm going to get *downright ballistic* in about *three seconds* if you don't help me find my damned kids."

The man let out a deep sigh, then squeezed his temples. "Look, lady. This day is really getting out of hand for me. I'm understaffed, and almost 100 percent of them are clueless and incompetent. I've got the Coast Guard and police — and a SWAT team waiting outside — all breathing down my neck, asking about what happened out there."

"What *did* happen out there? We heard an explosion or something on board, and then the ship slipped to the side, and —"

"And then stopped. Yeah, I can see that." He pointed over to where the huge luxury cruise liner sat perched in the waters.

"My husband and I were on a lifeboat," she continued, "but he sort of freaked out and jumped off, and then I came to shore, and I've been trying to find my kids ever since."

Howard seemed shocked by this last revelation. "He *got off the lifeboat* before it left?"

She nodded, frowning. She was surprised this bit of information seemed to mean more to him than news of her missing children had.

"Where is he now?" Graves asked Kate, starting to walk back toward the docks again. Kate kept pace with him. "Did he get on another lifeboat?"

She shook her head. "No, he's still on the ship."

He whirled around at this and stared, slack-jawed, at Kate. "He's *still* on board? I was told that *everybody* — passengers and crew — had disembarked, either on a lifeboat or one of the inflatable life rafts meant for the officers. Hell, that's where I'm heading right now. I need to check in with the captain and make sure he's okay. Believe it or not, most of my job is just babying these captains, who are apparently celebrities around here."

Kate ignored most of what he was saying, but she followed as he led them toward some of the inflatable lifeboats closest to the Port Authority buildings. She saw the crisp whites of some of their uniforms, but she didn't see anyone wearing the captain's hat. Of course, he probably had just removed it or lost it at some point during the cacophony.

They walked side-by-side for a few more seconds, Kate wanting to punch the guy for not picking up his pace, but once again reminding herself that he was the first and only person she had seen so far who seemed to actually know a bit about what was going on. Or, at least, able to do something about it.

One of the ship's mates ran over and met Graves. They shook hands, but Graves was barely paying attention to the younger man.

"Have you heard from our captain yet?" the man asked.

Graves frown deepened. "The cap — what the hell? He's not here?"

The man shook his head, then looked back at the others as if he had just forgotten to notice the captain. "No, he wasn't on our boat. None of us saw him before we left — he was off-duty anyway, so we figured he just came to port and skipped protocol." The young officer started to sweat. "I mean, it's not exactly illegal, but it does make things difficult when —"

Howard held up the same hand he had used to stop Kate earlier. "Yeah, I know the protocol. Captains and crew are supposed to check in here when they reach shore. But these assholes 'forget' all the time," he added, throwing up some finger quotes around the word *forget*. "As I was telling her, they're like celebrities around here. Kids even try to get their autographs, so I'm not surprised that he would have tried to sneak through before anyone noticed."

He let out a deep breath, apparently catching his breath, then went on. "But... it's... a little weird."

"What is, sir?" The man asked.

"I wouldn't have missed him if he *did* come ashore before everyone. Sure, they never check in and let us know what they're up to, but we've got cameras everywhere. Besides, our morning crew would have seen him show up. We don't miss a boat coming from way out there, ever. Even if he had hailed a private charter to come grab him, someone around here would have noticed it leaving, or when he landed."

The man mumbled something else, but Graves seemed to already be done listening. Kate waited to see what the man would say next, but instead Graves just spun around and stared at her. "You're telling me your husband is on that ship, right now?" he asked. The words were strained, rushed.

She nodded again. "Yeah, that's what I told you before. He's looking for our kids. There were a bunch of kids, I'm assuming, in the Kids' Zone area. We had just dropped them off when —"

"Yeah, explosion, right," Graves snapped. "Anyway, he have a phone or anything? And what's his name?"

Kate pulled her phone out of her pocket. "Jack. And yeah, he does. I've been texting him from this one. It's not mine, but —"

He snatched the phone out of her grasp before she could respond. "It's this first number here, right?"

She nodded again, but he was already moving the phone up to his ear.

CHAPTER 31

JACK

JACK AND GIUSEPPE had made it halfway down the Deck 2 hallway on the starboard side of the ship. There were a few rooms Jack opened and checked in, finding neither mercenaries nor kids, and they had just ducked into a crew lounge area Giuseppe had shown him when the phone vibrated in his front pocket.

He pulled it out and looked at it. It was Kate again. He glanced around — there was one more door on the other side of this room, but it only led to a large walk-in closet. He felt safe knowing no one was nearby. He answered the phone. "Kate? What's going on?" he asked, rushing through the words. "Did you find the kids?"

But rather than his wife's voice, he heard a strained, lower male voice. *"This is Howard Graves, Director of Security here at the Port Authority and the cruise company."*

Jack let out a deep sigh of relief. "Oh my God," he began. "There's — I have so much I need to tell you, but did you find our kids?"

"Negative on the kids, Jack," Graves said. *"But we're working*

on it; you have my word." Jack nodded along as Graves continued. *"Listen, I need to get a status update on just what the hell's going on over there, and so far you're the only person I can get a hold of. Mind telling me what happened?"*

Jack squeezed his eyes shut, then looked at Giuseppe.

"Listen, uh... Howard. We don't really have time to get into the details. I'll give you a full debrief when I'm off the boat, once I got my kids back. But you need to know something — I don't think this whole thing was an accident."

"The hell are you talking about?" Graves asked.

"I mean guys with guns have been chasing us around."

There was a pause. *"Guys with guns? Who are they? And who's us? Are you with someone?"*

"Yeah," Jack said, nodding. "Kid named Giuseppe, from Florence, Italy."

He looked at Giuseppe, covering the speaker with his hand. "What do you do here, kid?"

"I cook."

Jack smiled at him. "He's a cook. I ran into him down on the crew decks."

Graves ignored this. *"We're still doing a headcount out here, but it seems pretty clear to me that not everyone got off that boat. Can you confirm?"*

"I just told you — there are guys with guns who were apparently acting as crew so they'd go unnoticed, running around and killing everybody. Whatever crew members or staff *was* still on board... Graves, I'm sorry to inform you. They're probably dead."

"You've got to be shitting me. Who the hell are these guys? And what are they doing? What do they want?"

"Hell if I know," Jack said. "But they're trying to make sure no one else gets back to port and they seem to be doing a pretty good job of it. I took down two of them, but I think —"

"What? Are you insane?" snapped Graves. *"You're not — who the hell* are *you anyway? You some kinda cop?"*

"I work for the state," Jack said calmly. In case there *was* someone monitoring communications on the ship, Jack didn't want to reveal exactly who he was — or where he was.

There was a longer pause this time.

Jack pressed on. "Is my wife there? I need to talk to my wife."

"Yeah, hold on, give me a second," Graves said. *"Listen, Jack — thanks for the heroics and everything, but this is some serious shit you're into. Can you get off the ship and back to shore?"*

"Yeah, I could. But I'm not going to. I still don't know where my kids are, but if they're on this ship, I'm going to —"

"What?" roared Graves through the phone, cutting him off. *"You're going to what? Kill everyone else, like Rambo? You're going to take out whoever this other group is? You don't even know how many of them there are. All you're going to do is get yourself killed."* He paused, breathing heavily. *"Come on back, and let us handle it from here."*

"Where are my kids, Graves?" Jack asked. He waited for a beat, but Graves didn't answer. "Yeah, you have no idea, either. Like everyone else, you have *no clue* what's going on. And you're even farther away from my kids than I am right now. So I'm going to stay put until I find every last one of them. And yeah, if I have to kill some of them to get to my kids..."

Jack closed his eyes again and breathed. He needed to stay calm, stay focused. His kids needed him to come through for them. If they *were* anywhere on the ship, Jack couldn't imagine leaving them behind.

"You think you're some hot-shit cowboy or something?" Graves asked, finally back. *"I've got the Jamaican Coast Guard standing by. Get somewhere cozy and just stay hidden until they find you. That's an order."*

Jack frowned. "I don't work for you, Graves. Send in the Coast Guard and let them deal with whoever this is on board, sure, but I'm not done looking for my kids."

He glanced up at Giuseppe again and tried to gauge the kid's reaction. At this point he must have known that Jack was serious about staying behind, although Jack knew he probably didn't like it.

A new voice came onto the phone and he put it back up onto his ear.

"Jack, are you there?" Kate asked.

He felt tears immediately come to his eyes. "I'm here, babe. I'm safe, for now."

"For now?" she asked. *"I heard him say something about another group of people? Jack, who are they? Are they* hurting *people?"*

Jack wasn't sure what to say. He had wanted to put this conversation off as long as possible, to keep his wife from worrying any more than she had to.

Too late now.

"Yeah," he said. "They're hurting people. I haven't found the kids yet, so my guess is they're keeping them somewhere."

Kate shrieked then, pulling the phone away from her mouth. When she returned to the line, Jack could hear the sobs in her voice. *"Jack, I can't... Jack, how do you know —"*

"The kids are safe, I'm sure of it," Jack said. "Trust me." He *needed* her to trust him, to believe his expertise and experience. *He* needed to believe it. "They want something, but I don't know what it is yet. I'm not going to worry about that, though — I'll let the Coast Guard and the police deal with that when they get here. You just stay safe and keep your eyes out for the kids. If they're on some other lifeboat or something maybe —"

"They're not on another lifeboat, Jack," Kate said, her voice strained. *"You* know *that they're on the ship... and those people are holding them hostage, aren't they?"*

Jack was not sure how to respond. He did not want to lie to his wife, but he could not dodge the question. "I don't know, Kate," he said. "I don't know yet. But I'm going to find out."

AS SOON AS Jack had put the phone back in his pocket, he heard footsteps out in the hallway.

"Giuseppe," he said quickly. "Get in the closet."

He followed Giuseppe over to the large closet, and both men entered. Jack knew it was a horrible hiding spot, but if these people came into the cafeteria lounge room just to see if anyone was inside, there was a small possibility they wouldn't check the interior closet.

Then again, there was a possibility they would just shoot a few holes through the thin hollow-core closet door they were hiding behind, too.

He backed up against the far wall, sliding Giuseppe beside him as well.

The footsteps stopped, and Jack heard a keycard click. His heart rate rose. *They're coming in.*

And they *were* coming in — more than one, judging by the different voices Jack heard.

"You said there were snacks in here?" a high-pitched male voice asked.

"Yeah," another voice, in South American-accented English said. "There's a Coke machine there, and then right next to it there's a —"

Jack heard the sound of smashing glass and then laughter.

A third voice registered. "What the hell, man? I didn't know you were going to break into the damn thing!"

"I ain't gonna pay for this shit," the high-pitched voice said.

"Whatever, just hurry up. We need to get back."

"Let me just eat it first, okay? Won't take that long."

Jack was holding his breath, and he hoped the men would just take the Doritos bag or whatever and leave, but apparently they wanted to stay and lounge a bit. *Makes sense,* he thought. *It* is *the lounge, after all.*

"Victor is going to be pissed if we're late," the deeper third voice said.

"Late for what?" The high-pitched voice asked in return. "We're supposed to be looking through all the rooms, right? Well, that's what we're doing now. And besides, it's not like he's treating us to a nice dinner or something later. He's just a control freak."

"Control freak or not, he'll kill you if you're late."

There was a pause in the conversation, and Jack heard the crinkling sound of a chip bags opening. *Doritos, good guess.*

"Yeah, you're not wrong about that," the high-pitched voice said. "He's a schmuck."

"But he's a scary-ass schmuck," the deeper voice said. "I heard one time he hung a guy from a tree using shark hooks through his ears."

"Gross. The hell did he do to deserve that?"

"I guess he heard Victor and his girl going to town in a tent nearby," the man answered. "He wasn't supposed to be over there, or something. Victor caught him, and apparently asked him if he wanted to hear *everything*."

"Not the end of the world I guess," high-pitched voice said. "I mean, now the guy just has gauges, right?" He laughed. To Jack, his laugh sounded like he had just pulled air from a helium balloon.

"Nah, man," the accented guy said. "He slit his wrists too, so he got to bleed out the whole time. Victor watched, saying he got to hear his screams louder than anyone with those big 'ol ears."

Jack winced. *Victor sounds like a great guy,* he said to himself. He wondered if the deep gravelly voice he had heard earlier belonged to Victor.

"Hurry up, dude. This is your first op with Victor, but I've been on three so far. He's a real bastard if people disobey him. And he told us to be back in an hour."

"I know, I know," the chip-eater said. He crunched on a few chips while the others started talking again.

"How they going to get the stuff out, now?" one man asked.

"I don't know — maybe like a helicopter or something? There's a pad on the front of the ship."

The first man scoffed. "Helicopter? Are you joking? How the hell are we going to carry it all up stairs? They won't fit through the elevator doors. And they would have to lift them one at a time, too."

The chip-eater pitched in through a mouthful of chips. "Yeah, man, and a helicopter is, like, traceable. Can't be flying around out here — everyone in Jamaica would see them."

"Got any better ideas, then?" The man asked. "Victor's

boss was pissed to hear about those assholes stealing from him."

"Yeah, him and Victor got a plan for sure," one man said. "I don't know it, and neither does anyone else, of course."

"Because he's a bastard."

"He's smart, though, I bet it's good enough."

"Hopefully, it's good enough *and quick,*" high-pitched voice said. "I'm ready to get off this damn boat."

"You and me both, amigo."

The chip-eater finally finished, and Jack heard footsteps walk toward the door. "How much longer we got down here?"

"Just to the end of this side of the hallway," the other man said. "But who's counting? I say we just go up early. Tell Victor we looked in every room and be done with it."

The voices drifted away as they left the room and ended abruptly when the door slammed shut. Jack let out a breath he had been holding, and he heard Giuseppe doing the same to his right.

"Okay," Jack said. "Time to move."

Giuseppe was already on his feet, walking toward the closet door. He opened it and stepped out, followed by Jack. "Stay behind me," Jack said.

He walked through the lounge to the outer door and waited next to it for three minutes, counting the time down in his head. The waiting was excruciating, but he knew it was worth not getting caught. This Victor fellow sounded as though he did not take kindly to insubordination, and the fact that he and Giuseppe were still alive was very likely something Victor would consider *insubordination.*

He heard the distant *rat-tat-tat* of burst gunfire as one of the three men apparently found some poor soul still alive in one of the rooms. After that, he heard loud laughter coming from the same direction, and then silence. He waited another two minutes, then opened the door and peered out.

It was all clear in both directions.

CHAPTER 33

CARLOS

CARLOS KICKED through the center most space of the blasted hole in the side of the ship, careful not to cut himself or his fins on the twisted, charred metal of the hole itself.

Whatever had caused this explosion had blown through the hull completely, starting from the *inside* of the ship — not just something embedded in the foot-thick walls of the ship. Even from here, Carlos could tell from the remnants of the blast that it had to have happened from an interior room. The walls around him also showed signs of the blackened, fired carbon remains from an obvious explosion, and the blast itself had pushed the hull outward — along the edges of the circular hole, the walls of the ship bent outward slightly a few feet.

But what had caused all of this? he wondered.

His job was not to perform a forensics report on the explosion — even if he could — it was simply to *observe* and report back to Graves. Whatever he found here would be handed over to his boss back at port. At that point, he assumed, Graves could order a more in-depth report, perhaps even send another crew down, this time with cameras and lights and forensics or demolitions experts, to better understand exactly what had happened. It was strange to Carlos that Graves had put this little mission together so quickly — seemingly almost moments after the explosion itself — and then had sent Carlos alone to the ship. He had told Carlos there were other divers he was prepping, but then when it came time to enter the water, he had instructed the others to wait behind.

It was as if Graves was afraid of being seen, afraid to tell anyone that he had sent someone to investigate. But why? Surely they would *want* to know what had happened here?

And then he had not sent Carlos with any sort of equipment, not even a cheap underwater flash camera, the type ubiquitous in the gift shop and other souvenir shops around the island.

If he had to guess why, he assumed Graves was simply too busy. The man was trying to juggle many balls, including keeping the Coast Guard at bay while making sure everyone on shore — all the passengers and crew and the news agencies that would undoubtedly show up at some point — remained calm.

It was a tall order, and Carlos was glad he was not in charge of that. He would stay in his lane; he would swim to the blast, try to figure out — to the best of his abilities — what had happened, and he would report back.

So he swam through the hole into the interior of the ship. He immediately recognized this section as one that was usually closed off to the rest of the boat. It was a buoyancy safety mechanism, a sub-room meant only for taking on water in case of a breach.

He was in a small-ish compartment, perhaps twelve-by-fifteen feet. He knew there were more compartments exactly the same size on the other side of this one, running the length of the ship. He recognized this partition because it was one of many used to store the crates and gear that he and the crew at port loaded onto the boats.

While cruise companies would have preferred lining every last square inch of space with passenger accommodations to pack more people on board and extract more money from tourists, regulations prevented this. These partitions surrounded the ship, usually one or two partitions deep all the way through the first two decks of the boat. Cruise companies could not store *people* in these safety compartments, but they could — and did — absolutely store gear, food, supplies, and anything else they wanted to keep out of sight but needed to have on board.

On the other side of the wall directly in front of him, he figured there was either another compartment like this one, or a larger space that could be partitioned by huge metal doors in case of a breach. These larger spaces were multi-use — sometimes beneath stages, crew-only gathering places, or just storage warehouses, and in the case a ship started taking on water, the larger space would be quickly turned into many smaller spaces, to help keep water out.

Or, it was possible that behind this wall were crew quarters. Cruise crew members and staff were given these below-the-waterline rooms, since they were a hard sell for tourists, and the crew needed a place to sleep anyway. Passengers did not like the feeling of being helplessly underwater if something were to happen.

Carlos was prepared to examine every corner of this small room, in the interest of being thorough — and because he enjoyed the dive — when he caught motion to his left side, just over his shoulder

Schools of fish and the occasional ray had popped up to see the newcomer during his journey here, but other than these regulars, he hadn't seen much in the way of marine life.

He squinted as the dark shadow soared toward him. His eyes widened as he realized it was a shark.

No... not a shark.

The object drew closer, and as the sunlight caught it he knew it could not be a shark because of the way it swam. It did not flick left to right, darting its tail sideways to propel itself forward.

Instead, this creature sailed toward him smoothly, in a straight line.

It sailed toward him like something that was *not* alive.

Carlos began to panic, but where could he go? The object was just outside the ship's hull now, and it was moving ever closer each second. It moved with an uncanny speed, and as it grew to fill his vision, he saw that there were long streams of bubbles trailing behind it.

He recognized what it was then — a submersible. Specifically, a human-operated, two-man submersible, a personal propulsion system that divers held onto while it pulled them along. He had seen machines like this, but he had never used one.

This system was carrying two humans, and they were heading right toward him.

The machine, dragging the two divers behind, flew through the hole and entered the room Carlos was in.

He swam upward, but his foot caught on the craft as it stopped just beneath him. He twisted around in the water, coming to view them from straight above.

The two newcomers also wore dive suits, but their regulators were attached to the propulsion system itself.

Who are these people, he wondered? *And what could they possibly want?*

He had initially assumed they had come here, like him, to investigate the damage. Perhaps they were members of the cruise ship crew itself, or from a small Coast Guard unit that had been sent out to survey the cruise ship's hull?

But something about their speed and the way these men moved, the way they seemed to be targeting him...

The person farthest from him worked to release something attached to the side of the propulsion craft while the other one moved upward inside the room, directly toward Carlos. The man's air hose extended about six feet, and Carlos saw there was still more of it coiled around where he had been holding onto the propulsion system, allowing the diver to maneuver in the water away from the semi-buoyant machine.

The man grabbed Carlos's arms and held them in place. If they were trying to coerce him to go back with them, he would need to point out that their propulsion system was far too small to be of any real use. Two men was likely the maximum load — three would bog it down.

Then Carlos' stomach fell. He knew in the next instant that they were *not* here to bring him back to their boat with them.

They were here for something far worse.

Just as Carlos was about to pull out his own regulator to mouth words at the other man — a crude but effective pseudo-language for many divers, the man who had been working with something on the propulsion craft finally broke it free. He lifted it up and pointed it toward Carlos.

Carlos's eyes widened even more. It was a harpoon gun, the same type used for illegal whale fishing and hunting of certain protected species.

And the man was aiming it directly at his chest.

The second man still had Carlos' arms in his hands, and his grip had tightened even more as he tried to break free. The man twisted Carlos' hands over each other as if preparing to put on cuffs and then swam sideways, getting out of the way…

Just as the second man fired the gun.

The next few seconds were almost completely silent. He heard the swishing and swirling of water around him, the thunk of the faraway harpoon cannon as the trigger was depressed, and then the sickening crunch as it pierced Carlos' chest cavity.

Carlos's mouth fell open, the regulator spitting out and flying away. Bubbles flew around him as confusion and terror set in.

He needed to grab his regulator; he needed to breathe. And yet the pain in his chest was like a cold dagger, driving him backward ever so slowly. The man released his wrists.

It was surreal, as if he could feel everything and nothing all at once. His mouth opened and closed rapidly, and his eyes darted frantically from one person to the other.

Neither of the men staring back at him wore any expression whatsoever on their face. They were completely devoid of emotion. Watching. Waiting.

It didn't take long. Between the blood loss and Carlos' own gasping as he choked seawater deep into his lungs, it was only a few seconds before the men's faces — and everything else around him — faded.

CHAPTER 34

JACK

THEY WERE ALMOST at the stairs that met Deck 2 when Jack heard the crackling sound of an overhead speaker. He stopped Giuseppe with a hand and unlocked the Deck 2 stairwell while he listened to the announcement.

"Hello..." the ominous voice boomed over the speakers. Jack knew instantly it was the voice of the grizzled man he had heard down in the Theater Access area. *"My name is Victor. I hope you have enjoyed your stay on the ship so far, but I'm afraid all good things must come to an end."*

Jack swallowed as he realized the message was directed at him. Somehow this man already knew he was on board. Somehow he knew he was the only stowaway on board.

"My men have searched every room of this ship by now," Victor continued. *"They have informed me that behind every closed door is either no one at all or someone dead on their bed. All the remaining crew members or passengers are no longer with us, which leaves* you.

"I do not know who you are, but I do *know you are working*

with the CIA. I find that quite interesting — and I would like to have a conversation about it."

Giuseppe's wide eyes stared at Jack, a look of fear on his face.

Jack felt the same. *How in the hell could he possibly know this? How was Victor pulling these strings?* Upon jumping off the lifeboat and coming back on board the ship, Jack had not known what exactly to expect. Worst-case scenario, he had thought, would be that the kids had simply been forgotten in the chaos, passed over by a crewmember who had forgotten to alert their supervisor as to the status of the kids in their zone on Deck 10.

But his subconscious had known there was more to it than that. No cruise ship had boxes of weaponry stashed away. No cruise line would allow for such a thing to even be considered.

His subconscious had been right. *Almost.*

Now, he realized the extent of his mistake.

He had walked into something far larger than a personal quest to find his children.

And now this Victor guy is going to kill me for it.

"I do not know your name yet, friend," Victor continued, *"but I will find out soon. I have the manifest in hand, and my men will be informing me of which passengers and crew have reached shore safely. As well, we have identified most of the bodies left on the ship. So by process of elimination, I would assume that anyone on the manifest who has not reached shore yet is... you. Now, we can expedite this whole thing and make it easier on both of us."*

Jack waited for the ultimatum he knew was coming.

"Come to the bridge, where I will be waiting. From there, we

can move the conversation down to a more private area, where the captain might be able to join us."

The captain? thought Jack. *The captain is still on board? And he's involved?*

Was Captain Phillips somehow corrupt and part of this whole thing as well, or had he just been unlucky enough to stay behind, and now Victor was using him as leverage?

"I am giving you fifteen minutes get here. I am not a man who appreciates or humors excuses, so if you are injured, I suggest you better find some way to pull yourself up and make your way to the bridge. For your convenience, I have reactivated the elevators on the ship — but as I mentioned, they will be shut off promptly fifteen minutes from this... moment."

Jack pulled Giuseppe inside the second deck's stairwell. If any of Victor's men were here, they too would have heard the transmission. That meant that for the next fifteen minutes, Jack and Giuseppe were safe to move about the ship. Victor would not have his men shoot until he got eyes on him.

Not great news, necessarily, but silver linings and all that...

"I look forward to meeting with you in person," Victor's voice said through the tinny speakers. *"We have much to discuss."*

He heard the audio click off as the transmission ended.

Jack raced up the stairs, no longer worried about stealth. He needed to act, needed to figure this out. There was no way he would subject himself to the torturous and murderous bastard up *there*, but that did not leave him with many good options down *here*. What would happen *after* fifteen minutes? They obviously knew he was still on board, so would they just continue to search for him? Why not just hide somewhere and wait it out? Or even try to move around and take out his men a few at a time, like he had been doing?

No, that was no good. That strategy had gone out the window as soon as Victor mentioned that he knew he was CIA. He had no idea how they knew he was with the Agency, but it meant that Victor likely had other leverage on him as well.

Hiding, or skipping out altogether, was not going to be an option that ended well for Jack.

He would have to elude Victor if he wanted to stay alive, and Victor had just given him a fifteen-minute window to do just that.

But what could he possibly accomplish in only fifteen minutes? Jack had taken down two of Victor's men, and if he believed the ones he had heard discussing it, there were only thirteen or so left.

One against thirteen — not to mention having to guard Giuseppe the entire time — meant the odds were still stacked greatly against Jack.

And no matter what Victor might think, Jack wasn't *that* kind of CIA agent. He was a desk jockey, and ironically for this exact reason. He had never wanted the type of job that left his wife and daughters in fear, wondering if they'd ever see their husband or father again.

"Come on," Jack said, urging Giuseppe to hurry up.

"Where are we going now?" Giuseppe asked. "We will go to the bridge?"

Jack shook his head as they reached the entrance to Deck 3 landing. "No way," he said. "Victor will just kill you immediately and probably torture me. Worse, I have no idea what sort of information he's expecting me to have — I don't know a damned thing about his mission or what he *thinks* I know about it."

"You are *not* CIA?" Giuseppe asked.

Jack sighed as he clicked the keycard over the Deck 3 landing. He didn't want to burst out of these doors loudly, making an entrance. Just because he didn't think Victor's men would kill him on sight did not mean they would treat him well. He assumed they would harass him and force him up to the bridge after stripping him of his weapon.

He did not like that option — so for the time being, he needed to hurry, but also remain out of sight.

"I *am* with the State," Jack said softly. "But... I'm not that kind of agent."

CHAPTER 35

VICTOR

VICTOR FROWNED. This was a puzzling development. About an hour earlier, his navigation specialist had informed him that a human-sized foreign object was making its way slowly toward the ship.

His navigator had been watching the monitor he'd hooked up in the bridge, keeping tabs on the data from the 'dipper' in the water below them. It was essentially a sonar system, though it was capable of tracking much smaller objects than a typical maritime array, with the trade-off of only being able to see about a half-mile around its location. They called it a 'dipper,' as it was literally just a dipstick on a cable, dropped into the water, from which point the data was gathered and sent to a receiver and displayed on the bridge. Victor's navigator had set this up earlier that morning, almost immediately after the explosion, when he and his men had taken control of the bridge.

Victor had been told that the data was accurate, though the extrapolation from it was averaged. In other words, he had been told that they couldn't trust the data at face value. Just because it *said* there was a torpedo-like object making its way toward us did not mean that there was.

Besides, torpedoes moved fast — and this object was *very* slow.

Before it had even gotten close to the side of the ship, the object had stopped, slowly moved around, then wiggled and turned in the water as if alive.

And his navigation specialist had told him that the most likely scenario was that the object was, in fact, alive. Since it was clearly swimming from shore directly to the ship, it told Victor that this was a *human* diver, sent by someone onshore, against Victor's orders.

And they were trying to examine what had happened.

He had shaken his head in disgust. Whoever had done this would pay. He had explicitly ordered everyone — above *and* below the waterline — to stay back a half-mile. Any breach of this trust would end poorly for whoever had ignored his orders.

Still, the news had not been terribly troubling for Victor. A single diver was hardly enough of a problem for Victor to worry about: he already had a contingency plan in place for this very thing. Divers were standing by for the last phase of Victor's larger mission, but he had told them to be prepared for anything.

When his navigator had told him about the breach, he had simply passed it on to his second-in-command, Raul, instructing him to take care of it.

The man had answered succinctly. "Our divers will be in the water in under a minute."

Victor nodded, though he hoped these divers were as capable as Raul insisted. Working with his own teams back in Venezuela, there would have been no question about their loyalty or capabilities. All of them operated as he did — with total authority to do what they felt was right in the moment, and he could trust that it was the right thing, explicitly because he had trained them and worked with them personally.

But here in Jamaica, working with a crew of hired guns he did not know, things were different. He had to verify all of these things, one step at a time. He had to make sure his plans did not go off the rails, certainly not because someone failed to do the correct thing at the correct time.

So Victor had watched as the two scuba divers — men he did not know or trust — had snuck toward the ship, launching only moments after the first man. These two men left from a small boat that was currently anchored out in deeper waters, right at the half-mile mark he had previously designated. Not wanting to attract undue attention, Victor had ordered these men to anchor the small fishing boat at this location, placing the vessel facing north so that when and if his divers needed to leave the boat, they could enter the water unnoticed by all the other small boats gathered in that area, the large inbound motor house closing off the sightline.

Victor knew that any submarine the Coast Guard deployed would be spotted miles away and could easily be tracked on every boat's radar, including his own. But smaller, personal propulsion systems like the one his men were using — propulsion systems that were a mere speck on the most discerning sonar — would easily be dismissed as just some aquatic life, and only seen for what they were under great scrutiny.

The two men, showing as just a single dot on the screen, pulled forward by the powerful underwater jets, reached the side of the ship without slowing down. He knew they aimed directly at the hole that had been blown in his ship's hull, but he was surprised that they sailed straight through to the interior at seemingly full speed.

At that point, they simply disappeared, becoming just a part of the mass on the monitor that was the ship's body.

They had no cameras down in the space, and there were no other people in the water taking stock of what was going on. Was the person down below hostile? And if so, what had they brought along in terms of weaponry? Were they going to try to gain access to the ship?

Using explosives to gain access to the ship Victor knew would be impossible, but it was an idea he still did not want to entertain. If a blast like that didn't kill the person trying to sabotage their work, the onslaught and never-ending barrage of incoming seawater certainly would make it hard to get past the compartments.

Even then, one man was not enough to pull off something like that.

So it *had* to be something else, but what? It seemed stupid for anyone to send a single man into the fray unless they had taken pains to approach under the utmost stealth, and climb aboard another way.

But they had not — they had simply come to the ship like an estranged tourist, a diver excited to explore what might be the next shipwreck.

That was unacceptable.

It was over within seconds.

His two divers — the larger dot once again reappearing on his navigator's monitor — exited the space in the hull with their submersible. Just as they had entered, they made a beeline back toward the boat they had come from. No words had been spoken, no congratulatory cheers had sounded, and no praise was given.

No praise was needed — these men had done their jobs flawlessly, and that would be praise itself.

Victor watched the screen for a few more seconds, then allowed himself the briefest smile.

Things are progressing well, he thought. *Things are moving along as planned. Mostly.*

He filed the incident away — it was something to look into later, as he would have to know who had come to visit his ship and why.

But that all could happen later. That was something he could worry about at another time.

For now, he needed to get back to the main attraction — getting the area prepped for these divers, and then getting his prize off the ship.

And he *really* needed to figure out what this CIA agent was doing on *his* ship.

JACK FELT RELATIVELY confident the kids were not being held on Decks 1 or 2; while he had not checked every last door and interior closet, he also had not seen any of Victor's men guarding any rooms. He knew if the kids were down there, Victor would not leave them unattended.

But he had no time to check every single deck above him. There were a few spots on Deck 3 he wanted to look into, namely the larger kitchens and service stations that handled room service for the staterooms on Deck 3, as well as the large doorways he had seen on the aft of this deck that led down to the engine rooms.

He had no idea what a cruise ship's engine rooms might look like, but a ship this large was bound to house its engines and technical areas in a space large enough to hold a few dozen kids.

He raced toward the aft section of the ship, stopping about halfway when he heard a door opening up ahead on his left. He heard the dinging of an elevator as well and pulled Giuseppe inside one of the staterooms with him. He kept the door cracked while he listened to the men marching in his direction. He had no reason to suspect they knew exactly where he was, so as long as he didn't move the door at all, they should not notice him and Giuseppe inside. He had kept the light off for this very reason.

"...Guy's some sort of special agent, probably," one of the men said. He was pockmarked with acne scars and looked to be in his late forties. His hair was salt and pepper gray, and he carried the same assault rifle Jack was now holding.

"So what? It's just one dude," a far younger man next to him said. He also held an assault rifle and looked to be of South American descent. "Once we find him, Victor will figure out what he knows and then kill him. It's just a minor setback."

"It's wasting time, and Victor is pissed as hell about that," the older man said. They passed directly by Jack's and Giuseppe's hiding spot and continued on down the hallway. Jack strained to hear as much of their conversation is possible.

"Even if he knows something, he'll be dead soon. We don't need him."

"Yeah, true," the first man said. "The kids are the real leverage."

Jack's heart rate intensified.

The kids...

This was the first time he had heard verbal confirmation that the kids were still on board. He had suspected as much, but this information now solidified his mission. He wanted to know where, and he needed to keep listening.

He turned to Giuseppe and put a finger to his lips. "I need you to stay here for a couple of minutes. Do *not* make a sound, got it?"

Giuseppe nodded. As carefully as possible, Jack pulled the

door open and stepped out into the hallway. The men were not worried about their surroundings, not on high alert. These guys were simply walking down the hall, discussing him and what he might be up to. Jack crept silently behind them, doing his best to hide in the four-inch recessions at each doorway he passed. They were not much of a hiding spot — he knew that if they did turn around, they would see him immediately.

For that reason, he kept his M4 gripped tight, set on three-round burst mode.

"Yeah, but it's not like he's going to kill kids, right?"

"No, he's got a better plan I'm sure," the older man said. "I've worked with him before, and he's ruthless, but he's very smart. He won't kill the kids — at least not all at once."

The younger man nodded and seemed to accept this answer, but the older man continued. "Say what you will about Victor, but he gets results. And he doesn't care what he has to do to get them. I was on a mission with him once, in Caracas. There was a village near the route the cartel used for trafficking. They started to grow, and they asked the cartel if they could move their route around their village, because their kids had grown fearful of the nasty men who would come through each week."

The young man glanced to the side a bit, not enough to see Jack in his peripheral vision, but enough that Jack could see a surprised expression on his face. "What did Victor do?" The younger man asked.

The older man smiled. "He rounded up the families in the village and killed their kids, brutally, right in front of the parents. Said something along the lines of, 'now your kids have nothing to be fearful of anymore.'"

The younger man didn't respond. They just marched side-by-side toward the same doors Jack previously entered this deck through.

They reached the end of the hallway, Jack successfully staying behind them and out of sight. He had not made so much as a sound as he walked on his tiptoes, but his calves were growing tired of the exercise. He had an urge to let these men get through the stairwell door and move on, but as the older man reached the keycard access point, he turned slightly to stretch the card from its belt clip and place it over the door.

And then he spotted Jack.

He started to shout, but Jack was prepared. He lifted his rifle and put three rounds into the man's chest, one missing over his shoulder. The man fell as the younger kid was fumbling with his own weapon. Jack put him down as well, one round hitting him in the neck and two rounds smashing through his right arm and into the stairwell door.

The gunfire was deafening in the closed, reverberated corridor, but Jack didn't care. They already knew he was here, and they likely already knew he was armed. There was no way Jack was going to let these two assholes get back up to Victor and help strengthen his forces.

Jack ran over to them, both to make sure they were dead, and to make sure they didn't have any communications devices on their person.

Unfortunately, they did. The older man was still alive, wheezing and spurting out blood from a wound in his chest. But he pulled the walkie-talkie off of his belt and held it up to his mouth. His voice was raspy, but even. "Vic — Victor," he said quickly. "Deck 3. The CIA agent is armed. He —"

Jack put another round through the man's forehead at close range and he slumped back to the floor.

Jack's eyes were bugging out of his head. He was no longer operating in stealth mode, no longer moving around unknown.

But that ship had sailed. He was now the primary target on board this boat, and they knew *exactly* where he was.

Okay, shit just got real.

CHAPTER 37

JACK

THREE THOUGHTS RAN through Jack's mind simultaneously as he sprinted back down the hallway toward Giuseppe's hiding spot.

First, they absolutely knew he was here.

Second, they were going to be *pissed* he had killed more of Victor's men.

Third — and most importantly — Jack knew for a fact the kids were still on board the *Ocean Voyager* somewhere.

It was this third factor that caused him to slip in and pull Giuseppe out of the room forcefully, yelling at him to keep up. He barely stopped as he passed by the room, kicking it open and shouting while pulling Giuseppe's collar. "We have to move!" Jack shouted. "Now — toward the doors, then back down."

"Down?" Giuseppe stammered, already fifteen feet behind him. "But Mr. Jack — I heard the shots. Did they —"

"Pick up the pace!" Jack shouted. "Yeah, *down*." He smacked the keycard against the Deck 3 stairs and pushed the door open. "The kids are here somewhere, and we're going to either find them or one of Victor's men, and I'll beat it out of him. I'm not letting him get his hands on my kids."

The theory was simple, if a bit unsteady. By heading down to the bottommost deck, the stairs eventually would end. He would have quite the opposite of the high ground, but at least he would not have to guard *two* fronts — one above him and one below him — simultaneously. The older man he'd killed had given away Jack's position, so all of Victor's men would be corralled toward Deck 3 — exactly where he did not want to be right now. With any luck, he could peel off one or two of Victor's men and start trying to get some answers.

He tried not to think about the plan — the more he did, the worse it sounded.

But it was still better than nothing, his subconscious said. *But was it?*

He did not have long to wait. He already heard shouts coming from Deck 2 as at least two men ran toward his position just inside the landing. He pushed Giuseppe into the dark recesses behind him, between the wall and the large door, hoping the kid could stay out of sight long enough for him to get this done. He didn't want to stay here long — it was not a highly defensible position. The longer he waited here, the higher the chance Victor's men would pile up outside the doors. It was the epitome of the tower defense game he had alluded to earlier — and in those games, the tower eventually got overwhelmed, and the player inevitably died.

He heard the shouts clearer now as they approached the door. "He's up above us," one of the men said. "On Deck 3."

"Do we know which side of the ship? Aft? Port or starboard?"

There was no response, but Jack assumed the man had just

shaken his head. "No, let's just get up there and find them. That will tell us where he was at least, right?"

Jack heard the card reader click and the door started to swing open. He needed to time this correctly. He needed to wait until both men — and hopefully there were still only two of them, as he assumed Victor put his men in pairs or threes — and not more.

The first man stepped in, and Jack sucked in a breath as he hid directly behind the open door. He had to risk the door opening too far and bumping into him, which would immediately tell this man Jack was inside. One person hiding behind these stairwell doors was possible, but two was a stretch. Jack also had to wait until the second man was through the door, so that he wouldn't lose his chance.

He swung his rifle around the open door, hoping for a good shot even though he had to hold the gun awkwardly to do it. He pulled the trigger with his left index finger, two times, releasing six rounds in that direction, trying to spray the air on the other side of the door. He heard most of the rounds land where he had wanted them to — into the flesh of the oncoming mercenary.

But he kept moving, pulling his body out from behind the door and coming into full view until the second man was right there. The other mercenary's mouth was agape, a look of surprise on his face. He had his rifle swinging down from the carrying sling on his shoulder.

Should have been ready, asshole, Jack thought as he fired again.

But these rounds were not aimed at the man's core. It was a tricky maneuver, but thanks to the close range — a mere four or five feet — and Jack's training with firearms — he got the shot off perfectly.

The three rounds hit his right arm and shoulder, and his gun fell back to his side, dangling on its perch. The leather sling on his shoulder slid down, and the gun clattered to the floor. He groaned in agony as he both tried to clench the blood flow with his left hand and crouched down to retrieve his weapon. Jack stepped up to the guy and smashed the butt of the rifle into his nose, eliciting a shriek. Then he stepped over and kicked the rifle to the side, far out of reach. The man fell back onto his rear end and smacked the back of his head against the carpeted floor.

He immediately started suffocating on his own blood, his nose destroyed, and rolled over to the side, coughing and spitting.

Jack leaned down, the rifle pointed directly at the man's forehead, and growled. "Where are the kids?" His voice surprised him — there was no fear, no acknowledgement of the danger Jack was currently facing.

Just pure rage.

The man didn't respond.

Jack moved the rifle and aimed at the man's hand, continuing to surprise himself. "You've got ten fingers, and I've got way more than ten rounds. That's as long as this should take, but hopefully we get it done in less. *Where are the kids?*"

The guy opened his mouth and tried to formulate a response. "No habla ingles," he said.

"Wrong answer, champ," Jack said. He fired, having switched the firing selection mechanism to single shot. The NATO round pierced the flesh and bone of the merc's right index finger cleanly. After a second of shock, blood began pouring out from the empty knuckle.

The man screamed. "I do not — I do not know!"

Jack fired another round, another finger gone, another scream.

"Do you think you'll bleed out before I finish blasting off *every one* of your fingers? After that, we can start on the toes if you'd like."

"Vic — Victor will come for you," the man said, in perfectly acceptable English.

Jack took out another finger.

"Arrggh!" the man wailed. "In the captain's mess!"

Captain's mess, Jack thought, filing it away. "And where is that?" Giuseppe would know, and Jack was pretty sure he had seen it with his kids and wife earlier, but he wanted to keep this man talking. Perhaps he would talk himself out of being killed, but Jack was not going to bet on that.

The man didn't respond at first, so Jack shoved the searing hot barrel of the rifle onto the man's thumb.

"Okay — *okay.*" He coughed out another blob of mucus-laced blood. "Fore section, Deck 15. It's where they prepare meals for the officers."

Jack nodded. He did know the place — they hadn't been in the actual dining hall, but during their brief tour of the boat on their first day of arrival, they had seen the ship's officers' private dining hall on this level. He assumed the mess hall would be attached to the back of it somewhere.

As Jack stood to retrieve Giuseppe from behind the door, he heard the man on the floor start to chuckle. It sounded otherworldly, alien. There was no structure remaining in his nose, and blood was pouring out both sides of his mouth as he tried looking up at Jack. He opened his mouth to speak again, but no words successfully came out. Jack grabbed Giuseppe, who was looked horrified at having to step over two bodies, and as they passed, the guy on the floor finally got out a whisper.

"Victor..."

Jack brought the black, soft-soled shoe he had borrowed from Juan up and hovered over the man's emaciated nose. With as powerful a kick as he could muster, Jack shoved the heel down and across, as if aiming up the man's nose, where it lay limp on his face. The internal cartilage structure of the nose ended with a somewhat sharpened point, and it was this he tried to kick up into the man's brain.

Apparently, it worked. The man was now *very* dead.

"I — I heard him say Deck 15, fore section," Giuseppe said. "That is the private dining hall for the officers."

"Yep," Jack said. "Which means it's time to go visit our captain."

"But Victor's men are coming down here — they might meet us on the stairs. Surely you are getting low on ammunition, right? And he might have far more men than we know."

Jack nodded as he checked the magazine and replaced it with a fresh one from his pocket. He also bent down and grabbed the dead men's rifles, checking to see if there was anything worth taking.

"You're not wrong," Jack said. "We're heading up there, but we *are* going to take a brief detour first. I have to make a phone call."

CHAPTER 38

JACK

JACK PULLED the phone up to his ear and immediately heard the connection.

"Jack, that you?" A man's voice asked.

"Graves? Where the hell is my wife?"

"Easy there, buddy. She's right — "

"Get her on the phone, now. I don't have time."

Jack's patience had disappeared after his fourth brutal murder of the day, and he had no time for Graves' bullshit.

"I will, I will — just one second. I've been trying to call. I was hoping you could help me figure out a little bit about what's —"

"What's going *on?*" Jack yelled. He tried to his keep his voice low, but he knew they should be relatively safe from being heard.

He had hidden inside an internal closet in one of two conference rooms they had found on Deck 2, near the stairs. He had positioned Giuseppe just outside the closet door and told the man to knock three times — not too softly — if he heard anybody approaching.

"You want to know what's going on?" Jack continued.

"I've taken out *four* of Victor's men. They're all mercenaries, hired guns. Victor's some sort of cartel guy. I don't have a last name yet, but he knows I'm here. Doesn't know my name either, but he somehow knows I work for the CIA."

"Victor?" Graves asked. *"And you say he's with some sort of cartel?"*

"Venezuela, if I had to guess," Jack said. "I've been getting snippets here and there, but that's not what I'm calling you about — Graves, I think I found the kids."

Graves paused, then came back on the line. *"The kids? You found the kids?"*

Jack suspected this question was not intended for him, but for his wife and any others that were gathered near him.

"They're up on Deck 15. I'm going to go grab them, but I'm going to need some help after. Do you have assets in place?"

Graves stuttered. *"Yeah... yeah, I do, I guess. Coast Guard has been gearing up for some time and they're already in the water, about a mile offshore. Listen, we didn't want to send anyone in until we knew the ship was safe. You know... no more bombs and all that."*

"There are no more bombs, Graves," Jack said, not fully believing his own words but needing Graves to act. "But it doesn't mean it's safe. Don't send anything less than an entire army, you got it? I'm talking fully loaded, action ready. These guys *will* face open fire."

"Copy that, Jack," Graves said. *"I'll pass it up the chain."*

"How quickly can they be here?" Jack asked. "I'm in position, but I'm just one guy. I don't have unlimited ammunition either. I've taken out four, and my best estimate has the remaining force at around ten or eleven, plus Victor."

"Got it, yeah, I'll check into that."

"Check into... what the hell, Graves? You don't know who's ready to go, and where they are *exactly*? What have you been doing out there?"

There was a pause. *"You know, Jack, this isn't exactly... a* super common *incident,"* Graves said, his voice dripping with annoyance. *"I've been busting my balls trying to keep everyone happy — trying to keep them from all going to town on each other — but all the news stations found out about the missing kids, and they've been* hounding *me for answers I don't have."*

Jack sighed. "Yeah, sorry. I hear you; I really do. I'm just stressed as hell and scared out of my mind. If I could get a little bit of help — a few extra guns at least — we might actually have a chance."

There was a longer pause this time, and Jack knew Graves was running through the scenario in his mind. He had no idea who this man was or his experience, but he hoped to God it was enough to get something done.

"Keep that phone handy, Graves," Jack continued. "But let's just text from here on out, unless I call you. If I need to stay quiet, I can't be answering the phone."

"You got it. And Jack?" Graves asked. *"Good luck, and Godspeed."*

Jack hung up the call and immediately pulled up the messaging app. He had his boss' personal cell number saved and thought this would be a safer way to route the message than by trying to use the well-known CIA hotline plus an extension. Plus, he was not sure if his boss was even at the office now, so his personal cell might be the best way to reach him.

He had hesitated before, not sure he wanted to risk sending a text message that might be intercepted by the terrorists.

But now, after talking to Graves a couple of times, it seemed it would be safe. Plus, he wouldn't be giving his boss his exact location. And this was not Jack's op, so if his boss chastised him later for not keeping things 'in the official channels,' well... he could probably argue his way out of that one.

He typed quickly, trying to keep his sentences short but understandable.

> *Patrick — on the* Ocean Voyager. *Shots fired, explosion belowdecks. They know I'm CIA.*

> *Have any more information?*

He did not have time for another phone call, so this would have to do. There wasn't much Patrick, his boss, *could* do, so he hoped this would at least alert him to open an investigation and get the bureaucratic wheels greased and spinning.

He trusted Patrick; he was a good director. If anyone could help Jack navigate this situation, it was him.

He hoped.

AS SOON AS Jack had finished sending the text message, he heard a knock at the door.

Three quick taps.

He flung the door open and saw Giuseppe's startled face. "Jack," Giuseppe said. "I hear people coming."

Jack heard it, too, another pair of soldiers from Victor's army. They were walking in this direction, and though he couldn't be sure if they would stop in this room, he was ready to take matters into his own hands.

If Victor keeps throwing pairs of men at me, I will take them down until it's just me and him.

He felt the rage coming back, but he forced it back down so he could focus. He strode to the door of this room and waited near it. Pulling the handle now would likely be noticed, so he waited until the men passed the room completely, then flung it open.

He stepped out, firing three shots over the men's heads. The effect was instantaneous, and exactly what he had been going for.

The two men, stunned, heard the shots and saw pieces of the ceiling and light fixtures fall off in front of them, and they whirled around, arms already raising.

"Don't even think about touching those weapons," Jack shouted. "Keep turning, and keep your hands away from your rifles."

He hoped Giuseppe had enough sense to stay in the room, as he had forgotten to give the kid that order. By now, Giuseppe was probably used to the way Jack handled situations. He had never thought he was a 'shoot first and ask questions later' sort of guy, but this was not an everyday scenario.

Still, he was proud of himself for not just taking *these* guys out completely. He needed information.

"Where is Victor hiding?" he spat.

"Did you not hear?" one of the men said, a smirk on his face. "You are to meet him on the bridge."

"How do I know he's there, and that it's not just a trap?"

"Victor is a man of his word, unlike *you*, American spy."

The man spat at Jack's feet. He let the insults slide — he was not even close to a spy. But it still took him by surprise — was this guy that close with his mercenary comrades that he was so pissed off at Jack for offing a handful of them?

He got the sense this guy had taken it personally and hated the very sight of Jack.

"I told you he had a partner," the other man whispered.

The first man shook his head, silencing his friend.

A partner? Jack thought. *What the hell is he talking about?*

"What does Victor want?" Jack asked.

"*You.* He told you that."

"Yeah, I'm not an idiot. Let's move on, fellas. What does he *actually* want? Why are *you all* here, doing this?"

He wanted to add, *'and why do you have the kids,'* but he did not want to play that card just yet. *If they find out I'm a father of some of the kids on board, too...*

The man frowned. "Why don't you just shoot us? You're not going to get to Victor armed. It's hopeless, so just do what you're going to do and move on."

Jack shook his head. "Not good enough. I want to know what you all are doing here. Why the explosion?"

The man's eyes widened just a bit, but Jack caught it. "Playing dumb, I see. Good, you Americans were always good at that. What are we doing here? What are *you* doing here? How did you know about Victor's op?"

Jack was running out of time, and he was being faced with more questions than he was receiving answers for. He wanted to kill these guys, but if he could get anything at all from them, he would.

"Last time I'm going to ask you, boys," Jack said, aiming his rifle directly at the first man's forehead. "If you've seen your friends down there, you'll know I don't miss."

"Yes, you're right," the man said, slowly, sounding out each syllable. "That *will* be the last question you're going to ask."

Jack sensed the tingle on the back of his neck, the hairs there standing on end. Something had alerted his subconscious, but he wasn't quite sure what it was. He spun around quickly, seeing in a flash another man rushing toward him, who previously must have been moving stealthily through the hallway just as Jack had done earlier. He lifted his rifle and tried to re-aim, but it was too late.

The two men behind him had lifted the butts of their rifles, one of which he now felt driving into the base of his skull.

Jack hit his knees — then the floor — face-first, his rifle falling to his side.

He noticed Giuseppe's wide-eyed stare through the crack in the door as his world went black.

VICTOR PULLED the radio up to his mouth. He looked toward Roberto Flores, seated at the communications station. He did not know the man, but he had come highly recommended. Not just a fighter, he was smart, too. Victor had put him in charge of communication.

The first task Flores had completed had been the immediate and total shutdown of every ship-to-shore communication onboard, save for the cellular tower. That would come next, but it was a trickier operation.

But Victor had not needed him to worry about it — anyone still on board after Victor and his men assumed control was now dead — and dead people could not use their phones.

Flores nodded, letting Victor know that everything was set.

He was broadcasting both to the Port Authority onshore and any and all Coast Guard vessels in the vicinity. He pressed the *Talk* button to begin the message.

"Good afternoon," Victor began. "I hope you are all doing well. I apologize for the trouble I have caused, but I can assure you that if things go smoothly, we will all be out of your hair before the end of the day."

The two other men on the bridge with him stared as Victor explained his demands. They were simple, and he knew they would be met. It would be a small price to pay to end this. "I need a yacht — the largest you can find — preferably one at least twenty-four meters long, with enough space for fifteen men and supplies. It must be fueled up, with additional fuel loaded into five-gallon jugs held in the engine room.

"This vessel will be driven to the forward starboard side of the *Ocean Voyager*, by a single pilot alone. There is to be no crew, nor anyone else at all, onboard the boat. I cannot stress this point enough. Also, upon delivery of this yacht, I will allow the pilot to come aboard this ship. He will be handcuffed to a chair on the bridge but otherwise left unharmed. You may retrieve him after we are gone.

"You have one hour."

He released the button and waited, knowing that the Coast Guard and Port Authority were stumbling over themselves, trying to figure out who would get to talk to him.

Finally, a voice came on the line. *"Yeah, hey, this is Howard Graves, Director of Security for Port Authority here. So... I don't think we're going to be able to get a boat that big out to you before the end of the day."*

Victor shook his head and sighed. He hated people like this — people who tried to wield their own power for no reason other than to show others they had it.

He clicked the talk button again. "Mr. Graves, I am a man of my word. When I tell you that it *is* possible to get a yacht here within the hour, I *mean* it. Furthermore, if I tell you that disobeying this request will lead to severe consequences, I also mean it."

There was another pause. *"Right... consequences. Mind telling us a bit about that?"*

"Of course," Victor said calmly. "There were thirty-four children and teenagers checked in to the Kids' Zone this morning when our ship exploded, stranding us out here. Those kids are alive and well, as are the three staffers who did not get out of the Kids' Zone in time, and my men are making sure they stay that way. But if you know anything about me, you know that I believe in incentives. Raising the stakes tends to get things done in a much more efficient and reliable manner, wouldn't you say, Mr. Graves?"

He didn't wait for Graves to reply to answer his question. "I am not a heartless criminal. I merely want to get this job done and go home. Bring me the yacht in two hours. At exactly 3 o'clock, I will start killing the hostages. One at a time, every half-hour, starting from the oldest child and working down to the youngest."

Victor knew what effect this would have on everyone out there. Anyone listening to his broadcast would be horrified, but it would also snap them into action. Even now, he imagined this Howard Graves fellow scrambling to find a yacht that fit Victor's requirements.

Victor was a man of his word, and he was not above taking lives to see his mission to completion. When he had been sent here by the cartel's leader, he had not been sure about the endgame he would choose. However, as he had thought about it longer, working through variables and details, the pieces had eventually clicked into place.

Now the plan was flawless, and it would work.

He knew governments and groups around the world, in a situation like this, paid lip service to keeping hostages alive. But if they were honest, they would readily admit that every one of these situations came down to a risk assessment and cost-benefit analysis. What was at stake on both sides? If it were not enough, these people were more than willing to let a few hostages die to prevent someone like Victor from getting their way.

They would never *admit* it, but it was how the world worked.

But with kids — with *children* — all bets were off. He knew this first-hand. He knew how to tug at the emotional heartstrings of humans. He knew what made them tick.

He knew that threatening the lives of the children on board this cruise ship would light a fire under their asses. Every news outlet in Jamaica — and around the world — was probably watching this all unfold, listening to his broadcast, picking it apart, and trying to figure out what he would do next.

Trying to figure out if he *truly* was a man of his word.

And what he was about to do next was going to prove that to them once and for all.

But there was one thing he needed to attend to first.

CHAPTER 41

JACK

JACK CAME to with the worst headache he had ever experienced. He groaned, forcing his neck up. His head felt like it weighed a million pounds. His eyes adjusted to the bright light streaming in, and he attempted to rub them back into working order.

But he found that his hands were bound at his sides, and he frowned. He was sitting in a chair, his wrists tied to the chair's arms.

Everything around him was blurry, and he moved his head slowly as the blood flow returned to normal.

Where am I? And where is Giuseppe?

His heart sank as he realized the worst. Giuseppe was almost certainly dead — they would have killed him as soon as they had seen him.

He groaned again, moving his lips a bit as he tried to form words. "Where — where am I?" he mumbled.

He heard laughter coming from his right. He turned his head in that direction, his eyes struggling to make out the shapes.

Lots of bright rectangles, a larger square in the center, and a human-shaped figure far off on the side, seated in a chair. There were other human-shaped objects, maybe two of them. Seated, facing the other direction.

He forced his eyes to focus, blinking over and over again until he saw where he was.

The bridge.

He saw where the captain was supposed to stand as they piloted the boat, the numerous stations designated for navigation and communications, a weather module, multiple monitors hanging from the ceiling, and one screen showing the Jamaican coastline and the entire island on another screen. No foul weather in sight.

There were two other men on the bridge besides the man laughing. Both were seated in chairs, looking out the wide, expansive windows or down at their controls or monitors.

He focused on the person who had been chuckling. "Who are you?" Jack asked. "Get me... get me out of this damned chair."

It hurt to talk, and Jack knew he had been bleeding where the rifle had impacted the back of his skull. *Had they bandaged me up?* he wondered. *Or was there a scab there?*

The laughter grew, then was cut off sharply. "I must hand it to you, friend," the gravelly voice began. "I did not think your team was *that* well-informed. I thought we would have at least another hour before *you* contacted *us* from the shore, begging us to stop what we were doing out here and leave."

Victor. Jack knew this man's voice, and he put it together immediately who it belonged to.

"Team?" Jack asked.

"Yes, of course. Raul, the man who brought you up here,

told me that you were playing dumb, acting like someone from your spy movies. But you know who I am already, so let's cut to the chase. You know that I have no interest in deceit or bullshit, and I would like to get this job done and go home to my family."

"What *job*?" Jack asked, emphasizing the words with more confidence. "Look, I'm not who you think I am. I'm not some spy or secret agent or anything."

Victor's head cocked to the side as he took in this information. Did he believe him? Jack had to assume that he did not.

"I was impressed to learn that there were two of you on board, though I guess it should not surprise me. Your organization is good at what it does — at finding people like me. I put myself in an incredibly exposed position coming here, a position of vulnerability I do not appreciate. Was the man in the water yours as well?"

Jack's mouth moved, but no sound came out.

Victor waved it off, not interested in the answer. "But you *will* tell me what I need to know — you will tell me what *you* know, specifically. About my cartel, about me, and — most importantly — about what you told your people back at Langley. It is imperative for me to hear every last detail, my friend, so if I sense you are withholding information from me..."

"I don't know anything," Jack said. "I was just... a passenger. On the ship. I was here with my wife."

"Yes, of course," Victor said, frowning through a fake smile. "You were just taking a 'little vacation,' just enjoying your time on *this* particular ship. You — a government agent — chose this *exact boat* at this *exact time*. I do find that strangely coincidental. Do you not?"

"Think what you want," Jack said. "It's the truth."

"We'll see," Victor said. He motioned with his eyes, and Jack heard a door open. Two men entered — the two he had confronted in the hallway.

Dammit, Jack thought. *Should have just killed them when I had the chance.*

The man he now knew as Raul came over to Jack and yanked his chair around. He was now facing directly out the broad windows on the port side of the ship. He could see what must have been over a dozen boats of all shapes and sizes along the horizon. Yachts, fishing boats, and more than one large Jamaican Coast Guard vessel. A few helicopters whirred over the line of boats, but he noticed that none were anywhere near the *Ocean Voyager.*

In fact, it seemed as though they were all waiting behind a line, like runners waiting for a race to begin.

"I've informed the Coast Guard, as well as Port Authority, that we are not to be touched. If *any* boat or vehicle of *any* sort — on, above, or below the water — gets within a half-mile of our location, the children will die."

Jack stared, blinking, unsure of how truthful this man was being.

A radio crackled to life, the voice emanating from speakers throughout the bridge.

Jack recognized the voice as Howard Graves'.

"Hey, uh, listen. We're working on getting you that boat you asked for. You still there?"

Victor smiled. "Right on time," he said, looking at Jack. "I wanted you to hear this." He cleared his throat and began talking through the radio. "Yes, we are here. Anyway, I wanted to find a way of showing to you all that I *will* not be trifled with, and I *will* be taken seriously. As such, I want to direct your attention to the forward landing pad. I know you are all watching, so I know you can see this space."

Jack could also see the landing pad clearly. It seemed to hang over the ocean, a brilliant white punctuated by the bright red of the massive "H" on top of it.

As he watched it, two of Victor's men dragged out another person, carrying the smaller man between them. He looked to be in his early thirties, his mouth duct-taped closed and his hands bound behind his back. They pushed him roughly over the giant letter on the landing pad to the edge, the only area on the cruise ship not protected by a guard rail.

At Jack's side, Victor continued. "As I explained before, if you fail to deliver the yacht I requested in two hours, I will be killing one of the hostages, starting with the oldest, and ending with the youngest."

Jack's face twisted in rage.

But Victor was not finished. "The man you see with tape over his mouth out on the pad is named Darek Novak, from Poland. He has been a wonderful staff member, but his time on board the cruise ship has come to an end."

Victor watched out the bridge as one of his men pulled a pistol from behind his back and shot Darek in the temple. The man's eyes flashed open an instant before the bullet soared through his head, but it was far too late. He fell to the side, crumbling onto the deck and then fell headfirst off the side of the ship.

Jack closed his eyes, imagining the horrific shouts and screams from anyone watching on shore. *People knew this man,* he thought. *My* kids *knew this man.*

"I am a man of my word," Victor said. "I want you all to know that. If the yacht arrives in any shape *other* than what I told you, I will be killing the hostages, one at a time, until the situation is remedied. To recap: a *seaworthy* yacht, at least twenty-four meters long, room enough for fifteen men and gear, with extra fuel onboard. *No one* will be on this boat, except for a single captain."

Victor lowered the radio and smiled at Jack.

"Now, friend — can we continue our discussion?"

HOWARD GRAVES PULLED the walkie-talkie away from his lips, picking up another one he had in his other hand.

He barked into it. "You guys get that?"

The response came back immediately, Jamaican-accented English. *"Yeah, we copy. We've got three boats standing by, staying outside his designated circle. But we don't have a yacht. Can you get one?"*

Graves felt his headache swelling the inside of his skull. "Yeah, yeah," he said. "I'm working on it. Not sure how long it'll take."

"Well, it had better be fast. You saw what he did already. We know he's serious now. He's going to — "

Graves pressed the *Talk* button again to cut off the Coast Guard's response. He didn't want Kate Barr, wife of the man still on the ship, to hear. She had been hovering nearby all day, and she would not go away.

And already, he had heard from the crowd of bystanders and news crews that word had spread about the execution up on the helicopter pad. There had been screams, terrified shouts of surprise as the man's body hurtled down to the sea.

The news outlets were now champing at the bit to talk to him, and his team of rookie security guards and gift shop employees was doing their best to keep them behind the designated line.

The disaster was getting worse by the second, and Graves was now right at the center of it.

Not a role he wanted, and not a role he was prepared for.

He forced his mind back to the most pressing problem that seemed to be swelling his head: finding a suitable yacht for the man on the *Ocean Voyager* and getting it ready for him. Graves had already scoured through his contacts, working on getting something that might work, and he was now fumbling with his phone after clipping the other walkie-talkie to his belt.

He had to get out of this situation, and he had to do it fast. He needed to de-escalate it, but he also needed to make sure he didn't mess something up. Back in his police days, there was always support. There was always someone else who could take the blame, someone else he could shift responsibility to. Here, he had carved out a niche of being the only person in control — a fact that he now realized had backfired miserably.

He wished he were still on the force. They had access to professional hostage negotiators, detectives who thrived talking to criminals hellbent on killing innocent women and children. Howard was no such professional, and his experience was mostly in chasing down gangsters and thieves.

The Coast Guard surely had someone at least capable of handling this, but he could not let them get too close. He could not let them in.

He felt the stress growing but wasn't sure what to do. He

couldn't get a massage right now without being noticed by the cameras following his every move. He couldn't even manage the five-minute walk back to his office, where he kept a bottle of cheap rum. He was being hounded, his people trying to keep crowds to a minimum and away from him, but he had a feeling they were also listening to every word he spoke and leaking it to the news crews and local police who had gathered. He knew how it worked — cases like this meant promotions, more money, more attention. Rookies and veterans alike would want to participate in the festivities today, cashing it in for power and recognition back at their office.

The Coast Guard was a zealous bunch, as well. They had already threatened to fly in two Coast Guard choppers, totally ignoring Victor's threat. They had argued that the best way to handle the situation was to get out in front of it, to strike before Victor had time to put together a response.

It had taken Howard all of his mental acuity to hold them off, but they were still champing at the bit. *Let me try to get the yacht first,* he had told them in earnest. *Let's see if it works.*

He had a feeling this Victor person was, as he had explained, a man of his word. Howard knew that staying back, gathering intel, and waiting for the yacht was the best play. Best case, Victor and his cronies would ride off into the sunset with a free yacht, and the Jamaican Coast Guard or the cruise company would just foot the bill.

Money would exchange hands, like it always did, and that would be that. If he were *really* lucky, Howard could also paint himself the hero and end up with a slightly fatter paycheck.

But Howard sensed there was more to it. Perhaps it was the cop in him talking, but he *knew* Victor was up to something bigger, though he wasn't quite sure what.

That's why he had deployed his other line of defense — the one he had kept to himself. The one that was making him *very* anxious now.

Where the hell is Carlos? He should be back by now.

He had told Carlos to get in the water at the docks almost two hours ago, behind one of the parked lifeboats, out of sight and away from prying eyes. He didn't want anyone — cruise passengers, police, or Victor's men — to see him enter the water.

He had canceled with the other divers he had told to be on standby, for fear of causing too much attention. *One will have to be enough,* he had told himself.

Was that a mistake? he now wondered.

Carlos had confirmed that he could make the swim easily — in far less than an hour each way — and had insisted that he would stay beneath the waves the entire time. Graves knew there was no sonar equipment on board the ship that could detect something as small as a human diver.

He had wanted — *needed* — to get a man inside, to see what Victor was up to. It would help his cause later. It could be the key to Howard's success.

It was imperative that he know the full story before he made any more decisions.

THE MAN TORE against his restraints, screaming. "You *bastard*!" he shouted toward Victor. "I'm going to kill you!"

His hands had been tied tightly, and the best he could muster was shifting the chair around a bit. The other two of Victor's men turned and smiled a bit, then continued watching their screens.

Victor's smile grew as well, the walkie-talkie still in his hand. "No, friend," he said. "You are *not* going to kill me. In fact, *I* am going to kill *you* — something my men should have done long ago. But, as luck would have it, you might prove useful to me yet."

The man stared up at Victor, tears streaming down his face. He sobbed but didn't take his eyes off of him.

"As it turns out," Victor continued, "you still have information I need. Information that will help me figure out just what your government knows about me and my operation."

The man spat at his feet.

"Yes," Victor said. "Right. You Americans *always* want to play the hero, don't you? You always want to rush in and save things, like your dead friend down there. He tried to be the hero, and he got himself blown up." Victor wiggled his fingers in the air in front of Jack's face. "A one-man army — or, in this case, a two-man army."

The man tied to the chair frowned but didn't speak.

"And where did that get you? It's as I said before — I'm a man of my word. I threatened to kill you if you did not come to the bridge. Since you didn't, you *will* die. But let's discuss the topic at hand, shall we?"

He did not wait for the man to respond. "First — what do you know of this operation? I'm very interested to hear."

"Nothing."

Victor was displeased and felt his frustration growing by the second, but he held it together. "*Nothing?* Then how did you *know* about it?"

The man shook his head.

"I can see we are not going to get far here, are we?"

The look on this CIA man's face told Victor everything he needed to know. This man was an *exceptional* actor.

Tears streamed down the man's face, in between his sobs he tried shifting his gaze into one of rage and vitriol. It did not work, and Victor could see right through it. But this man *was* struggling, emotionally attached to his mission.

"What is your name, friend?" Victor asked. "And I don't want some spy bullshit — you're not James Bond or Jason Bourne."

The man stared up at him, his entire body vibrating.

"I will ask you only one more time."

The man hesitated, and Victor was about to have one of his men strangle the CIA agent. He was not quite ready to kill him — there was still information he needed, and he knew his men could probably beat it out of him — but he very much did not like this man's insubordination.

Finally, the man spoke. "Jack," he whispered. "Jackson."

Victor smiled, a sigh of relief falling from his lips. "See? Isn't that *much* easier? We do not have to play games here, Jackson. This is all hard enough without having to lie to one another. Without all the duplicitousness.

At that moment Raul returned, and Victor motioned for his right-hand man to grab the accessories they had retrieved from Jackson's person. A wallet, a crewmember's keycard — no wonder this man had been able to move freely around the ship — and one of the M4 carbines they had unpacked from one of the crates.

Victor had forgotten about this last item. "Jackson," he said, examining his prisoner's face. "It seems you have been busy. I've been told some of my men are dead. You wouldn't happen to know anything about that, would you?"

Jackson grumbled. "It's just *Jack*, asshole. Yeah, I know a bit about that. You're next."

Victor actually laughed at this, a hearty genuine belly laugh. *This man is too much.*

"Give me his wallet," Victor snapped. Raul handed it to him immediately. He flipped through it, finding what he was looking for. Not surprisingly, there was no identification badge or anything that designated this man as part of the United States' fleet of espionage workers. But there *was* an ID. "Jackson Barr, Jr." Victor looked up at him with a raised eyebrow. "So there are *two* of you in the world. Where is your father now, Jack?" Victor asked.

Jack spat at his feet.

"Ah, right. Passed away. Not two of you anymore, are

there? So here you are, invoking his spirit as you traipse around my corridors killing my men. Fascinating. But I need to know — *why*? What do you and your organization know about my operation here?"

Again, no answer.

He turned to the man nearest the desk along the side of the wall. "Hand me the manifest."

He didn't take his eyes off of Jack, and he was glad he didn't. He saw the surprise and fear ratchet up in the man's face. He did a good job suppressing it, but it was too late. Victor cocked his head to the side.

"You said you were traveling with your...?"

Jack shook his head. "Just me and my wife., Celebrating our fifteen-year anniversary."

Victor sensed the man was telling the truth. He was not sure, however, if he were telling the *whole* truth.

The communications operator, Brandt, handed him the manifest and he flipped through it quickly, happy Jack's last name was near the front of the tiny booklet. "B... Ba...," he said, sounding out the letters. "*There* we go. Barr, Jackson Jr. Looks like you *do* have a wife on board, as you said. Hopefully she's safely back ashore, no?"

Jack nodded. Victor could almost feel the displeasure growing in the man. He kept reading. "And — what do you know? Two *children* on board as well. Addison, eight, and Riley, eleven. Jack," he said, his eyes darting up quickly at his prisoner. "It appears you have not been *entirely* forthcoming with me. I don't need to mention once more that this sort of thing really does piss me off, do I?"

The man's chin fell to his chest, and the sobs came more quickly now.

He snapped his fingers at the man who had handed him the manifest. "Brandt, go check with the others and see if there is a kid named Riley Barr still on the ship. Eleven years old, from the looks of it. I would like to meet this young lady."

Jack screamed then, the bloodcurdling wail of rage almost deafening, even in the expansive bridge. Jack tore at his bindings, likely only causing rope burn around his wrists.

He began mumbling to himself, spittle and tears falling onto his lap. For a moment Victor wondered if he had been telling the truth — perhaps this man *had* been here just with his family? Perhaps he had no intention of getting embroiled in this fiasco?

But no, Victor realized. No matter what his intentions had been, he *had* become entangled in all of this. He was on this ship on purpose — and for what other reason than to retrieve his children and take down Victor and his men?

Suddenly, he had an idea.

"Where is his phone?" Victor asked. Another man handed Victor Jack's phone, and Victor tapped on the screen to wake it up. As expected, the phone was locked, but he had everything he needed right in front of him that it would take to get it *un*locked.

He strode over to Jack and ripped his hair backward, eliciting a wide-eyed expression and groan of pain. Almost immediately he held the phone out in front of Jack's face and then he saw the unlocking graphic on the screen as it registered the correct owner.

"Perfect," Victor said, releasing Jack's sweaty hair. He wiped his hand on his pants and then opened Jack's phone application. He swiped down a bit, not seeing any numbers he recognized, then moved over to his messaging app. "Here we go."

He read the next message aloud, for everyone on the bridge to hear.

"'Patrick,'" Victor began. "'On the *Ocean Voyager*. Shots fired, explosion belowdecks. They know I'm CIA. Have any more information?'" Victor paused, making a *tsk* sound. "Jackson, I was about to believe you. You *almost* had me fooled. Here with your family, just a week-long vacation in the beautiful Caribbean. I'll bet you even have flip-flops somewhere on board, don't you?"

He didn't wait for Jack to answer.

"But this last text message of yours is a bit... alarming. You see, whether or not you intended to get involved with my affairs, you now — without a doubt — have. Also, you've gotten *other* people at your department involved in my affairs. Make no mistake — I'm sure your organization has been keeping tabs on me and my cartel for some time now, but that does not mean I came all the way here expecting to be hounded by the CIA. Somehow *you* and your *partner* snuck onto my ship and have been anticipating my every move. Somehow you have been one step ahead."

He saw that the man was about to respond. About to deny his accusations.

Victor cut him off. "Until right now. Because this *ends* now."

Victor needed to be done with this man, but he needed to get the information he had first. His boss would want to know how the US government had seemed so... prepared.

After this, he would kill him. He had no more need for extra hostages, and a grown man would have far less leverage than the children. Like he had done with all the other crew members and staff — even officers remaining on the bridge — he would kill this man and move on. "Raul, Richardson," he said, talking to his two men standing sentinel nearby. "Take him back down to Deck 2. Show him what we've been working on. Let's see if that jogs his memory a bit."

Raul and Richardson — the two men who had nearly been killed by Jackson Barr, Jr., nodded at their leader. He watched as Jack's hands were yanked upward, causing the man to yelp in pain. Raul retied the man's hands behind his back.

"Don't show him everything, of course," Victor added. "We don't need him getting any ideas. Figure out if he's willing to talk — if you know what I mean."

"Sí. I know exactly what you mean," Raul said.

"Good. And then leave him down there with the captain, but make sure they are both guarded. I've got work to do up here, and I need to keep an eye on the Coast Guard ships and choppers. I expect our ride to be here soon."

Another nod, and his two soldiers left, Jackson Barr, Jr. in tow.

CHAPTER 44

JACK

JACK HAD NOT SPOKEN since screaming at Victor. He realized now that almost everything he had done leading up to this point — calling Howard Graves and his wife, sending a message to his director, killing Victor's men, and getting involved in cartel business — had backfired in a huge way.

Now Jack was being led to his likely death, all the way back down in the bowels of the ship, that much farther away from his daughters. Again.

And Victor was planning something with Riley. He focused his rage and confusion and fear and turned into a seething, smoldering anger, trying to push away any thoughts of what that might be. Victor had already played his hand, already proven that he was not above killing people in cold blood and sending them over the edge of the ship. So would he actually carry it through with children? And was he about to make an example of him through his daughter?

Jack shook his head, feeling the grip of the men holding him tighten.

"Almost there, *amigo*," the man named Raul said. The

other man chuckled, and Jack wondered what they had in mind. Surely this was not going to be as simple as the way Victor had made it sound — he was not being taken belowdecks to just "take a quick look around,"

He was being taken there to be murdered.

But the particular *flavor* of that murder eluded him. Were they going to torture him first? Try to extract information out of him that might help them understand what he and the CIA knew about their operation? Jack figured that was likely, but what then? Jack could not offer information he did not have. He had very little training in how to handle a torture situation, from either end. He probably could not even pass a lie detector test.

He certainly did not think he could handle whatever torture mechanism they decided to use.

I'm not that kind of CIA guy, he reminded himself. But he found that the sentiment did not help whatsoever. His thoughts reminded him of this. *You're going to* have *to be that kind of CIA guy, at least for a few minutes before you pass out.*

Yes — maybe that was it. Maybe he just needed to pass out and they would give up. He couldn't be tortured if he was passed out.

...Right?

All of these thoughts peppered his mind like bullets, each one searing through his thoughts and distracting him.

No, he thought. *I need to get* out *of the situation, no matter* what.

I need to get to my girls.

He knew where they were now, assuming Victor and the others had not been lying to him. So far, Victor had seemed adamant that he was 'a man of his word.' It was at least something to go on. If Victor had been telling the truth, it meant Jack had good information as to the whereabouts of his daughters.

But Jack was still alone — one man against a small army. Each of them probably better trained than him.

The elevator dinged, and Raul and Richardson pushed him out roughly into the Deck 2 hallway. Rather than turning right, working their way toward the *Theater Access* door, they turned left and entered another door hidden in the shadows. As soon as it opened, Jack smelled saltwater. The air in here seemed moldy, stuffy. They pushed him down a set of stairs and he realized he was on the opposite side of the same under-stage access room he had been in now multiple times.

This side, however, had been partitioned already, the metal walls splitting this half of the room into many smaller chambers.

He also heard a loud noise. He recognized it as the same humming sound he had heard before, only this time the device — whatever it was — was much closer. It sounded like a saw, metal on metal. The high-pitched whine and bright flashes of flickering light reaching his eyes in the open space solidified that theory.

Raul shouted something, and the saw stopped. Jack saw a man approach through a doorway a few seconds later, his hands raised in question. "Que paso?" He asked.

The man was wearing diving gear from the torso down, only his upper body free of the wetsuit.

"Victor told us to bring this guy down here. I thought you might want to help take some pieces off of him."

Jack shivered as he realized what Raul was implying.

Thankfully, the man seemed to have no interest in helping

cut Jack into tiny little pieces. "I can't, brother," he said. "We're on schedule; Victor wants this done within the hour."

"Yeah, yeah," Raul said. "I figured. He'll go ballistic if you don't finish by then, too. He gave the Coast Guard only two hours to get the yacht we need, so we have to have everything else ready by then."

"We're getting all this out on a yacht?" the man asked, a quizzical expression on his face.

"I doubt it," Raul said, laughing. "But *Victor's* got a plan — that's why we're here. We don't ask questions; we just do what he says."

"Right — which is why I need to keep going."

Raul waved him off and he and Richardson pulled Jack the other direction, through another doorway. Beyond this doorway was another small landing and then two small steps down. They pulled him off the landing and down these two steps — directly into six inches of water.

The murky seawater lapped against the stairs and around, smacking against all four walls before traveling back to the center of the room, repeating the cycle over and over again. He saw papers and objects littered beneath the water, some of the lighter buoyant objects floating and bobbing on the surface.

They must have closed the blast doors a bit too late, Jack thought. *And for some reason, they're sawing a hole through one of the doors.*

Raul and Richardson muttered to one another in Spanish, but Jack only picked up a few words.

Chair, fine, water.

Richardson left, and Raul slid the rifle off of his shoulder and pointed at Jack, whose arms were still tied behind his back.

"Don't move."

JACK STOOD THERE, not planning to move *or* talk. He was busy working through the new pieces of the puzzle that had just been revealed to him. He wasn't sure if he would ever get the chance to put it all together, but he couldn't help trying anyway.

Richardson came back into this room with a rickety wooden chair.

"That's the best you got?" Raul snapped.

Richardson answered in Spanish. This time, Jack heard the curse words clearly. From the other words he understood, he assumed the rest of the sentence involved something along the lines of, 'that's the best I got with the time I have.'

They forcefully shoved Jack backward onto the chair and Raul untied his wrists and then retied them to the chair arms. Jack clenched his fists as tightly as he could, turning them sideways. He hoped Raul wouldn't notice. It was an old trick, but if Raul and Richardson were rushed for time, perhaps this little trick would go unseen.

Raul finished, and Jack sat motionless while he waited for the next thing to come.

Unfortunately, the next thing to come was a massive blow to his right cheek, totally unannounced. It felt like his jaw had been shattered, and he realized Raul had used the butt of his rifle to do it. Jack's head dropped, his face aflame with pain. He gently worked the bones with his mouth, finding nothing out of place, but knowing there was going to be a massive bruise in short order.

"What else did you tell the CIA about us?" Raul growled.

Jack shook his head, having already gone over this with Victor. "I explained this already, I was just here with my —"

This time the blow came from his left side, from Richardson. *Dammit.* It struck his shoulder, this time knocking it out of its socket a bit.

Jack howled in pain. "Stop!" he shouted. "I already told you assholes, I wasn't here working on *anything*, I wasn't here trying to figure *anything* out. I came back on the ship to find my kids, that's it!"

Raul and Richardson discussed something briefly, away from Jack's ears, and Raul left the room. Jack eyed Richardson while they waited. If Richardson was going to attack him again, he at least wanted to see it coming.

A couple of minutes later he heard noise and shuffling as Raul — obviously lugging something heavy — came back into the room. Jack saw that it was a body, a man about Jack's height and build. He, too, was wearing the clothes of a crewmember.

Raul let the body fall into six-inch-deep water, and the splash got Jack's face wet, the saltwater stinging against an open cut he hadn't realized he had.

"You know this guy, right?" Raul asked.

Jack hadn't even seen the man's face, but he knew the answer was no. He shook his head.

"Come on, you work with him. He's CIA."

"Is he... is he dead?"

Richardson chuckled, and Raul smiled. "Oh yeah, he's dead. Funny story, though — *we* didn't kill him."

Jack wouldn't have called the story *funny* necessarily, but it was certainly interesting information. He had not expected this twist at all. When they had implied that Jack had a partner on board — another CIA agent — Jack had not thought he was already dead. And if he had thought that he would never have guessed that it wasn't Victor's own men who had done the deed.

"How did he die, then?" Jack asked.

Raul pulled back on the dead man's hair, much like Victor had done to him earlier. He activated a flashlight mounted to the top of his assault rifle and pointed it at the man's face, revealing its right side.

Jack saw blistering, the bright shine of burn marks on skin.

"An explosion," Raul said. "Your buddy here got too close when our bomb went off. Either the blast killed him, or he bumped his head on something else."

That is *interesting,* Jack thought. He felt for the guy, but he also knew that this could be an important clue.

"Victor was pissed about it, but you know why?"

Jack shrugged.

"This guy somehow got the bomb *off* the wall. He was walking around with the damn thing; we think trying to put it over the side of the boat before it could do its job."

Do its job, Jack repeated silently. *So the bomb* had *been*

Victor's after all. And it had been placed in a particular spot for a particular reason. A likely strategic reason.

Richardson jumped in. "Yeah, well, we found him right around the corner. Obviously he didn't get blasted apart, so we think he must have set the bomb down to do something and then started walking away. We're not sure why, or what he was really up to. But yeah, Victor was hoping you might be able to fill us in on the details."

Jack sighed. He wasn't sure what he could tell these men to make them believe him. He had no idea what was going on, nor who this guy was or what he was doing on the ship. He shrugged again, shaking his head. "Look, I really wish — for my own sake — that *you* could help *me*. I really wish I could tell you something that would convince you I'm either innocent and know nothing or guilty and just won't tell you the whole story, so you can just put a bullet through my head and be done with it."

"But you know us well, don't you?" Raul asked. "You CIA assholes. You all know Victor's reputation. You know that we *can't* do that. You know that we have to get whatever information we have out of you, one fingernail at a time, then one tooth at a time."

"Don't forget toes," Richardson said, chuckling.

Jack shuddered, but he glared at his two captors. *So that's the flavor of torture they chose,* he thought.

"Richardson here is a *very* capable doctor, if you know what I mean." Richardson chuckled again as Raul continued. "I need to check on our captain, to see if he has come around. How far along is he?" he asked Richardson. "Does he have any fingers left?"

Richardson smiled, and Jack saw three or four gold teeth lining the inside of his mouth amidst mostly black and decaying teeth. *Gross*, he thought. *No wonder the man smiled without showing his teeth most of the time. It would be torture enough to have this man breathe near his face.*

"He has plenty of fingers left," Richardson said. "Last I checked, anyway. We cauterized three wounds so that he wouldn't bleed out while we looked for this guy."

Raul nodded. "Did we get anything from him?"

"Nah, not yet. Nothing Victor didn't already know. But I *will*."

"You have the same deadline as everyone else, Richardson," Raul said. "If you don't do it in time..."

"I will, I will." Richardson swallowed, likely imagining what Victor would do to him if he failed, but then he looked down at Jack as he spoke. "But yes, you must leave me to it. I need to get busy if I'm supposed to get *both* these guys loosened up in time."

Raul left without another word, and Richardson pulled off his own rifle and set it on the back of the deceased CIA agent, trying to keep it out of the water. He walked around Jack slowly, a full circle. Kneeling in front of Jack's face, he let out a sharp, pungent breath. Jack winced, wondering if he had somehow invoked this himself just by the mere thought of it.

"Where to begin, my friend?" Richardson asked. "Mouth or hands? Teeth or fingernails?"

Jack thought of something. It was a long shot, but it was all he had. He groaned, ratcheting up the volume just a bit more than he had intended. He squeezed his eyes shut, rolling his jaw again and eliciting even more of a sharp pain from the right side of his face. "I — I think he broke my damn jaw," Jack began. "Just — just *don't* start there, please."

He opened his eyes and looked up into Richardson's, pleading. Richardson's disgusting grin widened. "Oh, your little face is in pain? Can you point to where it hurts?"

He waited a beat, like a comedian waiting the perfect amount of time before the punchline. "Oh, that's right. You can't. I'm *so sorry* about that. Here, let me help you."

Jack flinched as Richardson brought his left arm back, aiming directly for Jack's chin.

Jack pushed his head forward as far as it would go, hoping Richardson would take the bait.

Richardson swung, his meaty fist sailing quickly toward Jack's face. At the last moment, Jack whipped his head back again as far as it would go, letting the fist past pass mere millimeters in front of his face.

Richardson, now off-balance from the force of his punch not landing where he had intended, rolled sideways, his back now toward Jack.

Jack was not going to need a better opportunity than this. He kicked his legs out at the backs of Richardson's knees, sending the man down to the water. Then he stood up and raced backward, aiming for the nearest wall to him. He hit it full force, hearing the splintering sound as the chair broke into pieces. It fell around him, sprinkling the water.

His hands were still tied to the chair arms dangling by his side as he ran, but he forced himself to hustle. It was hard sloshing around in the six inches of water, but thankfully the room was small enough. He reached Richardson just as the mercenary was pulling his head out of the water. There was a startled look on his face as Jack's right foot caught him directly in the nose.

Richardson fell backwards, choking and coughing as he lay sprawled out on his back on the floor, the water violently churning around him.

Jack kept moving, immediately kneeing the man's neck, holding his head sideways and underwater.

Without water in the room, it would've been an unfair fight — this man could have overpowered Jack easily. As it was, his hands were flailing wildly, trying to gain purchase on Jack's arm and shoulder while also trying to push him off of his neck.

Jack held the man's head underwater with a chair arm, knowing that the broken nose, combined with his inability to control his involuntary functions would make quick work of him.

Sure enough, in about thirty seconds, the man's arms flapped once more and then lay still. Not wanting to leave anything to chance, Jack waited another ten long seconds, just to be sure.

After that, he could see the whites of the man's eyes, still open underwater like a spooky corpse floating up from the depths. Satisfied the man was down for good, Jack finally stood up.

Jack was soaking wet, but discomfort was the least of his worries. He saw the dead CIA agent on the ground, the right side of his face charred and burned under the water. He stepped over and grabbed Richardson's rifle from the man's back.

Then, thanking Kate for the idea once again, he snapped off Richardson's keycard from its holster on his belt.

He walked back over to the agent. *Rest in peace, friend. You've done well.* He wasn't sure what else he should do — it was not like he could carry a body around while fighting off Victor's men and looking for his kids.

He had a job to do, and once again, he was armed.

JACK WAITED by the open door that led up into the slightly larger partition. Most of the time he had been down here with Richardson and Raul the saw had been on, but toward the end of his struggle with Richardson it had died down.

He wasn't sure if Raul was still around here somewhere, but at least Victor's man wielding the saw would have heard the commotion.

It only took a few seconds before this man ran into the room.

The man jumped through the door and down into the water, standing right above the dead CIA agent. He stared down at Richardson next, and before he could turn around and wonder what had happened here, Jack fired three rounds into his back.

The man tried turning then, but fell, landing right on top of the CIA guy's legs. Jack put two more rounds into the back of his head.

Knowing that the shots would have been the loudest thing happening down here in a while, he turned toward the open doorway, prepared for more action. From here on top of the steps, he could see through into all three rooms — the main room they had entered into, and across from that the room where the saw guy had been working. He figured there might be another partition down here where they were keeping the captain, but it was impossible to tell.

Jack waited a few seconds, but no one came. He crept into the main room, then into the room where the saw guy had been working.

He was alone down here, for the moment. Wherever the captain and Raul were, there was no access to it from this third room.

Jack turned and saw what the guy had been working on. A large, rectangular hole had been sliced into the far wall. He tried to get his bearings, tried to remember where he was relative to the upper decks.

This has to be an exterior wall, Jack thought. He remembered seeing pictures online of the interior walls of these ships — they weren't solid, but themselves partitioned, wafer-like with plenty of air space between the outer and inner hull, both to improve buoyancy and to allow the bilge pumps to start working, in case of a breach. The individual tiny partitions would fill up, and many small pumps would work to expel the water before the ship took on too much.

He saw that Victor's saw guy had successfully removed the inner hull from the rectangle where he'd been working. He could see the struts of the outer hull and its cross braces, a bunch of thin sheets of sturdy aluminum. The man had been carefully working around the edges of this rectangle on the *outer* hull next, not pushing the saw deeply enough to pierce it completely, but enough to get close — to leave a scored line around the perimeter of the rectangle.

He also saw why the saw had stopped — the man he had killed had finished the cutting job and had begun working on wiring a bunch of little explosives up to the perimeter of the inner rectangle. The dozens of dots straddled this line, all connected together with a wired charge.

Compact C4, Jack knew immediately. The tiny little beads of explosive — by themselves — would do very little. But spread out over this rectangle in such a way, and thanks to the circular saw's action working most of the way through the outer hull, the charges would blow this entire rectangle outward. Immediately after that, however, it would fall back inside as the water from outside came in.

He suddenly realized what the larger bomb — the one the CIA man had accidentally detonated — had been intended for. Victor's men were simply going to blow a hole in the side of the ship and had partitioned off these sections to keep the water exactly where they wanted it.

But why?

In a flash, the answer came to him. *The crates,* he realized. *That was what this was all about.*

Victor was an arms dealer, one who probably dabbled in all sorts of other things considered unscrupulous. Victor was trying to get these crates off the boat. For whatever reason, he couldn't get them off the same way they had gotten them on — that is, he couldn't simply wheel them off the loading dock and into the warehouse, to be distributed later.

Jack assumed that was exactly how they had gotten *on* the *Ocean Voyager* in the first place — he had simply paid off a trusted third party — so why could he not do that here?

And then, how would Victor's men get the crates into the partitions that were already full of water? There was an infinite amount of seawater ready to come into the ship — how would his men get back into the partition holding the crates?

It didn't make sense, at least not yet.

But Jack's problems lay elsewhere. He still needed to get to his kids.

JACK

JACK GRIPPED THE RIFLE TIGHTLY, knowing it was his best hope of getting out of the situation alive. He turned right now, moving the direction they had come in from, then stopped.

He had noticed the door to his left, one that looked identical to the one they had walked into before. It was the only other door around, and Raul and Richardson had seemed to imply that the captain was nearby. He had Richardson's keycard from one of the men, so he figured it was worth the few seconds to check inside.

He slid his new keycard out and held it over the door's access pad. It clicked green and he opened the door, hesitant as he walked inside. He held the rifle tightly, expecting the worst.

Instead, Captain José Phillips stared at him, tied to a chair much like the one Jack had been in only minutes ago. There were lines streaking the man's face, from dried tears that had turned into salt. His wrists were bound to the arms of the chair and faced him, and Jack saw that three of his fingers, starting from the pinky, were completely missing. Cauterized scars covered the ends of the nubs, a move that would have been disturbingly more painful than the actual chopping off of the fingers itself.

Jack rushed forward, using his new M4's sling to toss it over his shoulder. There was tape over the captain's mouth, likely to muffle the man's screams, and Jack ripped it away. The pain of pulling against the man's whiskers would be the least of the pains he was experiencing right now, Jack knew.

He looked down at the captain as he worked against the man's bindings.

The captain wheezed. "Thank you," he said softly. "Thank you."

"I know this is going to sound stupid, but... are you okay?"

The captain just nodded.

Jack pulled him upward, careful not to disturb his pulped hand. "I need to get you off this boat, but we need to get to the kids first."

"The kids?" The captain asked, shocked.

Jack nodded. "Yeah, that guy's got all the kids corralled somewhere... including my daughters."

The captain chewed on this for a moment, still nodding. "Victor," he said.

Jack stopped working and stared at the captain. "You know him?"

"I do... but by reputation only." The captain swallowed, as if considering how much he wanted to reveal to Jack.

"Look, man," Jack said, suddenly realizing that there might be more to Captain Phillips' capture and torture by Victor. "I'm just here to find my kids. Any information you've got that can help me do that keeps us *all* alive longer. You understand?"

The captain's confidence grew, and he nodded harder. "Yes, I understand. I just... do not know what I can tell you."

"You can tell me how you were involved with Victor."

The captain's eyes darted away. "I know nothing."

Jack knew he was running out of time. "Listen to me," he said. He leaned in close to the older man and letting the M4's barrel touch right at the base of his wrist. The captain whimpered as he felt the searing pain of his missing fingers flare up. "I'm not here to make friends. I'm not here because I'm trying to lock you up, either. But I *will* leave you down here. I promise you that. I can do this myself, or I can do this with your help — and that way might save your life."

He paused to let this sink in. "Your call."

The captain swallowed, then nodded. "We were skimming off the top. The crates down in the Theater Access area, behind the stage? They are not for the cruise ship. They are full of weapons, manufactured in the United States, but on their way to Venezuela."

Jack's eyes widened. "Okay, so you *do* know Victor."

The captain shook his head profusely. "I've *never* met the guy in person. I promise you. That is why I did not recognize him boarding my ship."

"So you were skimming off the top? Meaning, you knew about Victor's little smuggling operation, but you were also stealing some of the stuff he was smuggling? And then doing what with it?"

"It's — it's not like that. We had a system — we bring them to port once every other month, and the deck crews would take all of the crates and stash them in the warehouse with the others, just like we always do for any normal cruise. But Victor's — the illegal contraband — would be marked. I have a few men who stack them in the Theater Access area, because it's rarely needed space."

"That explains the smuggling. What were you doing next?" Jack asked.

The captain continued. "And then I would have a few of Victor's crates set aside, away from the portion that were destined for Venezuela. The ones that would go to Venezuela get loaded onto a different ship that hails from that country. The few that we set aside each time, I don't know..." The captain shrugged. "I didn't have to worry about that part," he said, finally. "The money would just... show up in my bank account."

"Money?" Jack asked. "That's what this is about? Money?"

The captain nodded. "I am not proud of it, but yes. You think we are celebrities — you might think we are all making a great living, but we are not. Everything I have goes back home, to my family. You would think it would be enough, but it is not even close. It is expensive living your life at sea, even for us. *Nothing* is free anymore; they don't let us share in the proceeds like they used to long ago. And the perks are all but gone. No more treating us to the nice dinners you all get — if we want more than the scheduled rations they prepare for us, it comes out of our paycheck — at a premium."

Jack nodded in understanding.

"And retirement?" the captain said. "That is *impossible* now, at least if I hope to live a while."

At least in principle, Jack understood. Things had gotten more expensive lately due to inflation, supply chain issues, and of course corporate tendencies to extract every dollar they could from everyone, at all times.

"So, you pissed off Victor because you stole from him. *That's* why he's here? That's what this is all about?"

"I believe so, yes. We must have been found out."

"You keep mentioning 'we' — who are you working with? Who's 'we'?"

"I do not know that information either," the captain said slowly. "I promise. As I said, this was just supposed to be easy money. I bring the boat to port and allow for the deck crew to take the crates. They get *on* the ship because of me — I sign off on all of it — but it gets to where it is going up because of whoever is working the other side. My job really is to just captain the boat — that has never changed. As captain, I know every person and item aboard, at all times. But that is it — once we dock, the crates move on. It is out of my hands."

"So the cartel *needed* you on board, literally and figuratively. They needed you to know about the operation for it to have worked."

The captain nodded.

"And for this, you were compensated?"

"Yes, not much, but yes. It was a good stream of income."

"But not good *enough*," Jack said. "Which was why you decided to make a little under-the-table deal, *against* Victor's interests. Someone approached you and asked if you wanted to make a little bit *more* money. They could have just done it themselves, but since you would have had to know about the operation in the first place, they cut you in, as well."

Captain Phillips frowned, nodding. He let his head fall.

"And now, you're double-dipping — you get the cartel's money just by *allowing* the crates to be here in the first place, but then you get a little bit of side action, thanks to whoever's selling the few they are apportioning for themselves."

The captain looked up at Jack. "Exactly, yes."

Jack shook his head. "You're in a world of shit, man."

The captain looked up at Jack.

He sighed, then finished helping the man up. "But so am I, I guess. For now, we're on the same team. I want the kids, and both of us want to get out of here. You know the ship better than anyone, so right now you're my best bet."

The captain seemed enthused by this idea.

"I still don't know if I can trust you," Jack said. "But I don't have a choice. Stay in front of me and stay out of my way at the same time. You think you can manage that?"

CHAPTER 48

VICTOR

THE RADIO on the dashboard where Victor had placed it squawked to life. *"Hey, it's Graves. You there?"*

Victor rolled his eyes at this man's flippant attitude. He grabbed the walkie-talkie as the two of his men still on the bridge watched on. "Yeah, I'm *here*," Victor said quickly.

"Right," Graves said. *"I've been trying to hold the Coast Guard and police off, but the juggling act is getting old. They're not too happy with you."*

"I never expected them to be happy," Victor said. "Do you have information for me?"

"Yes, I was able to secure a yacht. Fully loaded; should have plenty of room for you and your men."

"That *is* good news; I appreciate your willingness to play by the rules."

There was a pause, and then Graves came back on the walkie-talkie. *"Look, man, I don't know what the play is now, but what the hell do you expect to do after you get on that yacht? You can't stay hidden forever — and the Coast Guard's just going to turn it over to the Army and Navy, who will be breathing up your ass until you run out of gas. They'll have your boat tracked by nightfall."*

Victor nodded, realizing that this man was somehow better than he had originally seemed. He was baiting Victor, trying to get him to reveal information that might help them track him down. To be fair, Victor had worried about this exact thing — how *could* he keep a luxury yacht out of sight for very long? But to that end, his trained navigator had assured him that he would be able to disable any communications systems that might let their location be actively tracked by an authority or another ship. While they would not be able to hide from actual radar pings, Victor had been told by his boss at the cartel not to worry about this, either.

After leaving on the yacht, he and his men would travel around the tip of Jamaica to a cove not far from here that was accessible only by boat and known only to locals. This would let them get safely out of sight for just enough time. There, another boat would be waiting for them, and *this* would be the actual vessel they would use to return to their home.

By having the fuel stored in five-gallon jugs, his men could easily and quickly transfer it to the new boat.

Victor smiled as he pulled the radio up to his lips. "That is indeed a good question, Howard," he said, knowing he was not speaking to just the Port Authority security, but all of the Jamaican Coast Guard listening in. "But I don't want to reveal anything too soon, for what is the fun of that? Rest assured — all I will tell you now is: pay attention. Pay very close attention."

Now *he* was baiting *Graves*. If Graves was worth his salt, he would not be fooled by Victor's attempts at misdirection.

It did not matter either way, of course — he would not

have time to play games with this man once the clock started ticking.

As if on cue, one of the boats broke through the line off on the horizon and started toward the ship. He did not recognize it, as it had not been among the dots he had counted earlier. "I see a boat approaching from the northwest," he said into the radio. "I assume this is my yacht?"

"Affirmative," came Graves' response. *"It's a 30-meter Jetliner, piloted by a single man and no one else on board. No funny business, just like you requested."*

Victor's smile widened. "I see, thank you. I hope you have also seen my demonstration from earlier," Victor said.

There was a longer pause, and then Graves' voice, weakened a bit, came back onto the radio. *"Yeah... Yes, we all saw that. You know, you didn't have to go to those lengths."*

"I did!" Victor said angrily. "Of course I did! You don't know how this works, do you? You think this is all cat-and-mouse, a game of negotiating. But I'm not here for games, Howard Graves. I'm not here for cat-and-mouse. I simply have a job I need to get done, that is all."

He released the talk button, annoyed. He looked over at his two men. "Go down and check on the status of the captain and our new friend, Jack Barr. Take a radio so I don't have to wait for you to come all the way back up."

One of the men nodded quickly and left the room.

He turned and directed his voice toward the other man. "You — go get the kids. Take them to our last lifeboat on Deck 10, fore section, the one we prepared for this. Get there and load the kids into it."

The man started to nod and walk away, but Victor stopped him. "One more thing," he said.

The man waited.

"I *am* prepared to release the children back to their families so long as what Howard Graves tells me is true. But before I give you the word, I still need to see if that girl is here. She is eleven years old, by the name of Riley Barr. I would like to meet her — if Brandt is still down there, help him look. Send him back up here with her."

The man rushed off without another word.

Everything so far was going smoothly — as smoothly as he would have hoped, considering his work down below had been sabotaged by that *damned* CIA agent. It was not something he could have predicted, but he knew it was only a matter of time before his men informed him that it was no longer an issue.

But there was one more unknown he had not been prepared for.

How had he missed the *other* CIA agent, Jack Barr, Jr.? How had this lone man eluded his men for so long? When they had found evidence that there had been a CIA agent on board, his men had scoured the manifest, and the man had revealed himself shortly thereafter with his sabotage — he had blown the bomb Victor's men had carefully set, killing himself in the process.

But Jack Barr had not so much as *spoken* with this other man, nor had they tried to communicate. It was absurd — even if they were undercover, two agents working the same case would surely have tried to coordinate their efforts.

So what *was* Jack's role in all of this? What was his new friend trying to accomplish, and why had he waited so long to reveal himself?

Victor watched out the bridge window as the luxury yacht approached their location. It was probably fifteen minutes out running at that speed, but that was perfectly fine — still plenty of time. Nothing like being a little early to give Victor confidence that Graves was upholding his end of the bargain.

Your move, Jack, he thought. He hoped his men had made progress interrogating him. He had extracted important information from the captain already, discovering that the CIA agent was not the only man who had sabotaged his cartel's mission here. The captain himself seemed to have gotten greedy and was likely working with at least one more person. Victor had been sent to clean up the mess, but it seemed the amount of sabotage was stacking up against him.

What are you up to, Jackson? he wondered. *What* exactly *are you working on?*

Victor's radio came to life a few minutes later once again. This time, it was the man he had sent to check on Jack and the captain. *"Bad news, sir.*

Victor squeezed the radio's lower half, his knuckles white. He gritted his teeth. "Go on," he said, forcing his voice to remain calm.

"The CIA agent escaped, and he took out Richardson and Elizondo. Looks like he got to the captain as well."

Victor cursed, slamming the radio down onto the screen in front of the navigator, cracking the LCD monitor in a thousand places.

"That's not all, sir," the man said. *"Elizondo was working on preparing the hole, and he was killed before he could finish."*

Victor squeezed his eyes shut. *Good move, Jack. Good move, indeed.*

"How far along was he?" Victor asked.

"Almost done, sir. Elizondo had just finished the cuts and

had started putting on the compact explosives. We've got almost one side of it ready."

"I see. That will be enough — the additional cuts to the outer hull he made were overkill. The C4 that's already there will do the trick, even without blowing the rest of it. I have the detonator here. Can you confirm that it is wired?"

There was a pause as the man checked. His voice sounded more optimistic when it came back on the line. *"Affirmative, sir. Looks like it's blinking and everything. All the other C4 is laid out next to the door, ready to go."*

"Well, in the interest of being thorough, I need you to continue the work Elizondo was doing. You can see how he was sticking the dots to the wall, yes?"

Victor waited, and the man confirmed. "In that case, stay down until it is done. I'd like a clean break if at all possible. Understood?"

"Yes, sir. Should not take me long."

It had better not take you long, Victor thought. He let out a breath, wondering how long he would have to deal with this surprisingly adept agent. He placed the walkie-talkie down gently this time, watching the yacht approach their location. He went through all of the events that led up to this moment — where had he gone wrong? What had he forgotten? How could this man have gotten the best of him?

He wanted to personally kill Jackson Barr *now*, but he knew he had more important things to do. The yacht would be here very soon, and he needed to ensure there was no trap awaiting them on board. Jackson Barr, Jr. would die today.

It may not be by Victor's own hand, but he *would* die.

CHAPTER 49

JACK

JACK RACED UP THE STAIRS, practically dragging Captain Phillips behind him. It reminded him of lugging Giuseppe, the poor kid, through the ship. He had failed him — he had let his guard down, and now the kid was likely dead. He hadn't seen the young Italian since getting jumped in the hallway on Deck 2. He could only hope the kid had stayed behind, hiding in the room and waiting for everything to blow over.

The captain groaned in agony, holding his gnarled right hand in his left. He knew the man was in severe pain and had not had any painkillers. He was sure that if they stopped and looked around, they could find some, but Jack didn't want to waste time. He needed to get up to the kids.

He tried to recall how many of Victor's men he had killed, and how many he had seen, but he was losing track. *Six? Eight?* Richardson was now dead, and so was the man who had been operating the saw in the room nearby. Raul, Victor's right-hand man, was still nowhere to be seen, and then there was the trio they had run into in the lounge room: the High-Pitched

Voice guy, the chip eater, and the man with the Latin American accent. He had not seen any of these men again since.

The odds were still stacked against him, but as long as he could move toward them without being seen, Jack trusted his chances against theirs with the rifle.

He focused on the weight of it now, heavy on his shoulder, as they ascended the stairs at the aft section of the ship. He knew Victor was likely still on the bridge, controlling and commanding everything from his captain-like perch. He wanted to stay as far away from the man as possible until he had gotten to the kids and gotten them to safety — however he could do that.

He wondered if there were any lifeboats remaining up on Deck 10, or if he would have to figure something else out. Could all of the kids even swim? Should he have been collecting lifejackets for all of them?

As he rounded the stairwell between Decks 7 and 8, Captain Phillips panting behind him, he heard the intercom above him click to life. Since these stairs were intended for both passenger and crew use, there were speakers in the ceiling above his head, so he heard Victor's words clearly.

"Hello again, Jack," Victor said ominously. *"My men have informed me that you slipped away once more. I find this surprising, but I hope you know this greatly disappoints me. I was thinking you would be willing to obey, considering I'm about to meet your eldest daughter."*

Jack swallowed, his heart in his throat. Surely Victor was lying? Surely he wasn't... planning anything.

He kept moving, plowing his legs upward, ignoring the captain's heaving breaths. He fought through the pain of overexertion, his thighs and calves already nearing their limits.

"And yes — I am *going to kill her, Jack,"* Victor said. His voice was even, confident. Jack wanted to scream, wanted to stop and cry out. But instead he kept moving, making his way up toward Deck 10.

"She will be sitting in the same chair you were tied up to before, and I find that somewhat... poetic. Before I kill her, however, it is important to me that I see you again. You have disobeyed me far more than anyone in recent memory. That is something I simply cannot allow; you must know that. I know you are not stupid; I am a father myself.

"Which means I know you will do the smart thing and come back up to the bridge, where we will be waiting for you. Me and your lovely daughter, Riley. See, I am not heartless, Jack. I want you to see your daughter one last time before you die."

Jack kept moving even as his heart accelerated beyond the limits of his body. No regular cardio exercise could prepare someone for this, could endure what he was feeling.

He reached the landing to Deck 10, the captain now dragging far behind, as Victor's voice continued. *"Jack, I am going to give you fifteen minutes again, starting immediately, because I do not know where you are on the ship. Consider it a gift. But if I don't see your face stepping into my bridge in exactly fifteen minutes or less, I will put a bullet into your daughter and toss her overboard, like her friend Darek."*

JACK RAN across Deck 10 like his life depended on it. In a sense, it did. His kids *were* his life, and theirs were in grave danger. He had almost completely forgotten about the captain, still working his way up the stairs.

Five minutes.

I'm coming, Riley.

He saw two men in the distance, both working on something at the railing near the front of the ship. He couldn't see what it was from here, but it didn't matter. He had a mission, and these two men were in his way.

I'm going to kill you.

It was a directed thought — targeted toward these two men, but it was his driving force, as well. *If you get in my way now, you* will *die.*

He needed to get back to the bridge, to his daughter, and he needed to do it in ten minutes or less. Everything had just gotten far more complicated, and yet nothing had changed. The kids were now separated, Riley on her way to Victor. He did not know where Addy and the others were, but Riley had become the priority right now.

Perhaps Jack was reading too far into it, but Victor's first words had been that he was *about to meet* his eldest daughter — which gave Jack hope that there was still time to get there before she did. He had no plan of attack, and there were, to his knowledge, only two entrances to the bridge. He assumed both of them would be guarded, and the heavy latched storm doors themselves impossible to break through.

If Victor wanted to funnel him in one door or the other, he could easily do it. Jack would be a sitting duck.

The captain was running on Deck 10 as well, picking up speed now that he was out of the stairwell. But he was now a liability to Jack, whimpering and running far too slowly for his liking. Jack slowed, needing to use stealth as he approached the fore section and the two men working.

He turned and faced Phillips as they reached the center of the massive cruise ship deck. "I need you to hide," he told him. "You can just lie low here, out of sight. I can't have you approaching these armed mercenaries without a weapon; it's suicide."

Then Jack had a thought. "You know your way around. My wife was always talking about 'secret passageways' and stuff — is there a way to get to where those guys are that's not... just walking across the deck?"

The captain nodded. "Yes, there is."

"Good," Jack said. "Do that. Meet me there as quickly as you can. You'll know I'm done when you hear gunfire. Got it?"

Captain Phillips nodded again, and Jack took off, not willing to waste another second. *He'll either make it or not,* he thought as he started his approach toward the two mercenaries.

He continued running, though slower this time, thankful that his soft-soled shoes gave great purchase on the deck and did not squeak. He needed to sneak up on these men, still busy working on something. They were both looking up and pointing at something above their heads, but neither was facing Jack.

Best of all, from what he could tell from here, they were not holding guns.

He crept along the long hallway now, one similar to the corridor at the aft of the ship, open to the ocean on one side and nothing but white walls and doors on the other. No hiding spots for him to slip into.

If they were going to see him, it was going to be during this last stretch.

He saw what they were working on now — one of the davits, still holding up a lifeboat — the only one he could see. They had been trying to get the mechanism to engage. It seemed like it might be stuck, and both men were busy fiddling with the switches and knobs on a control box next to the boat.

Jack lifted his rifle. He took in a breath, knowing that these shots needed to land. He was going to alert others to his position by firing, but he had no choice. He could not sneak past them completely.

But mostly, he needed them to die. He needed to reduce Victor's army by two.

He fired one burst of three rounds. The man on the left, working the controls, fell. He fired again as the other man spun around, surprised. One of his rounds clanged off the control mechanism's plating, but the other two sank into the man's side. He fell to the deck, grasping at something behind his back.

Jack sprinted now, directly toward him. He tried to close the distance as fast as possible.

The mercenary, writhing on the ground, pulled out a pistol that he had hidden behind his back. He fired, three quick shots. Jack dove to the side, but the third round hit its mark. Directly in the thigh, and Jack felt the hot lead barreling through his leg.

It was pain like he'd never felt before, excruciating.

He started to fall but caught himself.

Can't. Quit. He dragged himself along, hobbling on one leg, toward this man.

He fired one more burst, silencing the man as his pistol clattered to the deck floor. Reaching the lifeboat, still hanging from the davit above it, he approached the hatch. The boat was exactly the same as the one he and Kate had been shuffled into, large enough to hold over a hundred people.

He pulled on the latch as he felt his heart racing. His leg was bleeding, flowing freely now. He swung the door upward and open, hearing shouts of surprise from within.

The kids.

He pulled his head up and over, pain searing down his right leg as he stretched up on his toes.

He saw inside the craft, saw the tiny hands and faces. Tears streaming down cheeks, some whimpering, some sobbing.

They were all here. He looked at each face, all of them turned and staring at him, terrified.

And then he saw her.

She rose from her seat and ran over the floor of the lifeboat, her feet pattering loudly as she did. More screams and shouts rang out as the children, confused, tried to make sense of why she was racing toward the exit.

"Addy," he said, his voice cracking. "Addy, it's me."

She ran up the steps and threw her arms around his neck. He squeezed his youngest daughter as tightly as he could, then released her. "Addy, I love you so much. So much. Okay? But I need you to trust me." There was a confused look on her face when she pulled back. "Mommy is waiting on shore, okay? She's waiting there for you, and when you get there, you'll be safe. All of this will be over."

"You — you're not coming?" she whimpered. "Where's Riley?"

She started crying again, and Jack pulled her close once more. "She's still here, still on the ship. Which is why I have to stay. I have to go get her." His voice cracked again, the tears now flowing freely. "I'm going to find her, but I don't want to risk you and the other kids. I'm going to get you down into the water, and you'll float back to shore, okay?"

She swallowed, still confused, but eventually nodded. He pushed her gently back inside, looking at a few of the older kids — many of them Riley's age or slightly older by a couple of years, and all of them terrified. "It's going to be okay, I promise," he said, loudly enough so they could all hear.

The captain appeared behind him, having just popped out from a doorway Jack had not noticed.

He locked eyes with the captain. "I trust you can drive this thing, too?" he asked.

The captain nodded.

"Get these kids to shore," Jack said. He wasn't sure if he fully trusted this man — a man who had admitted to theft and sabotage — but he knew he was better than any of Victor's men. Besides, he didn't have a better option.

He closed the hatch and looked at the davit's control

station. The two men had been fiddling with knobs, but it seemed the machine was still not working properly.

"It's controlled from the boat now," the captain said, motioning toward the lifeboat. "There's a panel inside that controls the davit, and it will lower us into the water and release it. This row of lifeboats is designed to let the officers and crew board and control the lifeboats from inside, since they would be last off the ship."

This made sense to Jack — somebody would have to be the last person to get inside a lifeboat. That meant they would need to be able to control it from inside the lifeboat, not on deck.

He turned and nodded once at the captain, who approached the lifeboat and began to jump inside.

Before he could, Jack called out to him. "Wait!" he said.

The captain paused, staring at Jack.

"I just thought of something," Jack said. "I have an idea. But I need to *know* that I can trust you."

The captain frowned, but then spoke softly. "I have made many mistakes, my friend. Yes, I got involved with something I have no business in. But children?" He shook his head. "That is too far — that is beyond anything I could ever imagine. I *have* children. Please, know that you can trust me now, at least with this."

Jack waited, knowing that he had no better option. It was this man or no one, but he did not think the captain was lying to him. Why would he?

Jack sighed, knowing this was the only option. "Okay, here's what I need you to do."

AFTER TELLING Captain Phillips what his plan was, he asked him a few more questions regarding the layout of the mess hall below the bridge, then they parted ways.

Jack tried not to worry. *This will either work,* he thought, *or I'll be dead.* Not exactly comforting, but it was a plan, at least. Riley deserved any chance there was, and he certainly was not going to race up to the bridge and meet Victor face-to-face. The man was too smart for that. He would have planned for exactly that — and he would likely have his men standing by, ready to take Jack down immediately upon entering the bridge.

He raced to the nearest set of stairs, hoping against hope that none of Victor's men were guarding them. He had no time for stealth, no time for sneaking around. Victor had not just given him an ultimatum, but he had leverage.

He had Riley.

It was a ticking time bomb, and Jack could not afford to be late.

By now, Jack had taken down about half of Victor's men, by his count, though he did not know if Victor had more standing by. But now, whatever of Victor's men remained, he hoped they would all have much more important jobs to do than to simply guard stairwells and wait for Jack to appear.

He reached the top of the stairs unmolested, then pulled out onto Deck 15 where the captain's mess was. He needed to find the kitchen — specifically, the pantry. He hoped he had made the right call in coming here first; though he knew there was likely a larger cache of goods downstairs, trying to find what he needed in the storehouse of boxes belowdecks would be a losing proposition. He had no time to do that *and* race all the way back up the stairs and set things up in time.

Thankfully, he found what he needed only a minute later. Tucked behind the commercial kitchen, in a back corner near the walk-in freezer, he found a dry goods pantry.

His assumption had been correct — that a smaller subset of supplies and food would need to be stored well within reach of the chefs that kept the officers and captain happy. This kitchen — just like all of the other kitchens on board — had a supply of stuff from which cooks and chefs and staff could pick out what was needed, able to access it faster than having to wait around for it to be delivered from downstairs.

And what he needed was something found in every kitchen around the world: ingredients for making a bomb.

While he was on deck on the bridge with Victor, Jack had tried to take in every piece of information he could while listening to Victor's broadcasts. He had noticed papers and items from a desk bolted to the wall that had fallen on the floor — likely caused by a skirmish when Victor had barged in and taken over the bridge. He also thought he had seen bloodstains in a few places, another sign that there had been a struggle to overpower the officers who had been on the bridge at the time.

But another thing he had noticed was a small, rectangular door, set against the back wall of the bridge, straddled by two recessed areas where more computers and chairs sat.

The metal door sat in the center of the wall at about waist height, probably three feet tall by a couple of feet wide. He had seen the design before, but it had taken him a bit to realize what it was.

A dumbwaiter system.

It had not meant anything to him at the time, but now — since he was scheduled to meet with Victor once more — the dumbwaiter had given him an idea.

He plowed through the closet, looking on every shelf for what he needed.

He found the ingredients first, then the object he had *really* hoped would be present: a pressure cooker.

It was a long shot — he wasn't sure the strategy would even work, but he had to try. The whole thing would take him mere minutes, and since he had no better plan, he moved forward.

Once he finished, he shoved the entire thing into the dumbwaiter. If the system operated as he had suspected, this little elevator would pull everything upward when he pressed the button on the outside of it. He assumed it would move slowly enough so that it would not jostle any food or drink on the trays placed inside — or in this case, the bomb he had built.

The pressure cooker's journey would last for two decks, which he hoped would give him enough time to climb the stairs himself.

He also hoped the bomb would last longer than that — exploding halfway up the shaft was not going to be helpful to his cause.

He knew Victor would be waiting for him on the bridge —

he was, after all, a man of his word, as he had so often reminded everyone around him. But Jack assumed he would not be waiting alone on the bridge — likely some of his men would be waiting with him.

He also remembered Victor's words when he had heard them over the intercom last. *She will be sitting in the same chair you were tied up to before.* He needed that to be true. It was *crucial* to his plan.

He climbed the stairs, moving slower now that the endgame was in sight. Whether or not it would work was immaterial — he would see this through, for better or worse. There was no other alternative.

Jack reached the landing at Deck 17, still not having run into any of Victor's men. He had seen the yacht approaching and wondered if Victor had sent men down to check it out. The fewer the men up here, the better. While Jack had hoped to not run into any men guarding the stairs, he also didn't want many of them guarding his *daughter*.

He trusted his shot with the rifle, but he didn't want to have to put that skill to the test around his own kid.

The last stretch of stairs leading up to the bridge was outside. He climbed the narrow staircase and waited just outside the door. He assumed the door would be unlocked, as Victor had told him he would be waiting for him inside.

He had no doubt that whoever was in there was pointing their weapon at this very door, or his daughter, right now.

But Jack was waiting for the perfect moment to barge in. A moment he hoped would come to pass. It would signify that his plan had worked, at least to an extent.

The ingredients he had mixed together were common household ingredients, ones used to make low-powered bombs.

He had not put too many of the chemicals inside the pressure cooker, as he didn't want to blow the entire bridge — he just needed to make an entrance.

There was no way to time the pressure cooker and the ingredients inside — it was just a guess. There was no way to know if the bomb would even *work* properly — hopefully, he had added enough of the explosive ingredients inside to cause the sealed pressure cooker to blow. But he took solace in the fact that Victor had told him, essentially, exactly where he had placed his daughter in the room — that she was sitting in the same chair Jack had been in prior. That chair was the metal swivel chair bolted to the bridge floor, secured against heavy winds and huge waves.

That meant it could not be moved, so Jack was confident that Riley was now sitting in the same spot on the bridge where he had been tied up before. He knew that a small explosion from the dumbwaiter would be — he hoped — far enough away that it would not harm anyone sitting there.

As long as it explodes, he thought. He didn't need *size*.

He needed *surprise*.

In that exact moment, the makeshift bomb exploded.

Jack felt the pressure cooker rip apart the thin metal door it was hiding behind, sending pieces of it flying across the room. The door to the bridge he was currently hiding behind vibrated with the detonation.

He twisted the handle and pushed the door open quickly, not wanting to lose momentum. He pulled his rifle up and fired without second thought, aiming at the lone man in front of him, a man currently watching the devastation with a shocked expression on his face. The explosion had clearly done its job; it was not large, but it took the man by surprise enough for him to turn and face it — rather than the door Jack was entering through.

The man had no chance. Jack dropped him with a single burst of fire just as smoke and debris completely filled the upper half of the room. Jack sank to his knees, trying to see the room beneath the noxious fumes that had just flown out of the dumbwaiter.

He saw the chair. Saw tiny feet hanging from it.

"Riley!" he shouted. "Riley, can you hear me?"

"Daddy?" She screamed.

He felt the tears beginning to fall down his face again as he crawled forward on his hands and knees. He kept his rifle in his right hand, finger near the trigger, just in case someone else decided to enter the bridge.

But there was no one else here. The man he had killed had been the only man guarding Riley. That meant...

Victor was *not* here.

JACK REACHED Riley and immediately began untying her. His mind reeled. His little entrance had been a success, with one major problem:

Victor wasn't on the bridge.

He lied to me.

Victor had told him he would be waiting here with Riley. And yet he had left, leaving only a single man to guard the eleven-year-old.

That man was now dead, and Victor was nowhere to be found.

"Are we leaving, Daddy?" Riley asked.

Jack nodded as he wiped tears from his daughter's eyes, pulling her close.

"Yes, yes, we are. Are you sure there's no one else here?" he asked. "A man named Victor?"

Riley frowned, shaking her head. Jack felt another booming sound from far below his feet.

What the hell?

It felt like almost the same explosion as the first one —

when he and Kate and all the other passengers had rushed to the side to see what had happened.

This time, though, it had been slightly fainter, as they were now on the highest deck, as far from the blast as they could get.

And Jack knew exactly what it was.

They blew a hole in the side of the ship, he realized. *Victor detonated the C4.*

He had no idea what that meant to him, but a second later the ship groaned once more as it began filling with more water.

He pulled Riley up out of the chair, holding her hand gently but pulling her along quickly, back toward the door he had come into the bridge on. "We need to get downstairs," he told her. "Down to Deck 10, where we can wait for the Coast Guard."

Just then a voice boomed over the speakers in the bridge. *"Hello Jack,"* it began.

Victor. How is he broadcasting? Jack wondered. He must have been broadcasting remotely, as there was clearly no one else on the bridge.

"I hope you made it to the bridge. If everything is progressing the way I had hoped, you are waiting there with your daughter, hand in hand, looking at my good friend Raul. And looking at the barrel of his rifle."

Jack *was* looking at Raul — the man's eyes were open, staring straight upward as he lay dead on the floor.

Jack clenched his teeth as Victor continued. *"I want you to know, again, that your antics have not fooled me. You sent a diver to the ship — a man I am happy to report is no longer with us. But you* also *came here yourself, undercover — a fact I find humbling as much as I find frustrating.*

"At every turn, Jack, you deceived me or flat-out lied to me. I,

on the other hand, have done none of these things. I told you all full-well what would happen in the case of insubordination, and I take no pleasure in informing you that I will be proving to you just how frustrated I've become."

Jack listened with Riley, standing on the stairwell that led out of the bridge.

"As you can see out the port-side window from the bridge, my men have now launched the last lifeboat. The lifeboat that is currently full of children, as well as your *daughter, Jack."*

Jack felt his feet shift beneath him as the boat began taking on water. He knew in an instant this breach was larger than the previous one. He wondered what Victor had done — was he trying to flood the entire thing? Trying to sink him?

Everything in the bridge that was not bolted down slid to the side, some of the larger items — computers, books, soda cans. Up here on Deck 17, the movements of the ship far below were exacerbated. He saw another item crash to the floor and went to retrieve it.

My phone.

It was dead, but it felt good having something of his back in his possession. He searched quickly for his wallet, but could not find it.

Another groan, and he felt himself falling forward now. It seemed the entire front side of the ship was taking on water and beginning to sink lower into the bay.

"I hope your wife is watching from shore, Jack," Victor said. *"I know the Coast Guard and Port Authority listening in are anxiously awaiting my next move, as well. By now, you have probably felt the shifting of the ship, caused by the explosion my men rigged. I just detonated another hole in the side of the ship,*

which means that my work here is done. As such, I will be leaving now. Hear this: anyone trying to track my yacht will fail, and anyone trying to follow us out of the bay will be killed. That's all I will say on the matter — I trust by now you know how serious I am."

Jack looked down at his daughter, who was gripping him tightly around the waist, sobbing into his side. He wanted to leave, but he needed to know what Victor had intended.

"This entire day could have gone much more smoothly," Victor said, *"though I've gotten what I have come here to get, so I will — finally — be on my way. However, there is one last gift I want to give you, Jack.."*

Jack winced.

"Jackson Barr, Jr.," Victor continued. *"I told you numerous times what the punishment would be for your continued lack of concern for my instructions. The severity was to be intense, and I'm afraid now you will suffer the consequences. You think that because I am a man of my word, you expected me to be waiting up there for you? You should know better than that, Jack. You disobeyed me, so our little deal was no longer valid."*

He paused, and Jack felt his blood run cold. *"Once again, please note the lifeboat out on the waters. Are you watching? Very good."*

Jack saw that Riley had also peeked up as well, looking out the huge windows down into the blue waters of the Jamaican port. The lifeboat sat about fifty feet away from the ship, bobbing gently. The ship itself helped the view by slowly leaning toward it, moving inch by inch as it rolled over in the water.

And then the lifeboat exploded.

A massive fireball erupted from the center of the boat, engulfing it in flames and sending pieces of plastic and metal outward in all directions. Jack was stunned, choking as he held back bile.

He could not believe his eyes — Victor had planted a bomb on the lifeboat.

The lifeboat the kids had been on.

"I hope this has been a useful lesson for you all," Victor said. *"But especially for you, Jack. Goodbye."*

Jack was done listening before Victor had cut off the transmission. He pulled Riley with him through the door, trying to ignore the pain from his injured thigh. He limped down the narrow staircase one step at a time, then down the larger internal staircases to Deck 10. Riley protested the speed they were traveling, so Jack scooped her up and held her under an arm as they descended. She was heavy; he had not picked her up in some time, and his leg screamed in pain with the extra weight. But he tried to not let it slow him down. He needed to get down there as soon as possible, down to Deck 10.

At Deck 11, the side of the stairwell was glass, so he could see out over the waters as he passed over the landing. He didn't stop, but he did notice the yacht Victor was on, now moving full speed to the north and beginning to bend its way around the island. No Coast Guard ships, or choppers pursued the boat.

Instead, those boats were all racing toward *him* — no longer held at bay by Victor's demands. They were coming toward the cruise ship that was clearly sinking, leaning precariously to the side. It seemed as though the rate at which the ship was taking on water had increased, too, as Jack felt off-balance as he descended the stairs.

He saw the smoldering remains of the lifeboat, just now starting to sink beneath the pristine waters. Thick white smoke mushroomed into the air above it as the flaming wreckage sent off steam as it met the water.

It was this scene that was emblazoned in his mind as he continued down the last flight of stairs onto Deck 10. He reared back, Riley in his left arm, and kicked the door open with his good leg. He no longer had a rifle — no longer had a way to protect himself. It was too late, anyway. He didn't care about his *own* safety. He didn't care about his *own* life.

Victor had done the unthinkable.

He raced across Deck 10 and tried not to look out at the water as the Coast Guard vessels approached. He wondered what Graves was doing right now, watching the scene unfold, helpless from shore.

He wondered what Kate was doing, what she was thinking.

She would feel even more helpless than ever, as she had just seen the incident taking place out in the bay, watching from afar. He wanted to be there, to hold her and Riley together. He wanted to be there to wipe her tears and tell her it was going to be okay.

Because it *was* going to be okay. He could feel it.

He ran with Riley under his arm until the very end, until his left bicep he was carrying her with and the bullet wound in his thigh were screaming in pain, and he had to drop her. She hit the deck running as well, probably unsure what they were racing toward, but not willing to leave her father's sight.

It was growing difficult to run in a straight line, as the ship kept moving and sinking. He constantly adapted his gait, shifting his balance around, and finally reached the back corner of the deck a minute later, Riley about twenty steps behind him.

He turned, facing the same check-in stand where he and Kate had dropped the kids off earlier that day. He didn't stop but continued on down the hallway, finally turning left, the point where he had begun this journey hours ago.

He burst through the first set of double doors leading into the larger space, and then the second, interior doors, only stopping inside to catch his breath once he was nearly at the center of the room along the wall. Only then did he lift his eyes up and back.

Riley entered then, but Jack wasn't looking at her.

He was looking at all of the kids.

Spread out throughout the large space, he saw them. Every single child, all watching him with interest. Addy was sitting near the captain on the far side of the room, backs up against the wall.

The captain was smiling, his hand now bandaged in gauze.

He began to stand up as Jack rushed over. Addison saw him then, her eyes wide with delight. Her tear-streaked face brightened immediately, and she bounded toward her father, closing the distance in seconds.

They met near the far wall, where he pulled her in and squeezed her as hard as he dared. When he let her go, still holding onto her hands, he felt something tugging at his arm.

He pulled back and saw Riley there now, too, and he brought her into the hug as well.

He wanted to freeze the moment, but he knew they were working against a countdown. The ship *was* sinking, and it was only a matter of time before it fell over onto its side completely, making recovery and getting off the ship that much more difficult.

He wanted to be far away by that time.

And besides, his wife would be beside herself with grief, shocked and horrified by what she thought she had just seen.

HOWARD GRAVES PACED BACK and forth along the dock, near where the officers had previously gathered after arriving on their lifeboat. Kate Barr had been next to him, but for the first time all day she had extracted herself and gone somewhere else. He wasn't sure where, nor did he care.

All he could think about was what he had just witnessed. After seeing the lifeboat explode and sink out in the center of the bay, Howard Graves knew his career was over.

A lifeboat full of kids, he had thought. *Victor actually did it. Unbelievable.*

He could not believe his eyes, and he did not even *have* kids. He knew what she had been thinking — it was what they had all been thinking. Could this asshole, Victor, *actually* kill all of those kids? They had all certainly hoped not.

Graves had hoped not. His reputation was on the line, and thirty-something dead kids while he was in charge was not a good look.

He paced silently, wondering if he could piece together his

career once again, put something useful back together from the ashes of destruction.

Kate Barr had absolutely lost her mind. He thought her screams could have been heard all the way over on the *Ocean Voyager*, so he was glad when she finally left toward the docks.

He watched the radio in his hand, wondering if Victor was going to transmit anything else. So far he had told them that everything he needed here he had gotten — and so that he would be on his way. And so far that seemed to be true. Victor — apparently now on the yacht with whatever men he had left — was now sailing off toward the horizon.

The Coast Guard had informed Howard that they would not be chasing him, rather that they would find the boat later since it was registered and documented in their database. They were not sure what other leverage Victor might have had against them all, but they were too scared to find out.

Howard did not disagree with this assessment — he only wished he could have gotten on one of their boats to head out to the *Ocean Voyager* now, where they were all headed.

As Victor had claimed, it seemed the *Ocean Voyager* was finally finishing its journey to the bottom of the Jamaican Bay. It had rolled over on its side and was beginning to sink. On one side of the ship, it even seemed that water had completely filled the bottom three decks. The fourth was now just barely beginning to disappear.

He wanted to be out there. *Needed* to be. He needed to see it for himself.

When one of the Coast Guard boats had sidled up against the leaning ship, the men on board had gotten to work immediately. He used binoculars to watch as the Coast Guard men and women pulled passengers and crew — whoever was remaining on board — off of the ship and safely onto the Coast Guard vessel. He could not see individuals, as the Coast Guard cutter itself blocked the view, but it did not last long. The entire operation took less than twenty minutes, and before long the boat was sailing toward the docks, where Howard and everyone else was waiting.

The energy had changed to one of solemn realization, and after the screams and shouts of the bystanders — including those with missing children, like Kate — everyone seemed to be lost in despair. Even the news crews had quieted down as they realized what had happened.

Howard noticed Kate coming back over. She had seen the commotion and the Coast Guard boat picking up people from the ship, and she saw its trajectory — it would dock right where Howard was standing. She likely wanted to know if her husband would be among the people disembarking.

She looked terrible, as well. Her hair was a huge mess, and her eyes made her look like a drug addict, sunken into their sockets, dark marks around them. She came closer to him, but still stood away from everyone else, her arms wrapped tightly around herself, as if shivering from cold.

Howard gladly gave her space — he wasn't interested in the emotional collapse of this woman and her family. He had never been empathetic, never been one to console loved ones after a loss. That was for other cops, people who had experience with that sort of thing.

The Coast Guard cutter was approaching rapidly, and he walked forward to receive it.

The pilot performed a perfect maneuver, landing the ship within inches from the dock, turning it at the last moment so that it sat parked near the concrete edge of the pier. Two of

Howard's Port Authority employees raced out with gangplanks and tossed them up onto the edge of the cutter.

Two more dockworkers began tying off the vessel as children appeared on deck.

Howard's mouth fell open. *What the hell?*

Kate, standing next to him now, gasped and then screamed.

"How — how are the kids..." one of the dockworkers said, her voice trailing off.

He heard gasps from the crowd gathered just beyond the border of the Port Authority buildings as they all realized it as well, and he sensed all of the news cameras swivel toward this location.

He saw a man leave the inside of the cutter next. His face was a mess of grease and sweat with a bit of blood and tears thrown in, and his clothes were ripped in multiple places. He looked like a crewmember, wearing all black, complete with the requisite black shoes, but Howard knew he was looking at Jack Barr.

Kate ran forward and over the plank, nearly flying onto the boat. She scooped up one of the kids, and then another. She cried still, her wails reaching far past the shore. Finally, she stood up and hugged her husband, who seemed as shellshocked as everyone else.

Three Coast Guard officers were standing near Jack, and together the family and the officers all left the boat and met Howard onshore.

"Jack," Kate said, her voice a mere whisper. "I saw... I saw what —"

Jack squeezed her hand, then pulled her in for a hug. He raised his voice so that Howard and the others could hear him, likely not wanting to repeat the story too many times. "I believed Victor when he said he was a man of his word. He kept hammering that home, like it meant *so much* to him that we trusted him. So when he said there would be a severe consequence for not listening to him, I didn't want to trust that the lifeboat was a safe place for the kids. It was the only one left, and they were his leverage. There was nothing else he *could* have done, if things did not go his way."

"And apparently things did not go his way," Kate said.

Jack nodded and the officers watched him as he continued, solemn as they listened in.

"At the time, I had no idea if he had actually done anything to the boat or not — but I needed to make a call either way, and I decided to trust my gut. I wanted the kids off the ship more than anything, but I did not trust the lifeboat. At the last second, I told the captain to get all the kids out and hide them somewhere."

"Where did he put them?" Kate asked.

Howard watched as a man appeared from inside the Coast Guard vessel. *Captain José Phillips.* The man looked like he had been through hell and back, and Howard frowned when he saw his hand covered in gauze. *I guess he* has *been through hell.*

Jack smiled at the captain as he appeared on deck but continued his retelling of the events. "I sent them back to the Kids' Zone. I know it's probably a little twisted — that's where all of this began. And the kids knew that place — if there was anywhere on board that was comfortable for them all, I figured it might be there. But I had to act fast — that's why I had the captain help out. I couldn't take them myself, since I thought Victor was waiting for me on the bridge."

"But he wasn't there, I thought?" one of the Coast Guard officers asked. "He was already on the yacht?"

Howard stepped forward, naturally wanting to hear the entire story.

Jack nodded. "I thought this was strange as well. For someone like Victor, somebody who prided himself on being *so* truthful all the time, I thought it was weird. But then I knew it was all a part of his game — he didn't lie. In fact, I think he was prepared to..." He choked up as the words fell out. "I think he was prepared to *shoot* Riley because of what I did."

Kate gasped again, almost choking on the sobs.

"He's ruthless, but he did tell me what would happen if I did not comply. All bets were off when things started going south for Victor, so by not waiting for me on the bridge, he wasn't *lying* about it — he had changed the endgame.

"Either way, I didn't want to run up there empty-handed. I rigged up something that distracted the guy Victor left to guard Riley, and it worked. I wasn't about to just barge in there and let Victor — or the man he left behind — do whatever they wanted with me and my kid. It simply was *not* going to happen."

Jack looked then at Howard, a stern expression on his face, as if noticing him for the first time. Howard waited, but it seemed as though he was done with the story for now.

"And you must be Howard Graves?" Jack asked.

Graves swallowed, then frowned. This guy was surprisingly confident for a man who had just been through hell. He was used to being in charge around here, and today he had felt nothing but lack of control. It was emasculating, and this guy's actions seemed to drill the point home.

"Yeah, Howard Graves, in the flesh. Glad to finally meet —"

"I have no jurisdiction here," Jack said quickly, releasing

Kate and walking closer to Graves. He motioned to the Coast Guard officers. "But these men and women do. I'm asking that they put you under arrest, immediately."

Howard took a step back. "What — what the *hell*? Why? On what grounds do you have reason to suspect —"

"Corruption? Collusion? I bet we could dig up a few more, too. Did you have any idea that you were already under investigation by the CIA?" Jack asked.

Howard's mouth moved, but no sound came out. He suddenly felt very weak, his knees finally about to give out under the massive weight he had put on them for so many years.

He struggled to sound out words as the Coast Guard officers swarmed him, one of them slipping cuffs over his wrists.

Howard was not sure if he was feeling more shock or rage. This man — apparently a US government employee, operating *far* out of his jurisdiction — was trying to arrest *him?*

CHAPTER 54

JACK

JACK KNEW that Kate wanted to get away from all of this — *far* away, to start making it a memory, and not an experience they were currently going through. He had already made a plan — they would book a hotel in a faraway town, away from all this. If they stayed here, he was sure the news crews and media would hound them for interviews and pictures, pretending to want to respect their privacy but doing nothing to prevent breaching it.

And he wanted to get away from it all as well. It was time. Riley and Addy were hanging on by a thread, and he needed to get them the help they needed, whether it be therapy or just counseling.

But they were safe — *all* the kids were safe and were currently being reunited with their own families. Someone had let the rest of the masses of people outside the gates into the grounds, and the docks were filling up once again with grief-stricken passengers and crew members, as well as the growing posse of media types.

But he could not escape it yet. There was still an issue to

resolve. He had figured out most of it while running around the ship like a crazed assassin, taking out Victor's men as quickly as he could in search of his kids.

But the remaining pieces had finally clicked into place near the end of Victor's transmission.

At first, he could not figure out what it was that Victor and his men had wanted. He had no idea why they were here — what they could be after. He had racked his brain trying to figure it out.

Sure, there were weapons hidden down below on the *Ocean Voyager*. But Victor had seemed to not even care about them — and simply sailed away on his yacht.

When he had been offered a charging port from one of the Coast Guard guys, he had gladly accepted it. His phone came back to life a few minutes later, just as they were reaching the docks, and he had received a text message from his boss.

> *We already had an operator in place there; sorry you got swept into it. Jack, stay safe.*

> *Victor is with the Vínculo cartel, based in Venezuela. They buy and sell US-manufactured weapons to guerrilla armies in South America, among other lovely things.*

> *I'll send over a dossier to your encrypted email account, but again — stay safe. Call when you can.*

It wasn't much, and it certainly had not come in time for Jack to have done anything with it, but it was information, nonetheless.

Obviously, Victor was high up in a cartel that was engaged in dealing arms and weapons, through their base of operations in Venezuela. That much he had put together on his own, and his boss at the CIA had confirmed all of it. He had also learned that the other CIA operative — though Jack still didn't know his name — had been on a solo mission, undercover, to figure out what *exactly* Victor was planning next.

That particular mission had failed catastrophically, with the man dying trying to prevent the detonation of the bomb Victor's men had planted belowdecks.

So at first, Jack had assumed that Victor's entire goal was terrorism — he wanted to blow a hole in the side of the ship and freak everybody out, grabbing some hostages along the way and barking about some religious or moral high ground he believed they were taking.

But he had learned that Victor was *not* religious — at least not overtly, and it was not a part of their mission. There was no moral or ethical hill he was trying to die on. No reason to need hostages for whatever it was they were attempting.

So why destroy the cruise ship? Jack had wondered. *Why do all of this in the first place if he was just going to sail away safely, albeit down a few men?*

But then Victor had played his hand at the end of the transmission: *I got what I came here to get.*

That sentence had struck Jack as odd, so he pressed into it, putting his mind to work the last hour of his escapade on the ship, as well as the twenty or so minutes it had taken to get to shore.

Now, Howard Graves was stammering in front of him, growing more and more irate as the Coast Guard officers surrounded him and placed him under arrest.

"What's this all about, Jack?" Graves shouted. "You can't — there's no reason to —"

Jack held up a hand, which only seemed to piss Graves off more, but he interrupted, nonetheless. "I got to have a nice, long chat with Captain José Phillips of the *Ocean Voyager*,"

Jack said. "He would be here, but he's being treated for some nasty wounds at the moment. Anyway, he's not going to get off the hook, either. I believe he's a good man who just made some mistakes. But I'm not sure I can say the same about you, at least not yet."

"Mistakes? What the hell are you talking about?"

"Stop trying to save face, Graves," Jack said. "Tell me you *weren't* working with Phillips."

He waited, staring down Graves as the huge man continued to hem and haw. "Working with? I barely even —"

"Phillips tells me while he's never had so much as an in-person conversation with you, he does know you quite well, and vice versa. He says you've been working with him for almost a year now."

Kate appeared shocked, but she was listening intently, as were his daughters and the officers.

"Skimming off the top of Victor's operation, Graves? That's *next-level* stupid. Apparently, you guys had a deal with the cartel — get the weapons into Venezuela by way of a cruise ship. Brilliant, really: the only two guys who really need to know every single thing that happens on board a cruise ship are the captain, and the guy who puts all the stuff onto the ship in the first place."

Jack raised his eyebrows. "That's you, right?"

"I... no, I mean there are — I've got a guy who —"

One of the Coast Guard officers pulled out a small notebook and held it up to his face, reading from it. "We got word a little over an hour ago that you were going around and talking to divers you employed. SCUBA-trained. They were told they might have to investigate the wreck."

Howard's eyes widened. "That is a completely reasonable thing for me to do," he said, almost shouting.

"Perhaps it is," the Coast Guard officer said. "We've heard from five of them. Every single one of them, however, says there were *six* ready. Did you send a diver out there? And where are they, now?"

Now it was Jack's turn to be surprised. "The 'other man,'" he said softly.

EVERYONE LOOKED AT HIM, but he waited a moment before responding. "Yeah, Victor mentioned another man — a third person he thought was involved in sabotaging him. He knew about the CIA agent who was already poking around, and he eventually found out about me. But he mentioned a third guy too — a diver, specifically. Someone his men eliminated. I guess Victor had divers in the water, too, aside from the fifteen or so I saw on board."

Howard seemed to be in shock. His face had just stopped working. His eyes were blinking open and closed as if he were being electrocuted in slow-motion. His mouth flopped open and shut as well, his jowls shaking as they did.

"It's starting to make a lot more sense to me, now," Jack said. "All of it. That's the real reason you wanted to send divers out there, and that's why everything you said to me on the phone sounded strange. You didn't care about the hostages — you didn't give a shit about my kids or me — you wanted to know if Victor was somehow still trying to move his stuff. You needed to get out there fast to get eyes on the prize, didn't you? You thought he might be on to you, Graves."

There was a long pause, and Howard's eyes fell to the concrete pier.

"That's what I thought, Graves. But you sent a diver. You were too afraid to even make the move yourself. You sent someone to their death today, and all those other deaths on board might as well be on your hands as well — because you are why Victor was here in the first place. You were why one of the head honchos of a Venezuelan cartel had to come, in person, to check things out. And at least the captain owned up to it right away, recognized that he made a mistake. You're still vacillating between thinking you're right and hoping somehow you might be."

Jack took a breath and cleared his throat, then continued. "All the pieces fell into place about the same time I found the kids in the lifeboat. Of course Victor would need leverage — because he needed time. He needed to make sure he could get what was 'rightfully his' off the boat, in his own way, without needing it to go through port, since he could no longer trust them. Without needing to go through this guy."

He motioned at Graves. "He couldn't trust Captain Phillips anymore, and he certainly couldn't trust whoever Phillips was working with at Port Authority or the cruise company.

"Victor just knew that somebody was scraping a few boxes of stuff off the top — literally stealing money — from his operation, and he was sent here by the cartel boss to figure out who it was and put an end to it."

Jack was about to continue when someone interrupted

him. It was another Jamaican Coast Guard officer who had not yet spoken. "This makes sense," said the man, "but then, why did Victor leave? He had the leverage — he had the kids, and..." His voice trailed off as he realized the kids and Kate were still there, and he brought his voice down as he continued. "You know, what he said he would do... technically, he did do it, even though the kids weren't on the lifeboat anymore. All his leverage, gone. For what?"

Jack listened as the man continued.

"Anyway, it was working, right? He had us all held back past that half-mile line. We were all waiting for his next move. He had all the cards, literally all the leverage. And yet he just got on the yacht... and sailed away?"

Jack nodded again. "Yeah, I thought about this a lot as well — pretty much from the first time Kate saw those crates, I thought there was something fishy going on. It's too much junk to be hauled off on a yacht — I don't know exactly how many crates there were, but there probably had to be dozens of tons of weapons altogether."

"So he just left it all on the boat?"

Jack smiled, anticipating this question. "No, almost certainly not. That's the other piece I couldn't quite figure out at first: why in the world would he blow a hole in the side of the ship? But when I went down and found the captain, I also saw a man sawing another hole, this one in a different compartment. The first explosion happened because that CIA agent was trying to dismantle a bomb and move it to another place. It didn't work, and it opened a hole in the ship and killed him.

"But that wasn't where Victor needed the hole to be, which was why the first explosion put everything into motion, forcing him into action. It was why he needed leverage — why he took hostages. He needed to work as quickly as he could to make another hole now, this one in precisely the location he needed it to be in."

Jack could tell that even Howard Graves seemed curious, but it was Kate who asked the question. "And where exactly was that?" she asked.

"On Deck 1, between two seaworthy compartments. Victor manipulated the partitions as well, opening and closing doors so that the only section of the ship that would fill with water — the sections that just finished filling up now — were where the crates were stored. "

As he explained, he looked back at the *Ocean Voyager*, dead in the water. It seemed to have stopped filling and tipping for the moment, but it was leaning over at an impossible angle. Numerous Coast Guard boats and small ships had maneuvered over to the luxury cruise liner.

One of them had reached the docks, landing just in front of the larger boat Jack and the kids had been on. Jack watched, interested in why the Coast Guard crew all seemed so eager to get to shore.

And then he saw him.

Jack smiled as he ran over to the boat to collect the lone passenger.

"We found him belowdecks," a woman from the Jamaican Coast Guard said. "He was hiding in the stairwell, working up slowly as the water started pulling the boat down."

Giuseppe.

Jack stepped over the rope now being used to moor the boat, just as the young kid bounded down the gangplank. He ran over and hugged Jack.

"Mr. Jack!" Giuseppe shouted.

Kate and the others came over to join them, and Jack explained quickly. "This guy saved my life, more than once," he said. Then he pulled back from the hug and faced Giuseppe. "You're okay?"

There were tears in Giuseppe's eyes, but for the first time since they'd met, they were tears of joy. "Yes, yes, Mr. Jack. I am okay."

He extended a hand, and they shook, and then Giuseppe was whisked off by a Coast Guardsman, and Jack pulled another one aside. "He's going to be taken care of, right?" he asked.

The officer nodded. "We'll make sure of it."

"I'm going to hold you to that." Jack was not sure what they would be able to do for the poor kid, but he had made a promise to himself earlier that day that if they got out of this alive, he would figure something out. It would not be difficult at all to lean on his organization a bit and have them send something to his family.

Jack made a mental note now to follow up with it when they got home.

"He needed to fill up the large warehouse area Kate and I saw all those crates in," Jack said. "And any partitions that lay between the ocean and that warehouse."

Kate's eyes widened, and two of the Jamaican officers nodded along. "He's not going to move them," Kate said. "He's going to let the ocean do it for him."

Jack smiled at her. "Exactly," he said. "Coast Guard guys are on the boat right now, but I suspect it's too late. They'll likely be going room by room, door by door, working their way down to check for anyone still alive. It will probably be over an hour before they get there. But I'll bet if they looked in that room now, the entire area would be completely flooded. They wouldn't even be able to get in."

"And all of the crates will be settling on the bottom of the bay," the Jamaican officer said.

JACK NODDED. "It's still probably too late, but I bet if we get some divers in the water all they will find are empty crates. The boxes were metal, so they'll sink, but the lids were wooden. They'll float. We'll start to see them pop up to the surface soon, but whatever was inside of them will be long gone."

Jack turned to Graves. "Victor said he had divers that intercepted your man, Graves. Victor probably employed a half-dozen other divers as well, so all of them could work quickly enough to collect whatever was in those crates, put them in some nets, and simply drag them behind an underwater propulsion unit to wherever they needed to go."

One of the Jamaican officers, a woman, nodded. "I know of these systems. They are certainly powerful enough. They would not be able to run at full speed, but their range would be incredible once they got moving. And all of it would be underwater, so they'd go unnoticed."

"And it's too late to catch them?" another one of the officers asked.

"I'm afraid so," Jack said. "Victor's bold, but he's smart. He knew all eyes would be on the ship, on the hostages. Even on him. The whole time his men were working to make sure they could get his prize from the belly of the Ocean Voyager, he was engaging us, performing some sleight-of-hand and misdirection.

"And, right when I got to the bridge the second time with my daughter, he put his last phase into motion. He blew the hole and started flooding the ship — the plan he originally came out here for. Because the CIA agent rushed him by blowing up the bomb in the wrong spot, Victor felt he needed to take hostages in order to have leverage, to give him enough time to finish setting everything up.

"But as soon as it was all set up, his men were ready. All of the divers — men I never would have seen and no one else knew about — were already in the water the moment he did it, probably just out of range of the explosion. All they had to do was wait until the crates fell, one by one, to the bottom of the bay, where they could pluck out all of their stuff, stick it in nets, and send it on its way.

"So yeah, it's too late. Almost without a doubt, Victor's long gone. We'll still be able to look for him since we know about the cartel, but if Victor felt confident enough blowing the second bomb and leaving in plain sight, I'm sure it was because his men were in place and the goods were already gone as soon as we got to shore. He would not have risked it, otherwise."

"But they have to still be close," another officer said. "We should be able to —"

"You can try to look," Jack said. "And it's probably worth doing, just in the interest of due diligence. But trust me when I say: Victor will be prepared to be chased. He's ready for you and whatever you're going to throw at him now."

An enlist ran up and got the attention of one of the officers. All eyes turned to the younger man. "Sir, our chopper just found the yacht."

Jack waited for the explanation, interested in this turn of events.

"As soon as the yacht got around the side of the island, we sent our fastest cutter after it, but we also sent the chopper as high up as we could go, while still being able to see individual designations on the boats near shore," the kid explained. "We got lucky, but we found the yacht. It's parked just three bays over, in Local's Cove."

Jack frowned. "Parked? Like... anchored?"

The kid nodded at him. "Yes, anchored." His eyes darted to the left. "But... the chopper hovered for a while but didn't see anybody. They just called it in and said that they lowered a man onto the deck, a rescue swimmer, but he found no one inside."

Jack confirmed. "That must have been the plan all along," he said. "He warned all of you not to chase him, but knew that you would, anyway. All he needed to do was get out ahead, make sure you lost sight of him initially. He knew the yacht was easily traceable, that it would be on plenty of registries and databases — hell, you were the guys that gave it to them in the first place. So he probably had another boat waiting. The one that he's actually on now, probably already racing back toward Venezuela."

One of the officers shook his head. "We had him," he said. "We should never have taken eyes off of him."

Jack shook his head. "No, like I said, Victor's smart. He would've been prepared for whatever you would have tried, and it only would have led to more death if you tried intercepting him. I mean, he's carrying guns, remember? None of them — not even the ammunition they used — would have been underwater long enough for them to stop working, so he and his men could have probably held off an army. The best thing we can do now is start preparing our own attack. To start putting our own plan together of how we're going to bring him in."

Jack noticed Kate's eyes staring up at him. He looked down at his wife but didn't see fear for confusion there. He saw resolve.

Confidence.

Jack frowned as he realized what he had just said. The Jamaican Coast Guard officers had not corrected him, either.

"But Jack," his wife said, a smirk on her face. "I thought you weren't that kind of agent?"

He took a deep breath, looking at his wife and his kids silhouetted against the gorgeous Jamaican horizon, then smiled. "I'm not," he said. "But you know what? I think I might be considering it."

CHAPTER 57

GRAVES

HOWARD GRAVES SAT in the holding cell of the Jamaican parish precinct. This would not be his long-term accommodations — he knew he was going to be in and out of court over the next few years. The insufferable Jack Barr and his wife, Kate, had really thrown a wrench in his plans.

Hell, he had heard that even Captain Phillips had gotten off with just a fine and a few months behind bars, thanks to his willingness to come clean and help Jack with the kids. With the amount of money the man had likely saved already, however, he would get out with his proverbial slap on the wrist, able to enjoy his retirement for as long as he lived.

But Howard Graves was not going to be so lucky. The universe constantly was transpiring against him, it seemed. He had always felt despised, ostracized. No other cops had liked him at the precinct back in Miami, even though he *constantly* did their jobs for them. And then here, from the beginning of his second career as the director of security for Port Authority, his employees did not seem to appreciate his brilliance. They did not seem to *care* that he had the experience and knowledge and could lead them well, if only they would shut up and listen.

They did not care about him at all, judging by the fact that literally none of them had come to visit him.

Even here at the jail, the Jamaican police had treated him as if he were nothing but a low-level thug. A petty thief. They acted as if he were going to be here forever, as if he were going to *rot* in this jail cell.

He squeezed his fists together, the rage returning. *Jack Barr took it all from me,* he thought. *I was* so close *to washing my hands of all this.*

It was after hours now, and both guards that had been manning the station had left. He knew that there should be one more somewhere on the premises, but these officers were lazier even than his own employees back at the cruise port, and he wondered if the third cop had just decided to go for an 'extended smoke break.'

He heard a door open, and footsteps approach.

There he is, Howard thought. *Probably finished running his errands, and now ready to kick back and watch the football game.*

He waited, not hearing anything at first. Then they grew louder as they approached his hallway.

Strange. They don't usually come back here unless they want to harass me or ask me questions. He checked his watch, which they had for some reason let him keep. *And it's damn near the middle of the night. Why in the world would they want to ask me anything* now?

The hallway door opened, and a woman stepped in.

Howard was taken aback. She was absolutely gorgeous. South American, her long, dark hair flowing past her equally toned shoulders. She wore huge gold hoop earrings and dark lipstick, perhaps a deep maroon color or even purple, though he couldn't tell in the low light.

She eyed him, not saying anything at first. Finally, she walked closer to the cell door. "Come," she said in Spanish.

He stood, but did not dare approach the door.

She repeated the word more forcefully, and he once again ignored her. "Who the hell are you?" he asked.

"A friend of a friend," she said calmly, this time in English.

"And you're here... for me?"

The woman stared at him for a full five seconds, then smiled slowly. "*Sí*," she said. "I am here for *you*. Howard Graves, I presume?"

He nodded, his frown intensifying. "Are — are you going to get me out of here or something?"

She opened the clutch she had been holding in her right hand and pulled out a sick-looking 9mm pistol.

He shuffled backwards, his rear end hitting the wall near the bench as he found the jail cell suddenly even smaller than he'd realized.

"In a matter of speaking," she said. "Yes, I *am* here to get you out."

She lifted the pistol and fired, two quick shots. Her eyes never left his.

Both rounds hit Howard in the chest, and he felt his lungs collapse. His heart began to beat faster and faster, only working to shoot blood from the new wounds she had given him.

He fell forward, landing half on the bench, then slid off sideways as he felt the life leaving him. He was far too out of shape to attempt to get back up, but he pulled his head upward and stared at his assassin, blood dripping over his chin.

"Victor sends his regards," she said.

The last thing Howard Graves saw was the woman's shapely figure disappearing back down the precinct hall.

AFTERWORD

Thanks for reading! The next book in the *Jack Barr Thrillers* series can be found by clicking here.

If you liked this book (or even if you hated it...) write a review or rate it. You might not think it makes a difference, but it does.

Besides *actual* currency (money), the currency of today's writing world is *reviews*. Reviews, good or bad, tell other people that an author is worth reading. I'm hoping that since you made it this far into my book, you have some sort of opinion on it.

Would you mind sharing that opinion? It only takes a second.

Nick Thacker

BOOKS BY NICK THACKER

Jack Barr Thrillers

The Caribbean Affair (Book 1)

The Peruvian Exchange (Book 2)

Six Assassins Thrillers

Primary Target (Book 1)

Subtle Target (Book 2)

Unstable Target (Book 3)

Captive Target (Book 4)

Vendetta Target (Book 5)

Final Target (Book 6)

Mason Dixon Thrillers

Mark for Blood (Book 1)

Death Mark (Book 2)

Mark My Words (Book 3)

Harvey Bennett Mysteries

The Enigma Strain (Book 1)

The Amazon Code (Book 2)

The Ice Chasm (Book 3)

The Jefferson Legacy (Book 4)

The Paradise Key (Book 5)

The Atlantis Artifact (Book 6)

The Book of Bones (Book 7)

The Cain Conspiracy (Book 8)

The Mendel Paradox (Book 9)

The Minoan Manifest (Book 10)

The Napoleon Job (Book 11)

The Embers of Siwa (Book 12)

Harvey Bennett Mysteries - Books 1-3

Harvey Bennett Mysteries - Books 4-6

Harvey Bennett Mysteries - Books 7-9

Jake Parker Thrillers

Containment (Book 1)

The Patriot (Book 2)

False Allegiance (Book 3)

Standalone Thrillers

The Atlantis Stone

The Depths

Relics: A Post-Apocalyptic Technothriller

Killer Thrillers (3-Book Box Set)

ABOUT THE AUTHOR

Nick Thacker is a thriller author from Texas who lives in Hawaii and Colorado. In his free time, he enjoys reading in a hammock on the beach, skiing, drinking whiskey, and hanging out with his beautiful wife, two dogs, and two daughters.

For more information and a list of Nick's other work, visit Nick online:
www.nickthacker.com

facebook.com/AuthorNickThacker
twitter.com/NickThacker
instagram.com/TheNickThacker
bookbub.com/authors/nick-thacker

www.ingramcontent.com/pod-product-compliance
Lightning Source LLC
Chambersburg PA
CBHW051124190726
48290CB00006B/1674